Desperate Hope

by

Susan Leigh Furlong

Desperate Hope

Cover Art by *Lisa Dawn MacDonald*

The Wild Rose Press, Inc.
PO Box 708
Adams Basin, NY 14410-0708
Visit us at www.thewildrosepress.com

Publishing History
First Edition, 2022
Trade Paperback ISBN 978-1-5092-4597-0
Digital ISBN 978-1-5092-4598-7

Published in the United States of America

Dedication

This book is dedicated to all my former students and Power of the Pen writers who had the courage to put their hearts on the line and write down their stories, and to TR who gave this book a name.

"If there must be trouble, let it be in my day, that my child may have peace."

—*Tom Paine*

Chapter One

The Second Battle of Saratoga on October 7, 1777, in Saratoga County, New York, during America's Revolutionary War.

The British cannon shell screamed over their heads.

"No need to worry about that one!" shouted Alden through the noise and smoke of the battlefield. "It'll land well away." Some of the men still ducked their heads, but they all kept moving forward across the blood-soaked fields of the Freeman farm. The shattered pieces of bodies from both British and Continental soldiers littered the trenches and barricades along with spent cartridges and abandoned muskets from two months of fighting. The stench of death and gunpowder sickened even the hardiest, and it made the crossing a slow, treacherous struggle.

Short, earsplitting bursts followed, which meant another shell was coming in fast and would land almost on top of them.

"Cover!" shouted Alden. The men dropped into the mud and covered their heads.

Alden Carter pushed Gavin Cullane to the ground and fell on top of him. A sharp whoosh of air and vibrating sound waves gave way to the now-familiar pings and cracks as the shrapnel from the explosion showered over them. More shells soared over their heads.

Gavin's face slid into the mud. His nose filled with muck, and his ears rang from the deafening explosion, but he lay without moving a muscle or even breathing deeply for what seemed like an eternity as the dust and noise settled. When he lifted his head at last, he snorted heavily. Lingering wisps of smoke burned his nose and mouth as he searched the field for the ten men from his unit who had marched into this battle with him. Only five remained standing.

"Gavin, can you move?" shouted one of them over his shoulder as he ran to join the fighting. "What about Carter?"

"I'll take care of him. You take care of the redcoats!" Gavin struggled to heave an unconscious Alden off his back before running his hands over his own body, thanking the Lord he had only minor shrapnel wounds on his shoulders and the backs of his legs.

But Alden lay unmoving on the ground.

"Please, Lord, no!" Fighting for American freedom had bound them closer than brothers, and he couldn't face this war taking away the best friend he'd ever had. His voice cracked. "Alden, Alden, talk to me!"

As he lifted Alden onto his lap, streams of blood spurted from Alden's left arm, forming thick puddles of red on the ground. His bloody hand lay in the mud some ten feet away. Gavin ripped off his own jacket and shirt and used his shirt to tie a tight tourniquet around Alden's upper arm. The blood slowed, but not enough, so he grabbed that arm and held it up in the air, stopping all but a seep of lifeblood. Slipping his jacket back over his shoulders, he sat with Alden's arm in the air as the musket fire and commotion moved around them.

"We're driving them back!" shouted a passing colonial soldier. "They can't get reinforcements! We're driving them back!" More men bolted near Gavin and Alden, but none stopped to help them. No time when victory was so close.

Gavin shivered as the sun fell below the horizon and a cool autumn breeze blew across the battlefield, leaving only the moans of dying soldiers from both sides of the conflict, and these faded with each passing hour. Gavin looked toward the Freeman farmhouse for signs of help, but it stood empty and alone.

Only a sliver of moon lit the darkness when Gavin decided that Alden would die very soon if they didn't find some medical help. As he bent down to lift Alden into his arms, his friend's canteen fell out of his waistband. Scooping it up, he heaved Alden over his shoulder and started walking. Not knowing where the American and British battlelines started and ended, he wandered aimlessly for several hours until he heard the crackle of a fire and low murmurs of men's voices. He followed the sounds, only to discover he had stumbled into the camp of a small group of retreating British redcoats who immediately saw a chance to salvage a small victory out of defeat by capturing two prisoners.

The next morning, one of the weary Brits in a tattered red uniform pointed to Alden, saying in his stiff British accent, "We're moving. Leave that one."

"I'll carry him," said Gavin.

"Won't do any good. His hand is blown off. He'll be dead soon enough."

"What is it to you if I carry him?"

The soldiers prodded Gavin and Alden ahead of them as they joined up with other defeated British troops and their prisoners heading toward the Hudson River.

"Want a drink?" Gavin asked Alden when the redcoats called a halt. The still unconscious Alden didn't answer, but Gavin put the metal canteen to his friend's lips anyway and heard the familiar rattle. "Your wedding ring you pushed in here makes the water taste funny. I know, the rattle reminds you of your wife. Just swallow some of this, so you can take it home to Tansy yourself." Alden had feared a scavenger might steal his ring right off his finger, but they'd ignore a dented canteen. He had scratched his name on it with the hope someone would care enough to return it to the woman he loved.

Alden swallowed the water, and Gavin smiled for what would be the last time in a very long time.

****

New York City, October 1777

Tansy rubbed her ever-expanding belly as she rocked in the chair in the corner of her sister's kitchen. Her four-year-old niece, Mercy Hemstead, crawled up on her lap. "When can we see the baby?" asked Mercy.

"Sometime before Christmas," answered Tansy.

"Will Uncle Alden be here when the baby is born?"

Tansy brushed Mercy's soft brown hair out of the child's eyes, saying, "I sent him a letter telling him about the baby, but I don't know if he got it. When the war is over, he'll come here."

"Does he know where we live?"

"The man I leased the dairy farm to in

Pennsylvania will tell him that I came to stay with you and the family, and then Alden will come to New York City."

"How will he know the way?"

Daisy Hemstead, Tansy's older sister and Mercy's mother, stirred the stew on the fire and said, "Mercy, quit bothering your Aunt Tansy about things that can't be helped. Aunt Tansy couldn't take care of the dairy cows by herself, especially not when she was going to have a baby, so we told her to come here. It's safer and easier for everyone."

"Your mother is right," said Tansy. "The wartime prices of milk and butter are always changing, and Uncle Alden hadn't been paid by the army in so long, I just couldn't keep the farm by myself. I am thankful I could come here, even if it is a little crowded with your mother and father and you four children."

"I don't mind," said Mercy. "I like to cuddle close to Lizzie at night. She keeps me warm."

"She kicks me!" said her older sister, Lizzie, as she kneaded the dough for biscuits for the stew.

Mercy stuck out her tongue in her sister's direction before she asked, "Who will the baby look like?"

"I'm hoping the baby will look like Uncle Alden," said Tansy as she lifted Mercy to the floor and stood to walk around and ease her stiff back. "The baby won't be as tall as your father, but he'll have blond hair, like Alden's and mine. When he grows up, he'll have strong muscles and a quick grin. He'll probably like to tell jokes like Alden always did. I miss his jokes."

A pot of stew simmered over the fire, making the combination front room and kitchen of the Hemstead house warm and cozy, and Tansy felt a sense of peace and calm. She did so miss being able to see the horizon blocked by the tall buildings in the city. But the Hemsteads had made so many sacrifices for her, she never spoke her regrets to Daisy or Nate. She was glad to have a safe place to wait for Alden to come home.

****

Herded by the British soldiers onto an open barge, Gavin stumbled forward carrying Alden in his arms until he found a cleared spot to sit on the hard deck while the barge floated down the Hudson River toward a British prison ship off the shore of the British-occupied Manhattan Island.

As the barge passed by New York City, the once-bustling, active city stood dark and cheerless, especially when they came close to the burned-out section along the shore now known as The Burns. A fire had devastated nearly one-third of the city after the British invaded the island, but this twelve-block area had been destroyed beyond recognition. Little remained except the foul lingering smoke mixed with the stink of unwashed humans and the stench of their piss and waste from open latrines. Tents and lean-tos littered the ash-covered ground along with the gutted remains of former homes and buildings. This pitiful existence belonged to people displaced by the fire and those forced out of their houses that had been confiscated by British troops. The British, having made no attempt to rebuild, sent a message. *Let it remind the rebels that opposing the British king is futile!*

Gavin, his arms aching from Alden's weight, refused to let go of him. "There'll be help on board the prison ship," he whispered to a now-moaning Alden. "Just a little farther. You can make it." But Gavin soon discovered the British offered their prisoners no care of any kind. Red-coated soldiers drove the men who could walk into a crowded hold on the prison ship and, with rough hands, tossed in after them the ones who couldn't. Gavin pressed back against the harsh treatment but managed to carry Alden until he fell to his knees on the floor of the hold. Alden dropped out of his arms, landing in a mound of putrid waste, blood, and vomit from other helpless prisoners.

Gathering his friend up again, Gavin found a spot against the hull for himself and Alden, roughly shoving other prisoners out of his way until he could pull his friend up to sit with his back propped against Gavin's own chest. The wails of the men filled the hold until night came and those who could fell asleep.

Twice a day, guards lowered buckets of watery, maggot-filled mush into the hold, and Gavin had to leave Alden to fight others for a share. Gavin then dropped the foul-tasting gruel into Alden's mouth and rubbed his throat until he swallowed. He chased off rats trying to nibble on Alden's rancid flesh, but the fleas and ticks were too numerous to do much more about than just endure.

Alden's stump festered and turned black, yet Alden never complained of the pain or the choking reek of his rotting left arm. He simply sucked in his breath, closed his eyes, and whispered his wife's name, Tansy, over and over.

Chapter Two

Boredom in the hold of the prison ship took the lives and the minds of more men than the food, but Gavin and Alden never seemed to notice. Gavin asked Alden the same questions every day, and it distracted both of them from the death and disease around them.

"Remember the first thing you ever said to me?" asked Gavin every morning when the sunlight peeked through the cracks in the hull.

"Why did...General Washington ride his horse into...camp?" murmured Alden in gasping breaths.

"You got me into so much trouble. We were supposed to be at attention." Gavin rubbed the shoulders of his friend, hardly recognizable as the once sturdy light-haired man he had known, the man with strong arms and legs whose head only came as high as Gavin's nose.

"That...was the...whole point. Come on, take a guess. Why...did General Washington...ride his horse into camp?"

"I don't know."

After a gagging cough, Alden said, "Because the horse was too heavy to carry!"

Gavin's chortling laugh that first day in camp had brought the inspecting captain's nose right next to his. "Something funny, soldier?"

"No, sir!" answered Gavin as he blinked the

captain's spittle out of his eyes.

Following a grueling appraisal of his lack of fitness as a soldier, and how the British would serve their afternoon tea in his head, came the order for Gavin to march for four hours around the outskirts of the camp carrying a full pack. "That will give you plenty of time to think about how many men you get killed when you don't maintain company silence!" Surprisingly, Alden escaped all censure as the officers moved on down the line to the next poor soul.

"Why do you think the captain didn't yell at you?" asked Gavin.

"He'd heard the joke before." Alden may have been smaller in size than most of the men in the company, but he had a personality that touched the sky, and nothing had changed despite his desperate situation. Alden shifted in Gavin's arms and closed his eyes. "Hey, Gavin, what does King George call us?"

"I don't know, what?"

"Revolting!" Choking on his own laugh, Alden rolled to the side and spit out bloody phlegm. After his coughing eased, Alden asked, "Have you got your pack with you?"

Lying to his friend as he did every day, Gavin said, "I do. It's loaded down with my musket, my cartridge box, a musket tool, and a supply of flints. I've even got my bayonet and what's left of the food rations. The canteen is yours though, the one you're going to give to Tansy."

Digging his fingers through his own filthy hair, Gavin tugged the loose strands of his buckskin-colored locks out of his eyes. He groomed Alden the same way. What he wouldn't give for a bucket of water and a bar of soap.

Gavin reached inside his sock, feeling for Alden's pocket watch where he'd hidden it right before the Bloody-Backs searched him. No one wanted to touch his mud-and-blood-covered shoes or the open sores on his feet, so Alden's precious watch stayed safe.

"Want to see something beautiful?" said Gavin. He held out his empty hand and repeated, "Want to see something beautiful?"

The watch cover held a portrait of the most beautiful woman Gavin had ever seen. The woman's round, misty blue eyes sparkled against her milky skin and her lightly rosy cheeks as her hair caressed her shoulders and surrounded her face like the petals of a flower in full bloom. It shone the most exquisite shade of sunshine gold. She didn't smile in the miniature, but Gavin imagined her smile to be demure the first time she met someone and then become animated and beaming every time she laughed.

Alden reached out for the watch that wasn't there and said in a faltering voice, "Her name is Tansy, and she's my wife. She gave this to me on our wedding night."

Gavin had no words. *The most beautiful woman I've ever seen is named after a flower. Perfect.*

"All the Johansen kids look alike," said Alden, retelling the story as if it were new. "Their folks are Swedish immigrants and own a dairy farm in New Jersey in a place called Swedesboro in Gloucester County. Daisy's the oldest, and Tansy's the youngest. They're all named after flowers or trees. Don't know why. Her brothers are Birch, Ash, and Linden. Tansy's the only one with freckles. What do you think?"

"She's really pretty. How'd you meet her? How did a joker like you get so lucky?"

Alden smiled weakly, exposing straight teeth except for one tooth on the top row that turned outward ever so slightly. "I met her before the war when her brother, Ash, brought her with him from New Jersey to a dairy-cow auction about ten miles from our dairy farm in Pennsylvania. Ash was looking to buy a bull to strengthen his herd."

"Tansy's interested in dairy cows?"

"No, not much, but she wanted to see what somewhere besides New Jersey looked like. Ash didn't want to bring her, but, well, Tansy can be a pest, and once she sets her mind on something there's no stopping her. She kept at him until he agreed."

"Persistent, is she?"

"You never met one as stubborn as Tansy."

"She sounds strong-willed and independent. Good qualities in a woman, I think." Gavin wrapped his arms tighter around his friend in an effort to protect him from the wind blowing in through the cracks in the hull and from the cold river water seeping in at the bottom of the ship.

"Don't tell her I said this," said Alden, "but she's the youngest and kind of spoiled, if you want to know the truth, so she's used to getting her way."

Gavin interrupted as he always did. "But she's never mean about it."

"No, never mean. It took me a while to convince her to let me court her, but…" Waving his hand in the air like a magician finishing a trick, he said, "As you know I'm more charming than any living man."

"You still are." Even these rotting remains stayed

more charismatic than anyone Gavin had ever met.

Alden sucked in a jagged breath. "So I made three trips to New Jersey to see her on the pretext of getting her brother's advice on dairy farming, and I was grateful when she agreed to let me court her. We wrote letters and, believe it or not, I'm just as charming on paper as I am in person. I saw her a few more times before she let me kiss her, and that kiss made it all worth it."

Gavin, imitating Alden's magician-waving gesture, said, "I know, I know, you're as good a kisser in person as you are on paper."

Alden lifted his eyes. "She laughed at all my jokes, even the ones she'd heard before, and she..." He coughed from deep in his chest. "She was the first one to say 'I love you.' I'd never been so happy...until now, of course."

"Of course," said Gavin, even as his heart sunk at their dire situation.

"We talked about getting married, me more than her, and one Sunday we did."

"You're a lucky man. I've known some women, but none I wanted to marry. Tell me about her."

For the rest of the afternoon, Alden regaled Gavin with tales of Tansy he had heard so many times before, but each day it took longer for the fading Alden to tell the story. "She's only a fair cook, but she's a terrific seamstress. You ought to see what she can stitch together. Made her own wedding dress." He reached over to tug on his shirt sleeve, but it had been torn off in the battle. "See how strong these stitches are? But the best work she does is in the bedroom." He winked. "If you know what I mean."

Gavin nodded. Every day it crossed his mind that he, too, might like to know what Tansy was like in the bedroom.

As if on cue, Alden gasped, "I'm...tired. Your turn. Where are you from?" Alden closed his eyes and slept, only to jerk awake if Gavin stopped talking.

"I wasn't raised like you," began Gavin. "I'm an only child, not like you and your seven older brothers and sisters. My parents worked as servants in a big rich house, so I learned to stay out of sight and follow the rules. I spent a lot of my time with the house handyman. I even helped him design the plans for an outbuilding for the owner's art collection, the ones he didn't hang on the walls in the house. That's what I liked the best, figuring out where the windows and doors and the paintings should go. It was a good place to live until my mother died when I was seventeen."

Alden stirred. The first time Alden heard this story, he said, "I'm sorry," but now he couldn't respond.

"She was in a lot of pain, so in some ways it was a good thing, but with having to hire a new lady's maid whose husband would be the butler, the Duncans didn't have a place for me and my father. It's not that they were cruel, just no need to keep two sets of servants. We ended up with my uncle in Virginia.

"He gave us a small room in the barn in exchange for working me like an indentured farm hand without pay. After I left for the army, he kept my father on because he was good with the horses. If this war is ever over, I'm going back there and building a small house somewhere so he can live without having to work so hard." Gavin let his voice fade away, and Alden slept.

Eight desperate days later, Alden didn't ask his

riddles or talk about Tansy anymore.

Clutching Gavin's stained shirt with his right hand, Alden said in a gasping, brittle voice, "Fight back. Fight back and send the British home. Promise me you'll fight back."

"I will," said Gavin. "I promise you I will. Here, take this sip of water."

He put Alden's canteen to his lips, but Alden shook his head. In a voice as cold as the death that awaited him, he said, "Promise me, promise me you'll live through everything to come, whatever it takes, whatever!" He clutched Gavin's hand as he spit out black blood. "Swear it! I can die in peace knowing you'll never give up hope to win the fight!"

"I swear it! I'll never give up hope!"

After Alden closed his eyes and lived no more, Gavin whispered, "Death, I have seen you too often and too soon. You stole Alden's life, but I won't let you win. You won't win. I will do whatever it takes for as long as it takes!" He sobbed.

The next day Gavin wailed as the guards ripped Alden's lifeless body out of his arms and carried it to a scow anchored beside the ship. Gavin had watched too many dead prisoners thrown overboard into the river, leading to official complaints that the bodies created a health hazard to Americans and British alike. The more humanitarian approach now was to load the dead men onto a barge to dump them far out in the ocean, never to be seen again.

With Alden's body gone, Gavin concentrated all his thoughts on keeping his promise to the best friend he'd ever known, but first he had to get off this ship alive. His choices from now on would be ones he never thought he would have to make.

****

Two weeks later

The rocking chair creaked when a sleeping Tansy felt her sister's hand on her shoulder.

"Children, go outside to play for a while. Lizzie, take Gideon and Mercy out to the backyard. Charles, you go, too."

Twelve-year-old Lizzie said, "Yes, ma'am," but Charles, three years older, said, "I don't want to play with the babies. I'm reading."

Nate, standing beside his wife, snapped at his son. "Your mother told you to go outside, and that's what you'll do."

Charles jumped to his feet and followed his two younger sisters and his brother outside.

"What's wrong?" asked Tansy.

Taking her sister's hand, Daisy said softly, "Nate has news. The casualty lists have been posted."

Chapter Three

The day after Alden Carter's death, October 24, 1777

Gavin shivered without Alden's body next to his. He pulled his knees up to his chest, trying to warm himself. He had to get out of this hellhole to keep his promise to Alden.

Later that day, he held out Alden's watch, with Tansy's portrait removed, to a guard in a stained jacket with dusty boots standing near the hold. "Nice watch," said the soldier. "Worth a pretty penny. What do you want for it?"

"What can you offer?"

The redcoat closed one eye. "How about a piece of fish from the guard's mess? Maybe a walk around the deck once a day?"

"Sounds fair to me," said Gavin.

The next morning, Gavin approached the same man and whispered, "How do you like the watch?"

The Brit punched him hard in the face, sending him tumbling down the steps back into the hold. "If I see that pretty mug of yours near me again, I'll shoot you! Understand?"

Wiping the blood off his mouth, Gavin nodded.

Failure! I have nothing left to offer…except myself.

Two days later with a new group of guards hovering over the open hatch, Gavin moved close to a standoffish one with a look about him of someone overly qualified to be watching prisoners die.

"My friend died, and it's all that braggart General Washington's doing," said Gavin to no one in particular but within earshot.

"You think so?" answered the dark-haired man, never moving his eyes away from the other prisoners in the hold.

"I know so," answered Gavin. "We were fed a pack of lies about fighting for our freedom. We already had freedom plus the benefit of England's protection, and the king is entitled to his share, isn't he?"

"I'd say he is, but you bumpkins don't know anything about civilized society. No breeding I say."

Gavin bit the inside of his cheek. Retorts to these insults wouldn't get him out of this pesthole. "I've never been to England, mind you, but I've got ancestors from across the pond. Scottish on my father's side. I have a long-ago grandfather who was a laird of an estate in the southern Highlands, and a long-ago grandmother who escaped from pirates. The family name's Cullane. Know any Cullanes?"

"Nary a one. Get back below."

Gavin didn't move. "I know how to set a proper tea, even fold the napkins just right."

Today he swallowed a laugh. Gavin had been raised alongside the American version of nobility at a wealthy house in the city. He knew the proper manners and what to expect of people from the upper crust. To think that the impractical skills he'd learned as a servant might be of good use in this desperate place.

The guard curled his lip. "Bloody lot of good that does you here."

"No one here appreciates that I've seen what good British training can do. Your soldiers are orderly and clean." He pointed down into the ship's hold. "If the Brits were the ones in here, there'd be organization. Those born of higher station would be in charge, no questions asked. No anarchy, not every man for himself, live or die. The colonies would be different if we learned the proper order of things from the English, very different."

The soldier started to walk away.

"I'm Gavin Cullane," Gavin called after him. "What's your name?"

"Peter Wright," he said without looking back.

Every day Gavin found a way to stand near the hatch and talk with Wright, weaving a convincing story of admiration for the proper British culture and his hatred for the Continental Army. After three days, Wright handed him an extra slice of bread. The following day, Wright said, "Want to walk on the deck for a bit?" Gavin nodded and reached up his arm for Wright to lift him out. "It will have to be quick while the rest of the guards are below for the morning meal."

"If I had a strong needle and some string," said Gavin as he sucked in the fresh air, "I could mend that tear in the sleeve of your jacket. For a soldier to move up in the ranks, he needs to look like he deserves it, and a shoddy appearance isn't the way."

"We'll see," answered Wright, but later that afternoon the guard tossed his jacket, some thread, and a bent sewing needle at Gavin's feet. "Do what you can," he said, turning his back.

Gavin, having watched his mother sew dresses often enough, tacked the torn sleeve as best he could.

When he finished, Wright put the jacket on and walked away without a word. The next day he handed Gavin a small flask of fresh water, which Gavin drank down.

"Traitor!" shouted one of the prisoners as he grabbed Gavin's leg and dragged him back into the hold. The water flask clattered to the floor. Then came a swift kick to Gavin's ribs. As Gavin doubled over, another of the prisoners grabbed him by the hair, lifted his head, and sent a fist into his cheek. Gavin fell to the floor, but found a way to slide under the stairs and crouch in the farthest corner, making himself as small a target as possible. Curses and spit rained in on him, along with urine, but only a few fists hit their mark. When the food buckets lowered, the men forgot about Gavin and fought each other for the gruel.

Gavin didn't eat that night, but he stayed true to his promise. Whatever came, he'd fight back and never give up hope.

Four more days passed before Peter Wright called him up from the hold. "The captain wants to speak to you."

Gavin thought, *Now what? Is this my way off the ship or my way into the briny deep?*

The captain, a tall, middle-aged man, hobbled to his chair on a cane supporting a shriveled leg, still draining from a battle wound. The British army had generously allowed him to continue serving in the humiliating post as prison ship captain.

"Prisoner, you have survived this long, so there must be some mettle to you. Most prisoners rarely make it more than even a week, and Wright here thinks you have come to your senses about the foolishness of this revolution. He thinks you're willing to do something to end this war. Is he right?"

Gavin gave a curt nod. "Yes, sir!"

"Wright says you have lived in New York City all your life."

"Yes, sir."

"We are looking for someone to go among the colonists in New York and report back to us about what they are thinking and doing. Maintaining authority in the city requires that General Howe and his staff know exactly what is going on behind their backs. At the very least, we want to win over the remaining patriots or find out what they are doing so we can put a stop to it."

"I understand, sir."

"You've been through the mill, Cullane, but you need a clear head about the job we are offering you. No wavering. Are you prepared for your colonist friends and family to hate you?"

Gavin waited for a proper amount of time to indicate his reservations about turning traitor before saying, "Yes, sir. I know it won't be easy, but I'm convinced which cause is right."

That afternoon the captain bestowed the official title of colonial liaison on Gavin with the purpose of easing the burden of occupation on the citizens, but with the true intention of finding out what the rebel organizations were really doing. His job included gaining the trust of the people by doing favors for them. They would be small boons, like finding a piece of meat or a bag of flour or even a spool of thread not allowed during rationing, just enough to convince the people of the British willingness to be generous. Gavin's job was to first gain their confidence and then discover their secrets.

The captain introduced Gavin to a skinny forty-year-old officer with a sharp nose and buck teeth named Simon Duffy who would be his handler on shore. Colonel Duffy stood next to the ship captain's desk with arms akimbo and his nose in the air and bragged about being highly educated. However, Gavin, who'd been raised among the truly high-born, recognized the signs of his low beginnings by the frequent rubbing of his sweaty hands down his sleeves.

"What do you know about spying?" Duffy asked him in a scratchy, raw voice.

"I can learn," said Gavin.

"I am certain you can, but we British have been doing it for a thousand years, so you cannot outsmart us." Duffy sniffed. "You will be kept on a very short leash. One mistake and you will be back on the prison ship if you're lucky, and if not so lucky, shot or hanged. If you accept these conditions, you'll be a spy for the British, a turncoat, a traitor to your country."

"I'll do whatever I have to do."

A few hours later Peter Wright escorted Gavin and Simon Duffy on shore to a small cottage behind one of the mansions the British had commandeered. To rid himself of fleas and lice, Gavin shaved his entire body, including the hair on his head and his eyebrows, and then endured a toxic bath of coal tar, followed by apple vinegar. Nothing could be done for the sores, scabs, or rat bites on his legs and arms, now raw from the loathsome bath. Duffy ordered all his clothes burned and that included Tansy's portrait tucked into his tattered sock, not that he'd ever forget her face. In a vain attempt to fill in the cavernous look to Gavin's face and ribs caused by starvation, Duffy fed him better than he had been since he joined the army, but the lingering effects of poor food would forever change his face and the texture of his hair.

****

"You made a good choice with this one," said Duffy to the captain a few days later. "He is clever enough to be useful, but not so clever as to avoid the trap we will set for him. At the right time, this Gavin Cullane will deliver to us something that will change the course of this war in our favor, after which we will hang him. If, on the other hand, he does nothing of value for us, we will still hang him." Duffy gave a throaty laugh.

Chapter Four

Nine months later, end of July 1778

Daisy Hemstead opened the upper half of the split door at the front of the house, and a cold tremor ran through her. A muggy breeze, typical of summer in the city, floated in but did little to warm her.

Three British soldiers with dour faces stood on her front stoop in their red uniforms with their long rifles at their sides, along with one official-looking man in a white shirt, brown waistcoat, and buckled shoes. There in the middle of all of them, held tightly by his arms, was her oldest son, sixteen-year-old Charles.

Daisy muttered an expression she'd heard from her father to indicate trouble ahead, "And there be snakes."

"May I help you?" she asked, ignoring the emotions bubbling inside her. "Charles," she said, dragging out his name.

The man in the brown waistcoat clasped a red leather folder in one hand and carried a brown cloth mail pouch with a long strap slung over his shoulder. "Is this lad yours?" he asked.

What a ridiculous question! How could they not see the family resemblance? Same round face, same thick honey-blond hair, and both pairs of wide-set blue eyes flickering with alarm.

"Yes, he's mine," she answered.

Turning away from the door, she spoke sharply to three younger children seated at the table. "Lizzie, Mercy, Gideon, take the baby upstairs and stay there."

The oldest girl, Lizzie, picked up her eight-month-old cousin, Young Alden, and ushered her siblings out of the room and up the stairs. Reluctant to go, five-year-old Mercy dragged her feet as Lizzie tugged on her sister's arm. "Mama said to go!"

Before her younger son disappeared up the stairs, Daisy added, "Gideon, go get your father from the shop." Gideon, a bushy-haired ten-year-old, dashed out the side door to his father's print shop in the back of the house.

Daisy recognized the three soldiers on the step. They often patrolled in this neighborhood. One, a droopy-faced older man named Watson, was a career soldier, too incompetent for any other line of work. The man next to him tugged at his uniform as if his jacket didn't quite fit, but she didn't know his name. The third one standing in the back, called Wiley and not much older than Charles, wore a look of utter panic. Daisy smelled the nervous sweat coming off him.

She'd never seen the man in the brown waistcoat before, but he didn't have that pasty-faced Brit look about him. His hazel eyes set over a square jaw sparked with intelligence and curiosity, not like the other soldiers whose main goal was to get out of these blasted colonies and go home to Merry Old England. Spiky clumps of hair the color of maple syrup stuck out haphazardly from under his tricorne hat, and his cheeks sank into his face as if he'd been ill. Most alarming to Daisy, however, was his lack of British accent. Obviously, he'd been born in the Colonies, turned traitor when the king's men arrived, and now lined his pockets with plunder, goods, and money confiscated from colonists.

"Mistress Hemstead, we will be coming inside to talk to you about your son," said the man. "Step aside."

Daisy obeyed his order to step back but did not unlatch the lower half of the door. Moving up, the man banged his knee against the wood, making a cracking sound strong enough to rattle the nearby window. She bit her lip and tried not to smile at her subtle rebellion, but his expression never changed as he reached over the ledge to open the door.

The usually airy single front room closed in around her when the soldiers and Charles followed the man inside. Her heart raced, and she wanted to run up the staircase to the safety of the bedrooms in the converted attic or to her husband's print shop in the back of the house that could only be reached from the outside yard. But she would never leave her oldest child for even a minute to fend for himself with these men.

"Mistress, this boy has committed a crime that under different circumstances would earn him a lengthy stay in a British prison ship," announced the man in the brown waistcoat.

Daisy's breath quickened. The thought of her son in such a place terrified her. The British housed prisoners in ships anchored in Wallabout Bay along the East River, making their terrible conditions visible to those on shore to encourage the colonists to give up the fight.

She spoke evenly. "He's just a boy. What could the charge possibly be?"

Waving the mail pouch, the man said, "Stealing

British correspondence."

"Charles," she said again, very slowly.

The boy cringed, ducked his head, and rocked back and forth on his feet, making a floorboard creak every time he moved to the left.

"Stand still," Daisy snapped. The boy obeyed.

"He stole the mail pouch right off the carrier's shoulder."

Charles raised his head. "I did not! He laid it on the table at the café outside the brewery, and I just picked it up. No one was watching it."

The young soldier, Wiley, obviously the bungling pouch-carrier, said, "I was watching it! It was hot, and I needed to unbutton my jacket. I was watching it!" Drops of moisture on his forehead dripped into his eyes.

The older soldier, Watson, snarled at him, "We will deal with your negligence later. Mistress, the only reason your boy is not in the stockade is that I called out to stop, and he did. He raised his hands and handed the pouch back. We caught him red-handed." Charles and Wiley swallowed hard at his imperious tone.

At that moment, Nathaniel Hemstead burst through the side door, furiously wiping the printing ink from his hands with a rag. Before the invasion, Nate had made a good living printing novels, playing cards, and sheet music out of a printing shop on the south end of Wall Street until the British targeted it because he also printed pamphlets, essays, and posters to keep the local citizens informed of activities throughout the colonies.

The one pamphlet causing the British the most alarm was Thomas Paine's "Common Sense." Paine made a solid case for freedom in terms the everyday man could understand, but it, and similar publications, disappeared when writers became afraid of getting jailed or their property confiscated if they expressed their opinions. Even Paine had to publish anonymously in Philadelphia.

Daisy breathed a sigh of relief at the sight of her husband, her beloved Nate, a tall, lean man with a muscular build and a formidable personality. A thick strand of his coal-black hair came loose from the ribbon holding it in a queue at his neck, and he brushed it back, leaving a light ink smear on his cheek.

"What's going on here?" demanded Nate. "You already confiscated all but one of my presses, and I moved it here with your permission. I won't be able to feed my family with the little printing business left here in the city if you take it. You have no right."

"We have every right to enter your home, Mr. Hemstead," said the taller soldier. "You should consider yourself lucky that we have not boarded some of our troops with you. Four or five of our soldiers could bunk in this room."

Slowly, Tansy Carter stood up from the rocking chair nestled in the kitchen side corner. "We're sorry for the inconvenience," she said as she placed the skirt she'd been hemming on the back of the chair. She did sewing work for some of the neighbors and for a local dress shop to help provide for her keep, not that Daisy or Nathaniel ever asked it of her, but her pride required it.

Stepping into the center of the room, she said, "Your barracks must be crowded. Perhaps the king will see to your comfort and allow you to return home soon."

Daisy turned her head and winked at her younger

sister, a paler, more slightly built version of Daisy, with flaxen-blonde hair, smoky blue eyes, and a smattering of freckles across her nose.

The man in the brown vest looked down at his shoes for a moment before clearing his throat and looking up at Tansy. "I doubt the king will leave the city unprotected, but one may hope for a speedy end to the fighting." While continuing to look steadily at her, he said, "My name is Gavin Cullane, and I am the colonial liaison, charged with establishing a peaceful co-existence between the king's army and the colonial residents. This boy stole a British mail pouch."

Nate's eyes blazed at his oldest son, but his voice remained even. "I am sorry that my son broke one of the many lessons we have instilled in our children since the war broke out. He has been taught not to run the streets freely and to be polite, reserved, and above all cooperative with any of the king's men or soldiers."

"Those are important lessons, Mr. Hemstead, especially now that Charles is old enough to be conscripted into the British army."

Charles swallowed hard again.

"Is the British army so short of men, they need young colonial boys?" said Tansy. "That fact does not instill confidence in the occupying force."

Cullane took a step toward her. "Are you certain you want to test my patience in this situation?"

As Nate moved between them, Gavin shifted his gaze from Tansy to the man standing in front of him. Gavin's honey-brown eyes glowered into Nate's dark ones.

"I see that you have your mail pouch back," said Nate, "so no damage has been done. We're very sorry that you had to take time out of your day to bring this matter to our attention. We'll see that this kind of thing doesn't happen again. Right, son?"

"Yes, sir," said Charles, swallowing the lump in his throat.

Not taking his eyes off Nate, Cullane said, "I want to know why he did such a foolish thing."

"Well?" demanded Nate, shifting his eyes toward his son.

"It was a joke, sir," answered Charles. He struggled to speak and breathe at the same time. "I…I saw the pouch and I thought…well, it might be fun to see how far I could get with it."

"A joke!" said Nate and Cullane in unison, turning their heads to look at the boy.

Charles spoke in a rush, his voice shaking. "I'm very sorry, sir. I must have had a screw loose. I meant no harm. I swear I've learned my lesson. Never again, I promise!"

Wiley whispered to Watson, "What is 'a screw loose?' "

"It is one of those expressions they use over here. It means something like 'being a numpty.' "

"Oh."

Reaching around Cullane, Nate grasped his son by the neck, shaking him nearly off his feet as his ink-stained fingers left black prints on Charles's neck. "I'll see that nothing like this ever happens again, not by my son!"

Several long moments of tense silence followed before Cullane cleared his throat again and said in an imperious voice, "See that it doesn't." With a quick sweep of his hand, he indicated the three soldiers were to leave.

"Lad," said Watson, taking Charles by the arm, "come with us."

"The boy stays," said Cullane.

Watson's face turned a frustrated red. "I will have to report this."

"Do as you will. The boy stays."

Utter relief crossed everyone's faces as Gavin moved around Charles toward the door.

Tansy said in a low voice, "Mr. Cullane, if you will be so kind as to accept my thanks for leniency and my apology. My remarks were uncalled for."

"Apology accepted. War sets everyone on both sides on edge."

Just before ducking his head under the door sill and stepping out on the first step, he turned back. "Good day, Mistress and Mister Hemstead." Tipping his tricorne, exposing his bedraggled hair, he added, "Good day, Mistress Carter." And he was gone.

Daisy closed and latched both halves of the door. "Gideon, get to the window."

Chapter Five

Gideon, sitting on the sill of the window frame, looked like he was playing with his bilbo catcher, a wooden cup with a ball attached by a string, while in reality his eyes scanned the street, watching for redcoats or other people who didn't belong in the neighborhood. He wished he could still carry his slingshot in his waistband, but when the British declared it a weapon, he exchanged it for his bilbo.

So many things besides carrying a slingshot had changed since the British had taken over the city. The Hemsteads missed gathering on the Commons with neighbors and friends in the evenings to share news and watch the children play. Now people stayed indoors to avoid being arrested for holding a public meeting. No one could talk freely about their comings or goings with anyone, and they had to always keep their eyes on the alert for trouble in the form of redcoats and their guns.

Daisy and Nate had assigned each child a specific job to keep the family safe. Gideon served as the lookout no matter where they were. Lizzie, in the event of trouble, gathered the younger children and hid with them in the attic, which Daisy had stocked with foodstuffs, water, and blankets. If any soldier put a hand on five-year-old Mercy, she was to cry and say she was sick, and she didn't stop her tears until everyone came safely home. As the "actress" in the family, little Mercy had pulled this off several times already. Charles often ran errands for his father with instructions to go straight there and back. Today he hadn't learned the lesson well enough.

Now the family waited silently for Gideon to give them the "all clear."

A baby's whimper broke the silence. "I'll get the girls," said Tansy.

"We're here," said Lizzie from the bottom step of the stairs. Mercy clung to her skirt while Lizzie held the baby in her arms. "He was a real good baby until just now."

"I was good, too," squeaked Mercy.

"They're gone," said Gideon.

Tansy, taking her son from her niece, sat down in the rocking chair, pulled down the top of her blouse, and let him nurse. "He'll be quiet now."

"Well, I won't!" said Nate, standing menacingly over his oldest son. "Explain yourself!"

Charles's neck turned red as he gulped in air. "I saw the pouch lying there on the table at the café. The soldier wasn't even looking at it, so I grabbed it. I thought it might have something important in it."

"Important enough to risk your family's safety?" roared his father.

"But look what I have. I took them from the pouch before they caught me." Charles opened his shirt and pulled out a fistful of papers.

Nate snatched the correspondence out of his son's hand and riffled through the seven pieces. "And once Cullane realizes these papers are missing, he'll be back. For you!" Tossing the papers on the floor, he shouted, "And the rest of us. How did I get such a foolish son?"

Nate paced while Daisy scooped up the letters.

"I'm sorry! I...wasn't thinking," stuttered Charles.

"Well, I'll give you something to think about!" growled Nate. Grabbing Charles by the neck again, he started to lead him out the side door.

"Wait," said Daisy. "Don't punish him until I get back. There's only one thing I want him thinking about while I'm gone." She stepped very close to Charles. "I want him to know that his mother is willing to risk her life for her impetuous son. A son who violated our trust, but whose mother will do anything to rescue him. You think about that while I'm gone."

"Where are you going?" demanded Nate.

"I'm going to scatter this mail on the streets, so it looks like it fell out of the pouch before a foolish, reckless boy stole it. Charles, you think about whether I'll be able to come home to you."

"Ma, I'm sorry," said Charles, his eyes filling with tears. Seeing his agony, Daisy pulled him to her and hugged him close.

"I'll go with you," interrupted Tansy. "The baby and I could use some fresh air."

"It's too dangerous," said Daisy.

"It'll be less suspicious if I'm with you. I can be the eyes in the back of your head, and even the British will hesitate to arrest a woman with a baby." Daisy frowned, but Tansy added, "You can't dissuade me."

Briefly closing her eyes, Daisy recalled how her younger sister had been persistent and stubborn ever since she learned to talk.

Nate wrapped his arms around his wife, and she inhaled his familiar smell of printer's ink and lye soap.

"We've been married long enough for me to know

I can't dissuade you either," he said, "but remember this. If you don't return, I'll most likely kill your firstborn, so his life is in your hands."

Daisy's lips turned into a smile. Stretching up, she kissed his chin where the whiskers of his thick black beard tickled her lips. "I've listened to you bluster for the last seventeen years, and it hasn't changed a thing. I love you."

"I love you better."

"Better than what?"

"Better than everything."

"I'll be back," she whispered. Their kiss lingered.

Tansy tied a long, thick gingham scarf around her shoulder and across her hip like a sling, and nestled the baby inside. "We're ready."

So as to not wrinkle the papers, Daisy placed the purloined letters carefully underneath the baby. "Are you certain you want to do this? Charles is my son. He's mine to save."

Charles hung his head again.

"My Alden died for freedom in the Colonies," said Tansy. "He followed General George Washington into the gates of Hell in every battle, and I'll carry on for him. Lead the way, sister."

The baby smiled and gurgled his encouragement.

Once out in the street, Daisy's stomach clenched at the unaccustomed stillness of the city. "I can't stand that the streets are so empty," she said. "You might be used to the quiet of the country, but I loved the constant energy. Before the war, this city was growing, new homes and businesses every day, but now that's all gone. Pretty soon we won't be able to buy even the most basic supplies. Nate's having a hard time finding ink."

Tansy rubbed her shoulder against Daisy's. "It'll be over soon. The war can't last forever."

"I pray you're right."

About two blocks to the west of their Frankfort Street house, Daisy and Tansy approached the café on Ferry Street where Charles had lifted the pouch. Walking past it, they sat down on the low stone wall around a raised flower bed full of colorful blooming asters and mums. The house belonged to Myrtle Mason who had won prizes for her flowers at the annual city-wide fair held in the Commons every year. Daisy doubted there'd be a contest anytime soon. The British didn't like crowds.

"Isn't the sun lovely today?" said Daisy, gazing behind her. Through a stiff smile, she said, "Check for people watching from the windows."

Tansy adjusted Young Alden's diaper and pulled out two of the letters. "I see no one. Do you?"

Daisy shook her head and leaned closer to the baby to shield Tansy's movement as she placed the letters between the branches of two flowering bushes. The sisters sat there for a few minutes, and after making certain again that no one watched, they started across the street. Pausing as a wagon rolled in front of them, Daisy dropped another letter into a puddle and let the wagon wheel roll over it.

They dropped two more missives into a pile of cut firewood, and the last two found their way under the edge of the wooden step of a butcher shop that closed at noon after selling their limited delivery of meat. All the while Tansy and Daisy talked and tickled Young Alden.

Once relieved of their letters, they finally

appreciated the beauty of the day. People waved to them while sweeping their porches and front walks. Open windows on nearly every house let in fresh air in hopes that the breeze might cool the New York summer heat.

The two women were within a block of the Hemstead house when Lydia Packard, a long-time friend of Daisy's, waved to them from her upstairs window. "Hello, ladies!" she called. "Please, come in and have a cup of tea. I managed to find a bit last week at a dear price, and I've been cleaning all day. I need a rest."

"It'll give me a chance to nurse Alden while we sip tea," said Tansy.

"It's been a long time since I've had a conversation with anyone in the neighborhood," said Daisy to Lydia. "The patrolling soldiers are always suspicious of anyone talking to someone."

Tansy, after a few sips of long-denied tea, asked, "Have either of you ever been away from your husbands for long periods of time? Not just a few weeks, but for a year or more? Did you ever forget what he looked like?"

Lydia put her cup down and looked directly at Tansy. "My first husband died of cholera, and I was widowed for over four years before I married Eli, so I know what you're talking about. Maybe it will help if you tell us about Alden now."

Closing her eyes, Tansy envisioned the image of the man she had married. "He was quite handsome in a mischievous sort of way, medium height, shorter than Nate by several inches, but his quick wit always made me laugh. We only courted for about six months, and most of it by letter, but I fell in love with his charm and his doggedness to make me his." She paused. "But every day his face seems to fade, not from my heart, but from my memory."

Lydia patted Tansy's hand. "We understand, and it's all right."

An hour later, Daisy and Tansy headed home.

"Do you think Charles has had enough time to think about what he did?" asked Tansy.

"I'm certain he has," answered Daisy. "I just hope Nate has calmed down. He said he wouldn't kill Charles until I got home, but he made no promises after that. I must admit that this has been a delightful outing. I'm so glad you came with me. It reminds me of when we were children, and we'd go down to the creek and wade in the water and make little boats with the leaves and spend time just us."

"I remember," said Tansy. "It's been a wonderful afternoon."

As they turned the corner toward the house, they stopped walking.

On the front stoop stood the man in the brown waistcoat and buckled shoes with his hand raised to knock.

"And there be snakes," whispered Daisy.

Chapter Six

"Ladies," said Gavin Cullane, tipping his hat as soon as he saw Daisy and Tansy approaching the house. "It seems I have arrived at just the right moment of your return. I have news."

He had a wide, bright smile despite the "hungry" look to his jaw and cheeks, and he spoke intelligently and carried himself with authority. Tansy might have wondered where he came from or where he might be going in this world, but he threatened her nephew, and all she wanted was to get rid of him as quickly and completely as she would a rat in the flour bin.

Daisy spoke. "Your first visit was so pleasant. I'm certain this one will be as well."

The man scowled and cleared his throat.

"Won't you come in?" Daisy opened the door and stepped inside to a sight that made her feet freeze in place. Her mouth went dry.

On the table for all to see sat an eighth letter from the pouch with its wax seal broken open. A death warrant for her son!

Tansy made the terrifying discovery at the same time, but she moved into action. Bumping her transfixed sister hard enough to push her forward, Tansy darted around Daisy to the table where she set down the sleeping Young Alden. Untying the sling, she spread it out, covering the letter. "Lizzie, will you, please, take Alden and put him in his cradle?"

Lizzie did so while Tansy casually gathered up the sling, crossed the room to the rocking chair in the corner, and sat down with the blue gingham cloth clutched tightly in her arms. Only a ceramic pitcher of fresh water remained on the table now.

Gavin Cullane waited patiently on the front step for the women to get out of his way, but once inside the alarmed looks on everyone's faces, especially Charles's, alerted him to something amiss. "Have I come at a bad time?"

Nate moved to his wife's side and laced his arm around her waist as she sank into his grasp. "Absolutely not," said Nate in a deliberate voice. "What do you want?"

"I wanted you to know that it seems a mistake was made."

"Meaning?" Nate said it more like an accusation than a question.

"Meaning that the courier was far more negligent than first suspected. The pouch your son stole turned out to be empty. Clearly the correspondence had already fallen out and scattered along the street with the wind. We recovered the papers in various locations near the café."

Daisy's legs weakened. Nate's grip tightened to keep her from collapsing to the floor. "So, this entire fiasco was over an empty mail pouch? I assume we won't be receiving an apology."

Cullane's expression stiffened. His lips pinched and his eyebrows furrowed. "I am not here with an apology. I have no regret or remorse for my actions. You need to understand that the fact remains your son stole property belonging to the king's men. Empty or not, it's still a theft. I can arrest him in place of that apology, if you wish."

With a quick gasp Daisy regained her voice. "That won't be necessary, Mr. Cullane. You have your mail, and we have our son with a promise that he won't be so foolish again. Will that satisfy you?"

Cullane's face remained dark and guarded. "It will satisfy me, but my superiors may want to investigate further. It has come to their attention that the Continental Army is receiving secret information about British activities in this part of the city. General Howe views these security breaches as treason, so you understand why we acted as we did in your son's case."

Daisy paled.

Nate raised his eyebrows. "Do you suspect us of being spies?"

"Everyone is suspect, Mr. Hemstead. Everyone."

At that moment, the fire cracked a spark, and all in the room jumped, all except Gavin Cullane whose eyes moved from person to person watching their reactions.

"Will that be all?" asked Nate.

"Something on a totally different matter. Mistress Carter, may I speak to you about your late husband? If the subject is not too painful?"

"Is that necessary?" asked Nate. "She's been through enough."

"I understand that you are protective of her, Mr. Hemstead, but this is of a personal nature."

Tansy clutched the sling closer. "It's all right, Nathaniel. What is it, Mr. Cullane?"

Gavin's entire aspect transformed. His authoritative demeanor turned friendly and casual. He moved slower, spoke softer, and his shoulders slumped ever so slightly as a small smile crossed his face along with a slow intake of breath.

"I knew Alden Carter for over a year," said Gavin. "We became great friends. His sense of humor kept us laughing through a lot of desperate situations. He and I fought beside each other in a number of battles, and I was with him at the Battle of Saratoga. He showed me the small portrait of you pasted into his pocket watch, and that's how I knew your name the first time I came to this house."

Her heart raced. "I've had no news of him other than the posting of his name on the list of the dead that Nate tore off the wall of the British Customs House. Do you have his watch?"

"No, ma'am, I do not."

Her voice rose in pitch, and she leaned forward. "Were you with him when he died? Did he suffer? Did he say anything?"

Nervously fingering his hat, Cullane said, "I came to offer you comfort, not more pain, but no, mistress, I'm sorry to say that he didn't say anything." Then he lied again. "The cannon fire killed him instantly. We were standing right next to each other. He'd just handed me his canteen, so I could have a drink." He cleared his throat. "I'll never understand why he died, and I lived. I want to extend my condolences. He was a good man."

A wounded look sputtered across Tansy's face. "Did he get my letter? Did he know I was with child?"

"No, ma'am, he didn't. We hadn't gotten mail in a long time. I'm sure he would have been very excited if he had known."

A runaway tear slipped down Tansy's cheek. "He

41

sneaked away from camp three times and made his way home. Said he didn't have time to get a pass, and no one cared anyway. Men deserted and never came back almost every day."

"I know. I had to cover for him sometimes."

"The war changed him, made him angry and rough and selfish about every little thing. Did the war change you?"

"The war changes everyone in some way."

"But you said you were friends."

"We were good friends."

"Then I have to ask"—her tone hardened like ice on the pond—"how can you fight next to a man on one side of a war, and then come into this house as his enemy and threaten his family?"

All of Cullane's softness vanished. "Everyone makes choices. Whether those choices are right or wrong will be determined when this war is over, and a victor has been decided."

"Once an enemy, always an enemy, no matter what the outcome."

Cullane cleared his throat again. "I've been appointed colonial liaison to bring some level of cooperation and understanding to both sides, and it should count for something that I convinced the soldiers to bring the boy home instead of taking him to prison." He put his hat back on, covering his scruffy hair.

A crushing silence fell over the room.

"We are grateful," Tansy eventually said, "that you brought Charles home. We thank you."

With a curt nod of his head, Cullane turned toward the door but stopped to put his hand on the shoulder of the boy trembling next to the table. "Can I depend on you not to take such an unwise risk again, lad?"

Charles nodded. "What will happen to Wiley?"

"He'll be flogged for his negligence. It's a harsh lesson, but one that is necessary during wartime. Every decision has its consequences, and mistakes can be very costly. Remember that."

Tansy stood up, still grasping the cloth sling with its hidden letter. "If this matter is considered finished with us, can it not be considered finished with the young soldier? We would appreciate any influence you might have."

"Alden always said you had a kind heart for others, but I have no say in military actions." Abruptly turning on his heel, he moved out and down the steps but stopped and turned back to face the family. "I would burn that letter as soon as possible." Then he was gone.

Daisy closed the door, but no one spoke until Gideon said from the window, "He's cleared the block."

"He knows," said Daisy, her voice taut and edged with panic.

"He must have seen the letter at the same time you and I did," said Tansy as she unfolded the sling and laid the paper on the table. "He did tell us to burn it. He could have done far worse."

"He's a traitor, the worst kind of enemy," said Nate in a voice as sharp as nails. "Just because he knew Alden doesn't make him a friend to us. He fights for the English against us. The soldiers who took over the city are only doing what their duty calls for, but Cullane chose to betray his countrymen. Can't you see no matter what he does, he is dangerous?"

Daisy walked close to her oldest son. "He may

have done us a favor by not arresting you, Charles, but believe me, he will want some sort of repayment from us for that. He's not to be trusted."

"I'm sorry!" pleaded Charles.

"Everyone sit at the table," ordered Nate. "We have to talk."

"I don't think the children need to hear this," said Daisy.

Placing both palms on the table and leaning against them, Nate said, "I think they do, even Mercy. It's important that they understand what's at stake. Like it or not we're involved in a revolution." Looking directly at his oldest son, he added, "It is especially important that Charles know what we risk."

A blush rushed into Charles's cheeks as he swung his legs over the back of the bench and moved to lean with his shoulder against the wall beside the fireplace. After raking his fingers through his hair, he stuffed his hands into his pockets and stared at the floor.

"Listen carefully," said Nate. "We've talked about the way our lives have changed since the British took over, but we haven't said much about the reasons why. We're fighting for our freedom, but the King of England thinks that we shouldn't have anything to say about what happens to us. We're an ocean away, but he still wants to control us."

"That doesn't sound fair," said Gideon.

"You think everything's not fair if it's not what you want," grumbled Charles.

"Shut your mouth."

"That's enough," said Nate. "The king charges us taxes on sugar, tea, and one that affects this family the most is a stamp tax. Every time I print anything, I have to buy a stamp for every piece of paper. It makes whatever I print cost more, and I get nothing in return, and I don't have the freedom to print what I want, no one does."

Mercy scrunched up her face. "That makes me as mad as a wet hen!"

"One of the worst things is the British have no respect for us as citizens. They enforce martial law which denies everyone a fair trial. That means we can't defend ourselves, even if we're innocent. Charles, if you had been arrested, you would be in prison, and we might never see you again."

"How many times do I have to say I'm sorry?" His voice cracked as he pushed back the tears.

"Sorry wouldn't help you in prison or make this war any easier on us."

"This war killed Uncle Alden, didn't it?" asked Lizzie.

Tansy who had been slowly rocking in the chair in the corner stood up and came over to the table, putting her hands gently on Lizzie's shoulders.

"Yes, Lizzie. This war killed Alden."

Nate said, "Not everyone can pick up a gun and go to the fighting, so we fight in a different way, with words."

Charles righted himself. "We all know what you do. You send secret messages. They're meant for General Washington, and I know where you put them so someone else can pass them on. There's a loose stone in the wall in the park."

"Charles!" Daisy exclaimed.

"You think we don't see what you do. We're all old enough to hear the truth. Well, maybe not Mercy."

"I am, too!" protested Mercy. "I'm older enough!"

Nate sighed. "Yes, you're right, Charles. Some of what I print are coded messages about what I've seen here in the city. It's things like how many troops General Howe has, where they are staying, how many boats are in the harbor, things like that. Then other people decide if General Washington needs that information, and they get the message to him. My hope is that what I do might help end the war sooner, but it's dangerous."

Daisy wrapped her arms around Mercy's waist and pulled her daughter onto her lap. "That's why none of you can do anything to bring the redcoats or Mr. Cullane back to our door again."

"If the British found out," said Nate, "I could go to jail or worse."

"What's worse?" asked Mercy.

Nate hesitated. "I could be hanged."

"No!" cried all the children at once.

"You're scaring them," said Daisy.

"They need to be scared. They have to understand that consequences are serious. This isn't a game."

After an overwrought moment, Nate held up the eighth letter from the pouch. "I'll be sending a coded message about what's in this letter. General Howe and his staff are having a party in three weeks at John and Matilda Duncan's house. I'll encode the date, time, place, and anything else of importance from the invitation into a flyer and send it on. Maybe someone can attend who will learn something of value for the patriots. I've memorized it, so Daisy, will you burn it completely, please?"

Daisy took the letter from him and tossed it into the

cooking fire, watching it until the flames consumed it.

"So, bringing that invitation was a good thing," said Charles, jutting out his chin, desperately wanting to repair his pride.

"We'll see if you still think that after I get done with you," said Nate. "Out to the shed, young man." Charles dragged his feet every step of the way to the side door and out, closing it softly behind him.

"He didn't mean any harm, Nate," said Daisy. "Do you have to punish him?"

Letting out his breath in a long sigh, he said, "I won't punish him, but he might wish I had after I get done talking to him." Nate followed his oldest son out the side door.

Chapter Seven

Gavin needed time to clear his head. Everything had changed now that Tansy Carter existed in real life! From the first time he saw the portrait in the watch, her face had filled his mind and his heart every night and then again at every sunrise. Imagining what it would be like to hold her in his arms had kept him going through the horror of war.

But the moment she stood up today and spoke to him, his heart started racing and the lump in his throat almost choked him like a piece of dry bread. The fantasy who crowded his every waking thought had come alive right before him, in an actual living, breathing woman, and she was far more beautiful in real life. Real life! He could hardly believe it! He had hoped, and even prayed, that the portrait was a lie, that in reality she had the voice of a crow and a disgusting mole with hair growing out of it on her chin, but it wasn't true. Her curves from her breasts to her hips were the epitome of womanhood. Her cheekbones balanced perfectly under round azure eyes with surprisingly long dark eyelashes for someone so blonde. The portrait didn't do her justice, and his body reacted accordingly, just as it had so many nights on the road between battles. He claimed he had to relieve himself when he left his bedroll and walked into the privacy of the woods to ease the throbbing in his groin from his dreams of another man's wife.

He remembered how his father often teased him that he would never fall in love because Gavin prided himself on being a thinker, a man who thought once and then thought again before making his decisions. But, by God, he had fallen in love with a portrait, a fantasy, who had come to life as the living, breathing Tansy Carter. Nothing short of a miracle!

Alden had told him she was a woman of courage and character, and today she'd proved it with her challenging remarks about the British. He'd seen that strength again when she risked arrest to toss the letters along the street. She was strong in body and spirit, just the kind of woman he'd been looking for all his life, but he could never approach her. Disguised as her enemy, daydreaming was all he had left, at least until he'd fulfilled his promise to Alden. That had to be his first obligation.

As colonial liaison, he'd learned a great deal that could be of value to General Washington, but so far he hadn't found a way to send the information on to people who could use it. His was a double-edged sword, a patriot pretending to be a loyalist, a man despised on both sides while pretending to be a man true to both sides. Someone could easily slit his throat, and everyone would be glad for it.

He stepped onto the stone path through a small park a short distance away from the Hemstead house. He'd been coming here about once a week for the last three months to review the lies he'd already told Simon Duffy and to prepare himself for the ones he would tell in the coming week.

How he wished Alden were here. Glib, clever

remarks came easily to Alden, and he could spin a tale faster than he could snap his fingers, but for Gavin, fabrications, at least the believable ones, were much harder to come by. He saw himself as a planner, an organizer, all of which took time, thought, and preparation. Going by the seat of his pants wasn't in his nature, but he needed to adapt if he was going to survive as the supposed colonial liaison.

This park, a familiar place for him, sat only a block away from the splendid house where he'd grown up as the son of the butler and maid, and he had memories of playing here with the other neighborhood servants' children. Today Gavin watched other children running through the park and saw couples strolling on the path, talking quietly to each other and even discreetly holding hands. Despite the war, none of them seemed to have a care in the world, and he wondered if they'd ever faced choices like he had, choices that changed their lives and their entire character.

A jagged stone wall ran along two sides of the park, separating the grassy area from the road. Along the south wall sat a stone bench where people often passed a leisurely hour or two in the sun, so Gavin settled there to sort out his thoughts.

What have I gotten myself into? I went back to the Hemstead house to be sure that my eyes hadn't deceived me. She was real! What should I do about the beautiful Tansy Carter?

He took a deep breath and let his eyes wander until he noticed a loose stone in the wall behind him. Reaching through the slats of the bench, he jiggled the stone and, surprisingly, it fell into his hand. Peering down into the now open space, he saw a small package of brown butcher paper tucked inside. After pulling it out, he opened it and read an advertisement for chicken and lamb sold at a butcher shop whose name Gavin didn't recognize. He wondered why anyone would hide an advertisement for a shop that wasn't even in the neighborhood.

Then it occurred to him. A coded message!

If George Washington had any hopes of reclaiming New York, he had to have some sort of communication network between himself and the captured city. Surely Washington had learned his lesson after the arrest and execution of Nathan Hale within three days of dispatching him, so whatever spy system he used now had to be complicated and very secret.

Could this loose stone and advertisement be part of such a plan? Could I use it to get messages to the patriots?

Gavin replaced the advertisement in the opening, shoved the stone back into place, and crossed the park to wait and watch from behind a growth of bushes.

An hour later a woman with two young children sat down on the bench to read while her young ones played with a hoop and a ball in the grass. Gavin grew tired of watching her, but just as he was about to leave, she reached behind the bench and took out the loose stone and the butcher paper and slipped the paper into her book. She replaced the stone so quickly that he might have missed it had he not been looking for it. Yes, this was a spy message drop, a place to leave and to pick up information, and this woman could pass it on to another drop location, and the message would eventually find its way to General Washington.

Now what could he do with this new information?

In his head he made a list of things that he already knew, and then a list of questions he needed answers to.

First, the things he knew. Nathaniel Hemstead, as a printer, could make such an advertisement, and his shop was very near to this park, making it likely that he had printed this butcher shop message and left it behind the stone.

Now questions he needed answers to. Why would Charles take such a risk to steal the mail pouch unless he knew those letters could be useful? Why hadn't Nathaniel burned the eighth letter unless he wanted to use the information?

This new knowledge put Tansy and her entire family in deadly danger. His promise to Alden to do whatever it took now became leaps and bounds more difficult. Still, he would fulfill his promise even if he had to confess it all and then dangle from a noose himself. And every day it became more likely that he would!

****

"I can do this," said Tansy two days later just as Nate finished printing the coded flyer about the British party at the Duncan house. "Cullane will be watching for you, Nate. He could follow you, and it's too dangerous for you or Charles or even Daisy to take this to the drop in the wall at the park, but he won't think anything about me and the baby out for a walk."

Nate shook his head. "I'm the one who got us into this, and now that Cullane is suspicious, the risk is too great. Besides, this is the last time we can use that drop. The flyer says as much, and I should be the one to put it in place. I can't let anyone else take the chance."

A flash of temper lit Tansy's eyes. "Nathaniel,

you're as stubborn as a mule! All of us are already at risk of losing you. I can do the drop. I'll be careful."

"But Tansy, you've never done it before."

"I'll make certain that no one is watching. I'll sit there all day if I have to. No one notices a woman with a baby in a park, but they'd surely see a man who acts like a stubborn mule."

"Hee-haw!" snorted Mercy, kicking up her heels. "Papa is a mule! Hee-haw!"

Nate, putting his hands on his hips, glared at his youngest daughter, but she kept dancing around, kicking her feet out and braying until he burst out laughing. She did do a pretty good imitation of a donkey.

"All right, Tansy, against my better judgement you can make the drop, but I'll be a block away at Johnson's Tailor Shop getting fitted for a new pair of breeches. I won't be able to see you, but I can hear you, so if anything, and I mean if anything, even looks wrong, scream and I'll be there. With or without my breeches!"

"Maybe after I make the drop, I can talk to Mr. Johnson about sewing some suits for him. He's asked me so many times if I could help him out, and it would bring in extra money."

"Tansy! This is more important than any work for Mr. Johnson. Pay attention to what I am saying."

After Nate reviewed his instructions on how to leave the message for the third time and again for the fourth time, he handed Tansy the flyer folded and wrapped in the protective brown paper, which she tucked under Young Alden who was once again secure in her gingham sling. She left the house, knowing Nate would leave for the tailor shop ten minutes later.

Tansy inhaled deeply. The air felt warm, but thick gray clouds filled the sky and a brisk breeze smelled like rain. She loved that rainy aroma with its heavy odor of sweet flowers combined with the scent of moss by the edge of a creek. The coming rain would also bring a sound she loved, one that had often lulled her to sleep in the house she and Alden shared, the rain falling on the roof.

Her mind floated back to those days before the war, before they were married, when she and Alden spent time together on his visits to New Jersey. He never told her she was too young or too little or called her "the baby." He made her feel capable and strong, and she loved everything about this man from Pennsylvania, now gone from her forever.

She arrived at the park to find it empty. *Other people must have smelled the rain and stayed indoors.* That meant no one would be around to see her.

She hurried to the bench, sat down, and unwrapped Young Alden from the sling, laying him on the seat. While keeping her hand on his belly, he kicked and cooed as she scanned the wall for the loose stone. There it was. Tickling her son with her left hand, she reached through the slats in the bench with her right hand and pulled out the stone.

Then things got complicated.

Young Alden cooed at being free of the sling, and he wiggled and squirmed until he started to roll off the bench. As Tansy moved to catch him, she dropped the stone, and the wind caught the brown paper package, blowing it up and away along the gravel path. Scooping her son into her arms, she stood to chase the message, but Young Alden, sensing she might soon trap him in the sling again, arched his back and pushed his hands against her shoulders, throwing his head up and out.

While struggling to get her son under control, she started down the walk, but her legs tangled in the dangling gingham scarf, and her knees locked. In a panic, she barely managed to lurch back to the bench to sit down and sort out the baby, the scarf, and the rock at her feet.

While she watched the brown paper message blow away, she hugged Alden close and hummed a song to calm him. He continued wiggling and kicking until she tossed the scarf over her shoulder, opened her blouse, and moved Young Alden into position to do his favorite thing, eat. When he was quiet and enjoying his dinner, she'd go after the message. Until then she picked up the rock and laid it on the bench.

"Are you looking for this?" asked someone standing nearby.

Gavin held out the folded brown paper.

Blinking wildly, she said, "And there be snakes."

"Let me help you," said Gavin, sitting down beside her.

The blood drained from her face as he tucked the message into his vest pocket and replaced the stone in the wall.

She couldn't speak, only gulp in air furiously. After recovering her voice, she stammered. "You...have to let me...take the baby home first. Please, the baby. You can't arrest me until I take the baby home to Daisy and Nate. You can't take my baby to jail!"

"Take a deep breath," he said. "Let it out slowly.

There that's better. I'm not going to arrest you."

She gave him a questioning look. "Why not?"

"I came to warn you."

Her voice quivered. "Warn me? About what?"

Raising his left eyebrow, he said, "Don't play me for a fool, Tansy." He patted his vest pocket. "This message is not for everyone's eyes. If it's decoded, it will expose everything Nathaniel Hemstead wants to keep secret. I don't think you want to be exposed with him."

She shook her head desperately.

"Spying is a nasty business. What would Alden think if he knew that you delivered rebellious messages? Wouldn't he be ashamed?"

Tansy pulled her shoulders back. "How dare you mention my husband? He would not be ashamed. He would be proud I found a way to help our cause. What right do you, a traitor, have to mention Alden who gave his life for something he believed in? You called him your friend, but what would he think if he knew you'd been false to him all along?"

Gathering Young Alden and the gingham scarf in her arms, she stood. Gavin stood up beside her, putting his hand on her arm.

"You think I have betrayed my friend, but I want to protect you. Being associated with a spy is dangerous." He narrowed his eyes. "You must stop participating in Nathaniel Hemstead's activities. He can do it without you, and he can take the consequences without you. Think of your son."

She tugged the baby closer as the quavering in her voice vanished, replaced by deliberation. "If you intend to arrest me, then do it. If not, I'll be on my way with the fervent wish I never see you again."

She faced him when she said, "You have no intention of arresting me, do you? You've got everything you need to capture everyone on the spy chain now that you have the message, and you know where the drop is."

Shaking off his hand, she strode away. She'd taken only a few steps before he moved in front of her, stopping her escape.

The rain fell in large, gentle drops.

"Listen to me, Tansy," he said. "You have to understand the danger. I've been lenient with your family. I overlooked Charles's theft of the mail pouch. I ignored the careless way you and Daisy scattered the stolen mail on the street, and I ignored the letter on the table at the house. I can't keep ignoring such obvious seditious activity. If my superiors found out, I'd be the one in prison." His voice turned icy. "Along with the entire Hemstead family. The adults would be in one of the Sugar Houses now used as a prison, and the children would be out on the street."

She looked away, but he kept talking. "Your carelessness today puts everyone in peril. If my British superior, Simon Duffy, found out, I might have no choice but to arrest all the Hemsteads."

Her hands shook.

"Don't allow Nathaniel to manipulate you into this business. Protect your child. Repay my kindness by persuading Nathaniel to stop. Do it for Alden. Do it for me, Tansy."

She gripped the baby even closer. "You? Do it for you? I hear your warnings, Gavin Cullane, but don't for one moment think I will ever be in your debt."

"You don't owe me anything," he said, placing his hands on her arms so she wouldn't lose her hold on the baby. "The debt is mine to pay. I owe Alden my life."

Her now teary blue eyes scanned his face. "If you think you owe Alden, why are you threatening me?"

The rain came harder, making sharp pings as it splattered on the gravel walk.

"I don't want you to be afraid," he said as he gently lifted a loose curl of her hair and tucked it behind her ear, letting his thumb linger on her cheek. "The portrait didn't show how beautiful your freckles are, like tiny angel kisses."

She stayed silent.

"Don't be afraid, please, not afraid." His voice carried an ache in it. "I wish I could tell you everything." *But I can't risk it. I can only risk myself.* "I just want to convince you that all I care about is your safety. I'm not your enemy."

"Are you telling me that you're a patriot in disguise?"

He didn't answer.

"Well, it's a hell of a disguise. No one would ever guess. Don't touch me."

"Please, Tansy, we can work together."

"Never!"

"We want the same things, we do. I want you to be safe. I want the whole family to be safe."

Tears overflowed Tansy's eyes, and she pressed her forehead against his chest. Choking sobs left her throat as he stroked her hair.

Lifting her head as her tears covered her cheeks, she cried, "We'll never be safe! We'll never be safe. This is a war! No matter who fights, no matter whose side anyone is on, it will never be safe. Every minute I'm afraid. I can't ever draw a gentle breath, and you…and you…"

"What about me?"

She wiped her eyes on his sleeve. "You knew Alden. You're the only tie I have to him now, the link that he truly lived. You wanted to bring me comfort, but instead you brought me pain. Alden is lost to me! You are lost to me!"

"No, I'm not," said Gavin. "I'm here for you."

He hesitated, and without thinking of the consequences, he lowered his head and pressed his lips against hers. He had wanted to do this for so long. He softly touched her lips with his tongue, and then withdrew before continuing again to press his mouth to hers.

He pulled back. As their lips parted, a cool breeze wafted between them through the dampness. "You taste like sweet nectar."

Then, despite the squirming baby between them, she put her free hand on his chest. He prayed she would let him show her the truth of his feelings, but in that instant, she braced and wrenched her head back.

Her breath turned ragged. Raising her hand, she wiped the back of it across her lips before lifting her arm and slapping him hard on the face.

"I don't fear you as much as I hate you!" she said. "And Alden would hate you as well!"

He rubbed his throbbing cheek, but it wasn't the slap that wounded him. Her words cut through his belly like a bayonet on the battlefield. She hated him.

He'd let his daydreams cross over into a reality that didn't exist. She didn't know that in her soft blue eyes, he saw the woman he'd been waiting for all his life. She didn't know how deep his feelings ran for her or how strong his self-reproach was over Alden's death, and she couldn't fathom his guilt about the way he had chosen to keep his promise to him. All she knew was that he threatened the arrest of her family and then took liberties and kissed her. All his hope crumbled the moment she wiped his kiss off her lips and slapped him. What a fool he'd been!

Releasing her, he stepped aside and watched her run down the street away from the park and away from him.

The rain came down in heavy sheets as thunder rolled in the distance.

Chapter Eight

She ran.

Somehow she managed to keep a hold on Young Alden as she skidded across the wet stones and splashed through the mud and puddles toward the tailor shop.

What have I done? How had a simple message turned into such a disaster? I made so many mistakes today. I delivered the flyer into the hands of the enemy, and then I slapped him! Any leniency he might have shown to Nathaniel or Charles ended with that slap. Why couldn't I have held my temper long enough to walk away when he kissed me? But, no, I had to slap his face.

Self-reproach and shame swarmed inside her like bees in the hive.

Rain fell across her face as Young Alden howled, struggling to be free. She clutched him tighter.

Gavin's lips on hers had been gentle and tender like Alden's kisses had been when they first married, before the war changed him and his lovemaking became stormy and selfish. He promised it would be different when the war ended. Did she miss Alden's kisses so much that any man's would do?

Yes, Gavin was a most handsome man with broad shoulders and strong ropy muscles, despite the lingering gauntness to his face, but was his appeal merely physical? Or was it the authority he exuded at the house and again in the park? Did she admire his self-confidence? Alden's confidence manifested itself in boundless energy while Cullane's revealed as quiet, steady, and certain.

Was she drawn to his compassion when he spoke about his friendship with Alden? Or the way he fingered his hat like a bashful schoolboy when he first asked to speak to her? Was this man as tender as he was strong? How could she have allowed him to kiss her for even one second? She'd taken a chance on Alden, knowing him only six months before marrying him, but Gavin was her enemy! A traitor!

A wail left her throat. Nate could be arrested or hanged for what she did!

She rounded the corner and fell into Nate's arms as he stood on the small, covered porch of the tailor shop, her tears falling as hard as the rain.

"Tansy, what happened? Are you all right?" Nate asked as he guided her and the baby through the door and into the shop.

"I-I…" she sputtered. "He has it!"

"Who? What? Let me take the baby." Nate lifted his screaming nephew out of her arms, unwrapped him from the soggy gingham scarf, and laid him on a table covered with bolts of cloth. Nate lifted up several yards of brown wool on the top of the pile, covering Young Alden with it and patting him dry. "There, there, little one. Enough noise."

Marcus Johnson, the heavyset, balding tailor and owner of the shop, dashed over to the table, his belly bouncing with each of his labored breaths. "Not with my best piece!" he said.

"I'll pay for it," said Nate.

"It's not only the price of the cloth. It's what can be made with it where I make my profit."

Nate swaddled Young Alden, lifting him to his shoulder while still patting him on the back. "Never fear, Marcus. Get something for my sister-in-law to dry herself with." The little man scurried off to the back room and returned with a yard of huckaback, a strong linen used for towels, which he handed to Tansy who still struggled to get her sobbing under control.

"I'll put both pieces on your bill," said Johnson.

Nate nodded. "You know I'll pay when I can."

"I made a terrible mess of things," cried Tansy as she wrapped the huckaback around her shoulders and dried her hair with the edges. "Please, forgive me, Nate. I've made things so much worse!"

"What happened? Tell me everything."

Tansy waited until Mr. Johnson went back into the storeroom before recounting the disaster in the park, most of it in one long breath. "Cullane has the coded message. He knew where the rock went. He said he'd been easy on us, but he couldn't be anymore. Then he kissed me."

Nate straightened up to his full height, and cocking his head, he stretched out his words. "He what?"

"He took me by the arms and kissed me."

"That bastard! Doing a job as colonial liaison is one thing, but now he's gone too far."

"He didn't hurt me, Nate. It was a gentle kiss, but I made it worse." She faltered. "I slapped him."

"Well, good for you!"

"No, not good for me. He'll be after you even more now. He could have you arrested or have the house confiscated." Her tears started up again. "Nate, you're in danger. All of us are in terrible danger!"

"The rain's letting up. We'll talk more about this after we get home."

Nate, with Young Alden in one arm, put his other arm around Tansy still wrapped in the huckaback, and together they stepped outside to the small stone porch.

On the corner stood Gavin Cullane with rain dripping off the edges of his black tricorne hat.

Nate's eyebrows knit into a savage line, and his teeth clenched until a knot bulged on his jaw. He didn't speak. His threatening expression said it all.

Gavin put up his hands in a sign of surrender. "I wanted to make sure she got home all right."

Gavin turned and walked back the way he had come.

Chapter Nine

After three sleepless days and nights, and no visits from Gavin Cullane, or worse an arrest, Tansy held out the tiniest hope they had escaped the danger. Daisy told her any man who would follow her to the tailor shop to see if she was all right wouldn't turn in the coded message or arrest anyone. "His was a bluff," she said, but Tansy couldn't stop worrying.

Tansy said prayer after prayer that Gavin was done with them. "Please, let it be true!" she prayed. "Don't let him be waiting to gather enough evidence to convict the entire family. Please forgive me for bringing this danger home."

Late one afternoon, Nate said, "Follow me. Maybe I can reassure you."

"Look," he said. "No evidence against any of us still exists within the print shop. I've memorized many of the code's 763 number patterns that substitute for the words. I used to keep a textbook where certain page and line numbers translated into words, but when the British closed my downtown shop, I burned it. As for the lettered and numbered tiles used to print the coded message, they are all back in their original places for storage. Not a single sentence remains."

"But Gavin still holds the coded flyer, and that's all he needs for conviction."

"It's not enough," said Nate. "He doesn't really

know where it came from. He only knows you found it, and since we haven't heard from him, we're safe."

Tansy hated herself for being so careless.

She tried to put her guilt behind her by reliving memories of Alden during every quiet moment. She concentrated on how she felt in his arms, how his voice sounded, and how he made her laugh. But Alden had fallen away from her mind much faster than she ever thought he would. Images of their time together grew shadowy, and the details that made them special slid into oblivion.

On the sixth day after the fiasco in the park, a knock sounded on the door in the middle of the afternoon. Tansy sucked in a raspy gasp of air. *Was this the end of life as she knew it?*

Daisy leaned to look out the window. "It's all right. It's a woman."

Tansy, putting her hand to her fluttering heart, sighed with relief.

"No need to get Nate," said Daisy. "He's in the print shop working on an order of materials for King's College, the first paid work we've had in a while. Besides, it keeps him busy so he doesn't think about tracking down Gavin Cullane and beating him senseless."

Daisy opened the front door to a maid dressed in a faded flower-print blouse, a gray skirt covered with a white homespun apron, and a ruffled cap on her head.

The young girl curtsied. "Hello, ma'am. I'm sent by Miss Harriet whose parents are John and Matilda Duncan. Have you heard of the family, ma'am?"

Both Daisy and Tansy exchanged looks. They recognized the name "Duncan" as the hosts on the invitation Charles had stolen from the British mail pouch.

"Yes," answered Daisy, keeping her expression steady. "Everyone in New York has heard of the Duncans."

"Well, ma'am," continued the maid, "Miss Harriet needs a dress for the fancy dress ball they're having in a few days, and none of the seamstresses can please her. She would like Mistress Tansy Carter to make her a gown. Does Mistress Carter live here?"

Tansy came to stand in the doorway beside her sister. "I do quite a bit of sewing for people in the neighborhood, and occasionally for the local dress shop and tailor shop, but none of these people go to fancy dress balls, so how did Miss Harriet hear about me?"

The girl twisted the tie on her apron around her finger. "I don't rightly know, ma'am. All I know is that she wants a fancy gown that has to be the fanciest one at the party. She already tore up four gowns that she said she wouldn't wear to a dog fight."

Tansy giggled. "I've heard that dog fights are rather swanky events in New York City."

The girl didn't get the jest, so she kept on talking. "Miss Harriet says that she'll buy all the material and pay you fifty pounds British to stitch it up since it's so close to the party."

"Fifty pounds British? Are you sure that's the amount she said?"

"I am, ma'am. Fifty pounds British plus all the material you need. She says you're to buy it from the shop on Princess Street." She leaned in closer to whisper, "The shop doesn't rightly have a name because they run the blockade with European cloth and other things. The sign out front says it's the Second Church of England, but I been in there, and it ain't no church. Miss Harriet wants only the best in the city."

Tansy reached out her hand to the girl. "Won't you come in, so we can talk about this dress?"

"Wait a minute, Tansy," said Daisy, pressing her hip against the lower half of the door keeping it closed, and speaking in Tansy's ear. "If she's already torn up four dresses, you could end up doing a lot of work and not get paid. Besides, I want to know how she heard about you. We're on the other side of town from the la-dee-da Duncans."

"It doesn't matter how my name came up. I won't pass up the chance to earn fifty pounds. Besides, if Miss Duncan can afford fifty pounds for one dress, she has money to spare, and it would take me three years to earn that much."

"You did hear her say British pounds? Nate won't like you working for the British."

"Nate can think what he likes. That's a lot of money, and I intend to take the job. Once it's paid to me, it becomes my money to do with whatever I want. It'll be a way I can repay you for all you've done for me and Young Alden. Come in, young lady." She opened the door while gently pushing Daisy aside. "What's your name?"

"Naomi, ma'am," she said, keeping her eyes on the floor. "Thank you for doing this. Miss Harriet would be upset if you turned her down. Here are her measurements, and she even drew a picture of what she would like."

Without looking up, Naomi handed Tansy three pieces of paper. One was the lady's measurements.

Harriet appeared to be a slender well-proportioned woman about five feet six inches tall. On the second paper was a crudely drawn picture of the basics of a gown with a laced neckline, a fitted bodice, and long loose sleeves.

Daisy took the drawing from Tansy and studied it. "This could be something very beautiful, providing you choose the right fabrics. Expensive fabrics could cut into your profits."

"I don't think that will be a problem," said Tansy, waving the third piece of paper. "This is an unlimited cost voucher for the Second Church of England on Princess Street. I have some ideas already. We could go this afternoon and get what we need. Lizzie could watch the children."

"Miss Harriet wants a fitting in four days," said Naomi. "She doesn't want anyone to see her dress before the party, so she'll meet you at the shop at three p.m. on a day you choose. There's a room in back where she can try it on. Miss Harriet said if you agree, you should write your X on this paper." The girl held up a fourth small piece.

"My X? She assumes I can't read or write. Hand me that paper, Naomi. Is the ink pot full, Daisy?" She walked over to the small table against the wall at the back of the room. On the fourth piece of paper, she wrote with the quill in her precise script, *"I will be pleased to make you a gown. I will meet you at the shop on Friday at three p.m. for your first fitting. I look forward to working with you. Tansy Carter."*

"That's a lot of words, ma'am," said Naomi. "Are you sure they're spelled right?"

"I'm sure," answered Tansy. "Just give it to your

mistress. Oh, before you go, is Miss Harriet a pretty woman?"

"I don't know if I should say, ma'am."

"You can tell me. I won't tell Miss Harriet."

Naomi took a deep breath and let it out through her nose. "She thinks she's very pretty, but she's getting old, and she won't be pretty much longer. She's twenty-five, and she's worried that no man will marry her. That's why her gown has to be so special."

"I see," said Tansy.

"But I think the reason she's not married is she's too persnickety about everything. She only wants what she likes, and she doesn't like very much." Naomi made a face and pinched her voice to imitate her mistress. "His eyes are too close together. His voice is scratchy. He's too old. He's too young. He passes gas." She leaned in close and whispered, "And she don't mind telling them to their faces."

****

Tansy and Daisy met Miss Harriet four days later. Naomi had not exaggerated the beauty of her mistress with her rich auburn hair and the strands of sun-bleached blonde marbled through it. Her green eyes highlighted a face with a creamy complexion and prominent cheekbones.

Her temperament proved another matter.

"Is this all you have finished?" asked Harriet as she stood in front of the mirror with her hands on her hips admiring her figure.

"It took quite some time to smock the silk organza bodice, which you can see fits nicely over your corset. Here is the layered cream-colored satin skirt that goes over the white underskirt and your padded rumps that will accentuate your shape," answered Tansy.

"I can see all that."

"The skirt is lightweight and drapes beautifully, and now that I know it fits, I'll stitch this overskirt onto the bodice. There are still two more layers of satin to drape from the waist. I also have a fine, glittering gold lace to attach to the sleeves."

"I will admit your stitching is quite good, but the dress seems so plain. I will look like a virginal queen."

"A queen, yes, but the virginal is up to you."

Harriet gave Tansy a scalding look before Daisy, always the peacemaker, interrupted, "She hasn't put on the trim yet. Gold ribbon will ripple down both sides starting at your shoulders and flow to the hem, calling perfect attention to your bosom and to your slender waist. It'll also emphasize the fullness of the skirt. By putting a thinner ribbon just like it above the elbow on the sleeves, the effect will be stunning. No one will have a dress like it."

"I should hope not!" retorted Harriet. "That's what I'm paying you for. What about the back? The back of this gown must not be boring. You must make certain people notice me from all angles, front, back, and sides."

"A narrower cut of the same ribbon will also go down the back on both sides here," Tansy said as she ran her hands down the back of the dress. "It's designed to make people want to see the entire gown and the woman who wears it. No one will be able to hold a candle to you."

"Of course not! Now I expect to see the finished product in three days."

"Except for the hem," said Tansy.

"The finished dress on Tuesday," repeated Harriet. "I won't pay for anything less than a fully completed dress on Tuesday." She untied the unfinished skirt, stepped out of it, and tossed it on the floor. "Unfasten this top."

After scooping up the skirt, Tansy put her fingers to unhooking the fitted smocked blouse and sliding it off Harriet's shoulders. Once she had the entire gown safe from Harriet's clutches, she said, "The dress will be ready on Wednesday. You will send the full payment to my house. Once I have counted it, I will give the gown to your messenger. If you wish it hemmed, you will include an additional five pounds, and I will meet you here at three p.m. You will wear the slippers that you intend to wear on the night of the ball, and I will hem it on Wednesday."

"I won't agree to such ridiculous terms. It is my money. You work for me."

"You will pay cash on the barrelhead, or I will sell this gown to someone else who wants to look like a queen that night."

"You wouldn't dare!"

Tansy's expression said she would.

Each woman stuck out her chin and pursed her lips. If looks were daggers, bloody stab wounds would cover both of them. Neither spoke a word for several minutes.

Daisy held her breath as her eyes flitted between Tansy and Harriet. Who would win this battle of wills? This rich spoiled brat or her sister? If she were a betting woman, she'd put her money on her sister. Tansy may have been the youngest of the Johansen siblings, but she'd always held her own even against her biggest brother.

With her hands on her hips, Harriet finally broke the tension. "Wednesday my messenger will be at your door by ten o'clock in the morning. And you will meet me here to do the hemming at noon. Are my terms understood?"

"I understand," said Tansy. "I will meet you here at noon if my terms are met. Will they be?"

Harriet gave a curt nod before she slipped her shift over her head. "But you can be assured that you will never get another recommendation from me or my mother or from Gavin Cullane."

Tansy's eyes flew open wide. "Gavin Cullane?"

"Yes, he used to work for our family and has just returned to the city on official business. He said he had it on good authority that you were the best seamstress in New York City." As Harriet stomped out of the room, after gathering her cape and her shoes, she added over her shoulder, "But I assure you, I will tell everyone about your atrocious manners and your unprovoked demands. No one will hire you. I will make certain of it."

Daisy grabbed Tansy's wrist with a look of horror on her face. "Gavin Cullane? What would he know about your sewing? Why would he give your name to the Duncans?"

Tansy sucked in a hard breath. "Alden. Alden must have told him. He said they were friends, and they must have talked about their families. I'm sure Alden would have mentioned how I loved to sew. But why would Gavin give my name to the Duncans? Why?"

"You can bet Cullane wants something from us, and it's not a fancy ball gown!"

Chapter Ten

Days and nights of stitching left Tansy's fingers and wrists stiff and cramped, but on Wednesday morning at nine o'clock, she completed Harriet Duncan's gown except for the final hemming, and what a stunning sight it was!

Daisy, holding it up in front of her, twirled across the room making the skirt and sleeves drift out in soft, elegant circles and the ribbon sparkle in the light.

"This will certainly be the most talked about gown at the ball," said Daisy. Humming her own dance music, she added, "Well, what do you think? Do I look like a fairy princess?"

"Far more beautiful than any princess," said Lizzie with a loving smile. "I'm so glad Aunt Tansy let me do some of my own stitching in places that wouldn't show. Aunt Tansy, will you make me a dress like that when I get married?"

"I'd like nothing better than to make one even lovelier, but it's the girl who wears it who will be the loveliest of all. Daisy, help me wrap it in the dress paper I picked up at the fabric shop so that it's ready before the messenger comes."

"Do you think Harriet Duncan will actually pay you?" asked Daisy as she laid out the large roll of white paper while Tansy protectively placed the gown in the center of it.

"She had better. I don't care if I have to stand on the street corner and shout out, 'Dress for sale!' I'll get paid for this gown one way or the other. Maybe not fifty pounds, but I'll get paid."

"It still worries me that Gavin Cullane gave your name to the Duncans."

Kneeling on the floor, Tansy folded the paper over the gown and started to tie it with string. "I don't understand why Gavin did it either. I don't think I've had a moment's peace thinking about it even when I'm sewing." She folded her lips in, remembering how his kiss tingled. She couldn't tell her sister how her emotions about Gavin tumbled around inside her like churning butter.

"Here, hold this down while I cut the string. Maybe his friendship with Alden was the reason. Maybe he's trying to make up for arresting Charles or for threatening me in the park."

"You're a lot more forgiving than Nate or me. No matter how you look at it, Gavin's a turncoat, and I don't trust him."

Tansy tied the last string around the dress holding the paper in place to protect her hard work. "If Alden saw something worthy in him, maybe we should, too."

Jumping to her feet, Daisy stood over her sister with her hands on her hips. "Don't be a fool, Tansy! Papa always said, 'And there be snakes,' because a snake will always be a snake. A snake hisses before he bites to warn you to get out of his way. Cullane has hissed, so take the warning, or you'll get bit and so will the rest of us."

Guilt wrapped around Tansy's heart like the ribbon on the gown. "You're right. I won't look for something

75

that isn't there. Everyone will be safer if I listen to you and Nate."

Gathering up the dress bundle in her arms, she laid it on the table.

A few minutes before ten o'clock, a knock sounded on the side door.

"It's probably someone looking for the print shop," said Daisy. "I'll send them around back." But after peering through the small glass window in the door, she gasped. "No! It can't be! Not again!"

Scooting out from under her mother's arm, Mercy tugged on the doorknob. "Who is it, Mama?" The door opened wide.

There stood Gavin Cullane dressed in a dark blue jacket with gold buttons, matching blue breeches, white stockings, and buckled shoes. He doffed his black velvet tricorne hat with one edge pinned back by a round blue ruffled ribbon. A traditional white wig with a roll of curls above each ear covered his own hair. A picture of British elegance.

Daisy pulled Mercy back against her and moved aside as Tansy stepped in front of both of them. At the sight of Gavin, she straightened her back and looked at him like the threat she knew him to be.

Fixing her gaze, she said, "Don't you look like the whole nine yards today, Mr. Cullane?" Not waiting for an answer, she added, "What do you want?"

"This is not official business," he said.

"So, what is it?"

In a gesture she'd seen from him before, he fingered the edge of his hat. "I have come to apologize for my behavior that day in the park. Even though I was only looking out for your safety, it wasn't necessary for me to frighten you the way I did. I regret my words and my actions."

"Apology accepted. Good day." She started to close the door, but he put his hand against it to stop her. "Wait, I have something for you."

"What could that possibly be?"

"It's two things really." Reaching into the black leather pouch slung over his shoulder, he pulled out a small metal flask. "This is Alden's canteen. I want you to have it." He hesitated before saying, "He handed it to me just before he was killed." Gavin held it out, and she took it from him.

Turning the battered flask over in her hands, she stroked the letters *A. Carter* carved on one side in an awkward script.

She lifted it toward Daisy. "Look, Alden touched this. He drank from it. His lips surrounded the raised opening. This canteen is a part of him." Her breath caught in her throat, and tears threatened.

"Thank you. This means a great deal to me," she said to Gavin in a trembling voice. As she continued to rotate the flask, she heard a rattle. Shaking it hard, she put it close to her ear and listened to the sound of metal hitting metal. "What's in here?"

"It's his wedding ring," said Gavin. "He didn't want to lose it during a battle or have someone steal it off his finger. He figured if someone found the ring, they'd sell it, but if someone found the flask, they might return it to him. That ring meant a lot to him."

Rubbing the cool metal of the flask over her cheek, the memories she thought she had lost flooded back.

"How did he get it in there?" asked Lizzie, peeking around the door frame. "The opening's too small."

"He held the opening of the canteen to the fire until it softened. Then he pushed the ring through. After that he let it cool until he could screw the cap back on. Every time he took a drink it made that clinking sound, and sometimes in the dark of night, it was the only way I knew where he was."

"Oh, Alden," whispered Tansy as Daisy wrapped her arms around her sister, and Tansy put her head on Daisy's shoulder. "Only Alden would do that."

"Thank you, Mr. Cullane," said Daisy. "This means so much to my sister and to all of us. We'll treasure it." She started to close the door.

"Wait, there's something else," said Gavin. Reaching into his vest pocket, he took out an envelope. He held it out just as Nate burst out of the print shop door and charged at Gavin, giving him a hard push to his chest, sending him to the ground. "You bastard! How dare you put your hands on Tansy? Stand up and take your beating like a man!"

"Nate!" cried Daisy.

"I don't care what authority he thinks he has. This is a matter of decency!"

Sprawled in the dirt on his back, Gavin came up on his elbows, his temper boiling like water on the fire. Raised as a servant and subjected to his employers' whims, he could never speak up or defend himself. The prison ship forced the same powerlessness on him, but here, right now, he would not be treated like anybody's whipping boy. Nathaniel Hemstead had a shock coming if he thought Gavin would surrender his pride to him or to anyone else ever again!

"I was wrong to kiss her without her permission, but don't think you can beat me like a whimpering dog," said Gavin. "I'll fight back. Believe me, Nathaniel Hemstead, I will fight back." Gavin stood and braced himself for Nathaniel's attack. "I have apologized to her. I've owned up to my mistakes. If that's enough for Tansy, then that's enough for you."

"Only your bloodied face will be enough for me!" shouted Nate as he lunged toward Gavin, swinging his fist. Gavin ducked to the side.

Nate reached out, grabbed the strap on Gavin's pouch, and, swung him around, flinging him to the ground again. As he fell, Gavin kicked out his foot, snagging Nate under the knee. Nate landed face down in the dirt beside him.

"Stop it! Stop it!" cried Tansy. "I mean it! That's enough! I say this is over!"

Both men looked up and stared at her in bewilderment.

"Stay out of this, Tansy," said Nate. "Don't put yourself in the middle of this."

"It's between Nate and me," said Gavin. "I don't need your help. I can take care of myself."

That was just enough time for each of them to catch their breath and jump to their feet for round two.

Nate and Gavin circled each other like wolves after a kill until Gavin stepped up and landed a fist on Nate's face. Nate stumbled back, tasting blood, and then, charging like a bear, sent both his fists pounding into Gavin's stomach.

Gavin fell on his backside just as Tansy moved between the two men, ducking under Nate's still swinging arm. "Stop it! Stop it!"

Daisy sprang off the step, wrapping her arms around Nate's waist to hold him back.

Doubled over, Gavin winced and came to his feet while Nate used the back of his hand to wipe the blood dripping down his chin while he heaved in deep gulps of air.

"Are you done acting like six-year-olds?" Tansy demanded in a voice that woke up the sleeping Young Alden who started to wail. "Brawling won't solve anything!"

Charles, who had bounded out of the print shop behind his father, said, "But Aunt Tansy, he dishonored you."

"It's my honor, so that's for me to decide," said Tansy. "He has apologized and any further discussion, and I said 'discussion,' not brawling, is between Mr. Cullane and myself. I consider this matter settled, over and done with. Now both of you brush off the dirt and walk away. Both of you!"

Like repentant schoolboys, the men grumbled as they swept their hands over their dusty breeches.

"Off my property, Cullane!" ordered Nate.

"I can't, not yet," said Gavin. Searching the ground, he circled until he found the envelope, which he handed to Tansy. "This is for you from Harriet Duncan. She sent me to deliver it."

"You?"

"I've known the Duncans since I was a child. I called on them recently, and the topic of the ball they're hosting came up, as did Harriet's trouble finding a suitable gown. I assured her that you would keep your word about finishing the dress, and she sent me to pick it up. Although, I tell you if the situation were reversed, she'd deliver it to you in shreds. You bested her, Tansy, and she won't forget or forgive."

"Just as long as she pays," said Tansy, opening the envelope. Inside were British notes. Rifling her fingers through the bills, she counted them. "There's fifty-five pounds in here."

"Yes, and I'm to escort you to the Second Church of England for you to hem the dress."

"The Church of England?" said Nate.

Daisy said, "It's the name of the fabric shop. I've been there with Tansy. It can't go by its real name since they run the blockade." Facing Gavin, she asked, "Have I just betrayed the shop owners to the British colonial liaison?"

Gavin shook his head. "No, Mistress. The British ignore their activities for the sake of getting high-quality goods to the island. Few colonials can afford the price, but a lot of the wealthy loyalists can. Tansy, I have a carriage out front. If you'll get the dress, I'll escort you to the shop."

Nate's neck flared red again. "You have proven you can't be trusted. How can we be assured of Tansy's safety? How can we be sure you won't molest her or cart her off to some prison?"

"You have my word that today I act on my own behalf. This is not official business, but personal. I am acting as escort, on my gentleman's word of honor."

Before Nate could answer, Tansy clasped her hands in front of her. "I'm confident that I'll be safe." Nate opened his mouth to speak, but she added with a set to her jaw, "It's my decision."

"No, Tansy, as the man of this house, it's up to me. I have a duty in place of your husband to protect you. I may make mistakes in doing it, but do it, I will."

"I'll go with her," interrupted Charles, flipping his

shaggy blond hair out of his eyes. "I'll protect Aunt Tansy's honor. I won't let him out of my sight." He glared at Gavin with cold blue eyes. "I want to show you I can do a man's job."

Gavin kept his eyes on Tansy as he stuck out his hand toward Nate to shake. "If it will make you feel safer, Tansy, I will submit to Charles's supervision."

Her voice hinted at defiance, but she spoke with sincerity. "Nate, you have taken me in and shown me more kindness than I can expect. It hasn't been easy adding me and my son to your family, but with your permission, I'm confident that I will be safe with Charles as our chaperone. I must take the gown to be hemmed, and riding in a carriage would be faster and more comfortable than walking with it in my arms. With your consent, Nathaniel."

Nathaniel looked from face to face while ignoring Gavin's outstretched hand. "Charles will ride with you there and back and will stay with you while you're at this church. Charles, you are not to let Tansy out of your sight. Do you understand your responsibilities?"

The boy nodded and thrust his shoulders back.

"Do you understand your responsibilities, Cullane? Anything untoward, and I will hunt you down, and no one will stop me from separating your head from your shoulders." He reached out and took Gavin's hand, giving it a quick, stiff shake. "Am I clear on that?"

"Yes, sir, you are," said Gavin. Sweeping his hand out toward the street, he added, "If you will bring the gown, Tansy, we can be on our way."

A soldier dressed in his red and white uniform with tall black boots and a white feather in his cap sat on the carriage high seat. He held the reins of a black horse with white spots on his flank, but unlike typical carriage drivers, he didn't jump down to open the door for his passengers.

"This is Jackson, my driver," said Gavin as he opened the door to the carriage. Jackson gave a sullen nod. "We're going to the Second Church of England on Princess Street." Again, Jackson gave a nod without saying a word.

Inside the carriage, Charles and Tansy sat on one leather bench with the wrapped gown laid out between them, Tansy holding the skirt and Charles with the bodice on his lap. Gavin sat on the facing seat.

They rode for the first minutes in silence until Gavin said, "Of what I can see around the edges of the paper, this dress is very pretty. How long did it take you to sew it?"

"No need for small talk," said Charles.

"I'm sorry, Charles. I thought a little talk might make the trip more pleasurable for all of us."

"We're not here for your pleasure. Aunt Tansy has a job to do, and so do I."

Tansy said, "Charles, I appreciate you acting as my chaperone. You have taken on a man's job, and your father will be pleased. However, I'd like to respond to Mr. Cullane's question."

Charles scowled, crossed his arms, but kept his eyes on Gavin. "All right," he said, "Go ahead, talk."

"Thank you, Charles," said Gavin. "Mistress Tansy, how long did it take you to sew this lovely dress?"

"About seven days and nights from start to finish with the help of my sister. I hope Harriet Duncan likes it, but come to think of it, it doesn't matter." She chuckled. "She's already paid for it."

"That got her goat." Gavin laughed. "She can be rather, shall I say, uh, spoiled." He laughed again from deep in his throat. "I used to call her Miss Limburger behind her back, you know, after that smelly cheese."

Charles rolled his eyes. "I can hardly wait to meet her."

Both Tansy and Gavin smiled.

"She said you used to work for the family."

"My mother was Matilda Duncan's maid, and my father the family butler. I did whatever chores anybody wanted done. My mother died of a rotting flesh disease when I was seventeen, so my father and I were dismissed. We left to live in Virginia with my uncle before I joined the Continental Army. My father's still there."

Silence returned to the carriage until Tansy leaned forward and asked, "Why did you give my name to the Duncans?"

He shifted uncomfortably in his seat. "Alden told me you were a great seamstress, and I was trying to make up for my earlier ill-advised interactions with your family. Now that I'm the colonial liaison, I carry a little more influence with the Duncans than I did as a servant boy, and I thought you might forgive me if you could bring in extra money, and Nathaniel might stop putting all of you in—" Before he could finish, Tansy burst into loud coughing while jerking her head toward Charles.

This didn't fool the ever-alert Charles who uncrossed his arms and said, "Have my father stop what?"

Turning toward her nephew, Tansy put her finger

to her lips. "The chaperone is to sit quietly and watch, not join in. I am still the adult here."

Charles's shoulders slumped.

With her finger still at her lips, she glanced at Gavin, indicating their conversation was over.

They arrived at the Second Church of England twenty silent minutes later.

Gavin carried the gown inside with Tansy and Charles right behind him, and as they entered the back room, they found Harriet already there, tapping her foot and sticking out her chin.

"I said 'noon.' You're late," she snapped.

Gavin said, "We aren't late, Miss Harriet, and even if we were, I'm certain that you will be thrilled with the final look of the work." He laid the dress on the table, tore off the paper, and held up the gown. "This dress will complement you as much as you will complement it. Would you like to try it on?"

Her eyes flitted between Tansy, Gavin, and Charles before she spit out the words, "Of course I would." She skimmed her hand down the front of the dress with the same delight as a child licking icing off a cake. "Help me get into it. Not you, Gavin, her."

Shooing Gavin and Charles out of the room, Tansy waited until Harriet removed her shift before opening the skirt and attached bodice to let Harriet slip her head into it. After Tansy hooked the back and closed all the ties with delicate golden bows to hide each hook, Harriet cocked her head to gaze at her reflection in the mirror. "It does fit well. As a seamstress you have skill, despite being a most disagreeable person."

Struggling not to roll her eyes, Tansy said, "I'm glad you like it. Shall I let Gavin and Charles see it?"

Without waiting for an answer, she opened the curtain and motioned for them to come in.

"Exquisite," said Gavin in such a solicitous tone that Tansy almost laughed aloud.

"Ma'am, if I can put in my two cents," said Charles, "a man would have to be blind not to want to dance with you at your party."

A smile crossed Harriet's lips, the first true smile Tansy had seen, but it quickly disappeared. "Hem it. I'm wearing these gold slippers. I want everyone to see the toes whenever I stand or walk, but in the back, I want the skirt to skim the floor. It seems simple enough. I hope you can do that."

"Of course I can," said Tansy. *A rabid dog had a better disposition than this woman!* "Please, step on this stool. Gavin, will you help Miss Harriet up there?"

"It will be my pleasure," said Gavin. Taking Harriet's hand, he helped her onto the step and then up onto the round hemming platform. Squatting, Tansy began pinning the fabric.

"I am very pleased with the fit," said Tansy without looking up. "Others will be sure to notice it as well." Hesitating for a moment, she added, "Perhaps others will want similar work done for them."

"I'm certain they would," said Gavin before Harriet could protest. "It will reflect well on you that you chose such an excellent seamstress. Don't you agree, Miss Harriet?"

Harriet Duncan remained silent.

Once finished with the pinning, Tansy eased Harriet out of the gown, saying, "It will take me about an hour to stitch the hem in place."

"I can't wait that long," said Harriet in her usual

terse fashion. "I have better things to do than wait for you. Have Gavin deliver the finished gown to my house, and since I've already paid you, there will be no need for me to see you ever again." With a quick flip of her hair, she left the back room of the Second Church of England.

After waiting until Harriet Duncan was out of earshot, Gavin said, "A most dreadful woman, but despite her behavior, I can tell she thinks the dress is the best she's ever worn."

"A thank-you might have been nice."

"I doubt those words have ever crossed her lips in her entire life."

Sitting on the hemming stool, Tansy began making small even stitches along the hem of the full skirt, leaving the final touch of a flat golden bow tacked at the top of the smocked bodice until she finished. "This is the most expensive dress I've ever made, and even though my mother would scold me for being arrogant, I'm proud of my work. If I could make these kinds of gowns all the time, I'd be a very happy woman."

"So would the ladies who wore them," said Gavin. He winked. "I don't mind being arrogant for you."

Just then a burly man with a scraggly beard, dirty white breeches, a long-sleeved white shirt stained with sweat, a blue vest, and a red kerchief tied around his neck pulled open the curtains.

"Hey, lad," he said to Charles, "my name is Cyrus. I own this place. How about helping me unload the fabric from our latest shipment? Me and the other lads got it here from the ship, but they left, and I need help getting it inside. I'll pay you."

His eyes brightening, Charles asked, "How much?"

Cyrus reached in his pocket and pulled out a collection of coins. "I'll pay you this much," he said, holding out his hand. He held a generous assortment of coins, one of which shone gold.

"I'll take it," said the boy, scooping the coins out of the man's hand and stuffing them into his own pockets, but as he started to follow, he stopped and turned back. "Aunt Tansy, I can't leave you alone with him. I'm sorry, Cyrus, but I have responsibilities here. I'll give the money back."

Putting a hand on the boy's shoulder, Gavin said, "If I give you my word of honor as a man and a gentleman that I won't in any way insult or molest Mistress Tansy, will that be enough for you? Until you return, I swear I will be as kind to her as you would. What do you say?"

Charles glanced at Tansy with a pleading look on his face. "I would like to earn that money, and I don't think it's shirking my duty if I'm close by, do you, Aunt Tansy? Please?"

A grin flashed across her face. "I promise to scream at the top of my lungs if Mr. Cullane even so much as gives me a wayward glance. Go on now."

"I won't be far away. Don't worry, Aunt Tansy."

"I won't." But she did worry. It would be the first time she'd been alone with Gavin since the park. She wasn't worried about how he'd react, but about how she would.

Chapter Eleven

With Charles gone, Gavin had so much he wanted to say to Tansy, but he wondered if he had the courage or even the permission.

"May I help you with anything?" Gavin asked as Tansy carried the now-hemmed dress back over to the table to lay it out.

"Yes, take the iron off the stove. I don't want it too hot, just enough to heat the cloth while I press it with my hand. I don't dare touch the iron to the material or I'll scorch it."

As Tansy held the hot iron just above the inner side of the hem, she smoothed it with her other hand. At the same time, Gavin lifted the fullness of the skirt to keep it moving.

"You work with such steady and precise movements. Even though Harriet treated you so badly, you don't let it affect your work. I'm not sure I'd be so tolerant."

"My work stands for itself. I can't let her make me less than I am."

Tansy creased the hem, and Gavin thought while Harriet may be beautiful, her character was as empty as his plate after dinner. Tansy, on the other hand, had character well beyond her beauty. How he yearned to hold her close and make her his own, and while kissing her in the park had given him the tiniest hope, her slap had taken it away.

She noticed him watching her and gave him a quizzical look. "What are you looking at?" she asked.

"A beautiful woman doing work she obviously loves."

Her expression drifted into a scowl. "Please, don't talk to me like that. I'll have to call Charles back in here." She continued pressing the hem. "Nate will have both our heads, and Charles's, if he finds out that we're alone."

He looked up at the ceiling and tried to gather his resolve. She didn't know the truth about him, and she was oblivious to the emotions that were so real to him and had been for such a long time.

"I'm sorry. I want us to be friends," he said.

Setting the iron back on the stove, she stiffened her back. "We'll never be friends. While I'm grateful you didn't arrest Charles and that you gave my name to the Duncans, you and I are on opposite sides in a war. If we had met under different circumstances, things might…well, I don't know how things might have been, but I can't be friends with a man who would abandon his country to work for the enemy, and I can't be friends with a man who threatens my family. We can be civil, but nothing more than that."

All at once he wished he'd never met Alden Carter. He wished he'd been killed in the fighting. It would hurt less.

"I want to explain, but—" began Gavin.

"There's nothing to explain," she said. "All is very clear. A coin can either fall on one side or the other, not both. If I'm heads, then you're tails. It's always one side or the other." Turning her attention back to the dress, she added, "Her gown is finished. Let me wrap it, and you can deliver it to Harriet Duncan."

Gavin's heart fell. She could never know the truth, so he planted his feet and held his head high.

As Gavin carried the wrapped dress to the carriage, Tansy called for her nephew. "Charles, it's time to go!"

She found him in the storeroom at the back of the Second Church of England carrying one end of a large bolt of blue cloth with Cyrus hefting the other end.

"Cyrus, I have to go," said Charles as he shoved the bolt into the bottom shelf with other similar material. "Have I earned my pay?"

"You have, so be off, lad," answered Cyrus, wiping his brow with the kerchief from around his neck. "You're a hearty worker."

"I think you could load the shelves faster and easier if you get the bolts in order by size and kind of material when they first come off the ship. Then it's just carrying them to the right slot on the shelves from the top down. There'd be a lot less time wasted climbing up and down the ladder."

Cyrus scratched his head. "You're right, boy. I just might try that. If your pa don't mind, maybe you can help out after school, just for a couple of hours. I'd pay you a fair wage."

"There's no school since the British came," said Charles. "They're afraid of what we might learn, so Ma teaches us at home, and she's harder on us than any schoolmaster ever was."

"Nobody can teach the way you can put things together, the way you see them in your mind. That kind of organization you have to be born with. Come see me when you're grown, and I'll hire you for sure."

"Thank you, sir!"

Charles followed Tansy out to the carriage, talking even faster than he had when he'd been caught with the British mail pouch. "This is the first time I've earned real money on my own, Aunt Tansy. I don't mind working hard, but you have to do it the right way."

"I'm certain Cyrus will appreciate your organizational advice."

Interrupting the conversation, Gavin said, "Tansy, would you mind if I ran a couple of errands before I take you and Charles home? It won't take long."

"That would be fine," said Charles before Tansy could answer. "I'll take care of my aunt."

"Thank you, Charles," said Tansy. "Mr. Cullane, that will be fine with both of us."

Gavin gave directions to Jackson, and a few minutes later the carriage turned into an alley and stopped about halfway down the narrow passage. Gavin, grabbing a large lumpy bag from under the seat, jumped out the carriage door and flung the bag over his shoulder, saying, "Wait for me. I'll be back soon."

"Where are you going?" asked Tansy. "You can't leave us here. We're coming with you." She stood and made her way to the door with Charles right behind her.

Gavin tried to block their exit through the partially open door with his body. "You'll be perfectly safe with Jackson. He waits for me here all the time."

"You will not leave us in this alley," announced Charles as he helped his aunt out of the carriage. "Who knows what could happen in this part of the city while you're gone. We're coming with you."

Despite thinking this might turn out to be a very bad decision, Gavin said, "All right, but be quiet."

Charles was right about it being an undesirable part of the city. So much had changed since the British had taken over New York and shut down the supply of incoming goods. They passed Cohen's Bakery and Marshall's Apothecary, both abandoned and now empty. At the next door, underneath the crossed-out names of "Croft and Dillard—Attorneys at Law," were those of the British legal team of "Lloyd—Solicitor, and Bennett—Barrister."

Tansy locked her arm through Charles's. "Mr. Cullane, are you certain you want to do business in this part of town?"

Gavin didn't answer and walked faster.

One block later, the trio turned onto Broadway Street that ran across from the devastated city blocks destroyed by a fire that had raged through New York City nearly two years ago. The blaze burned for two days in this area now known as The Burns, and in the years since, the British had abandoned the neighborhood.

Makeshift shacks and tents dotted the fire-ravaged ground. Gutted remains of the once splendid houses and buildings offered shelter to none but birds and rats. People wandered around dressed in grimy, ragged clothing that once must have been sophisticated outfits.

"Why are we here?" asked Tansy, holding her hand under her nose to try and block at least some of the stench coming from the area.

Gavin said, "Stay here on the street, and I mean it. Stay right here. I won't be long." He crossed the street and walked into the burned-out section. He hadn't gone in more than a few yards when a bevy of dirty-faced children and several adults greeted him.

Charles, from his spot opposite The Burns, asked, "How does Mr. Cullane know all these people?"

"I don't know," said Tansy.

"We're lucky the British didn't take our house."

"We're very lucky."

Gavin, reaching into the bag he carried from the carriage, pulled out a knotted handkerchief, untied it, and started passing out pieces of hard peppermint candy to each child. To one bedraggled boy, he gave two pieces. "Yancy, this one is for your brother. You be sure he gets it. Promise?"

"Yes, sir!" said the boy. "He's better today. He wanted to come, but Mama said he wasn't well enough yet."

To a girl who looked to be about Charles's age, Gavin handed a small vial. "This is the medicine for your father. The doctor says he should take one swallow twice a day until it's gone. Can you remember that?"

"Yes, sir. Here's your penny."

"I'll be back with more medicine in a week."

"Father says he can't pay you anymore. He sold the last of the jewelry and didn't get much for it. Mother cried, but she knew he had to do it."

"Then he'll be pleased to hear that after two vials, the doctor doesn't charge for the next two," said Gavin.

"Are you sure? We always had to pay for his medicine before."

"Your father won't go without what he needs." To another boy, he asked, "Where's your brother, Donovan? He never passes up candy."

"The soldiers took him yesterday. They caught him stealing from the garbage cans behind the butcher shop.

Nobody knows where he is."

Gavin frowned, looked skyward, and sighed, frustrated that he could do so little. He set his eyes back on the boy. "You tell your mother I'll find out where he is and bring him home as soon as I can."

"Thank you! We knew you'd help," shouted the boy as he ran off, jumping over piles of ashes and broken bricks.

"Mr. Cullane," said a small woman wearing a green velvet dress with a soiled skirt and sleeves and a torn hem. "I don't have any bread for you today."

"Not to worry. I already have two loaves at home, and I can't eat them both before they spoil, so I will pay you in advance for the next loaf. Here is one pound." She took the money from his hand and curtsied before shuffling back to the tents.

"That's too much to pay for a loaf of bread," said Charles to Tansy.

"He isn't paying her for the bread. He's finding a way to give her some money and let her keep her pride. These people once ran businesses and lived in grand houses, and now they're forced to survive here. No one likes to beg."

"He did the same with the medicine. A vial like that costs a lot more than a penny. Who is paying for all these things?"

"I suspect it's Mr. Cullane. I had no idea people lived in such wretched conditions. I wish we could help. I didn't bring any money with me. Did you?"

"I've got the money Cyrus gave me. I'll give it to them." He dug in his pocket and pulled out a handful of coins.

"I've got an idea." Her eyes lit as her eyebrows

went up. "My sewing kit. It's full of thread, needles, buttons. That woman could use all of it."

"Are you going to give up your scissors?" asked Charles. "The ones Alden gave you on your wedding day?"

"She needs them more."

Untying the sack from around her waist, she called to Gavin, "Wait, wait! Give this to her. She can repair her dress, and maybe sew something for the others."

She took several steps into the street, but Gavin held up his hand to stop her and ran back to her. "I told you to stay there." Taking the kit from her, and then palming the coins from Charles's outstretched hand, he followed the woman farther into the rubble. He handed her the sewing kit. She curtsied and waved a quick hand to Tansy before turning and walking away.

Tansy and Charles watched Gavin move from person to person engaging them in easy conversation and handing them needed supplies from his sack. Each person also got one or two of the coins.

"I don't understand," said Charles. "How can he be the same man who came to arrest me, and the man who kissed you in the park. Who is he really?"

Tansy's expression turned pensive. "He's the kind of man Alden would share his canteen with, and he's someone who would bring news of a friend's death to his widow, and someone who would risk defying his British commanders to help people in need."

"How can he be all that and still work for the enemy?"

"I don't know, Charles. I don't know."

After Gavin had given the last of the items in his bag to the women and children, he shook hands with several men who had waited before emerging from the tents.

"I heard that the Dickerson shipbuilder is looking for extra hands," said Gavin. "You'd be cutting trees for planking."

"That's no good. None of us have axes," said a tall, broad-shouldered man with a gray cast to his skin.

"I'll bring a couple axes tomorrow morning," said Gavin. "I'll leave them right here for you to pick up."

"Where will you get them?"

"There will probably be a few lying around tonight at the work site." Gavin winked, and several of the men returned very obvious winks.

"You expect us to work for the people that took our homes and put us here?" said another man in a hard voice. "Not me!"

A gaunt man said, "I never thought it would happen, but my family's hunger is getting the better of my pride, so even though I never cut down a tree in my life, I'll do it."

"I'll show you what you need to know," said the tall man. "Do you think a British shipbuilder will hire a man with no experience? Someone with no calluses on his hands?"

"I don't know," said Gavin, "but the least you'll get out of it is a brisk walk."

"My oldest boy and I'll be there in the morning."

Gavin shook all the men's hands again and strode across the street to Tansy and Charles.

They were almost back to the alley where the carriage waited before Tansy said, "Is that part of your job as liaison?"

His face turned as grim as the Devil looking for

souls. He pointed his finger back and forth between Tansy and Charles. "You can't mention this to anyone, either of you. If my superiors hear what I've been doing on my own time with my own money, I'll be..." He wanted to say, "back on the prison ship before I can blink," but he couldn't tell her that part of his story. "I'll be in serious trouble. The British don't want anyone thinking they have soft hearts or that they take any responsibility for these people ending up like this. Not a word to anyone. That's why I didn't want you to come."

"We promise, not a word," said Tansy. "Right, Charles?"

"Yes, ma'am, I swear."

"That was a nice thing you did for them," said Tansy.

"Nothing nice about it," Gavin answered. "Nothing nice at all. I can't go past them every day and not do something."

"I have material left over from Harriet's dress. The women can do some patching with it. I'll bring it the next time."

His voice came out like a harsh wind. "There's no next time for you! You can't come down here by yourself. It's too dangerous. The people in The Burns are hurting, and they're angry enough to hurt others. They bloodied my nose the first time I came." Pointing to a scar on his forehead, he said, "See this? A sharp piece of metal did it. Nearly took my head off."

"Then we can come together. I want to help."

"I want to help, too," said Charles.

"I said no. I can't let you come. Please, promise me you'll stay away."

He glanced back and forth between their faces. He had to convince them not to come here before she got hurt. He'd confess all to Duffy first rather than see her pay any consequences for his actions.

"Promise me."

Both of them lowered their eyes and nodded their heads.

"Thank you." He kept moving down the street.

"What does Jackson think you're doing?" she asked.

"He thinks I'm in here," Gavin said as he stopped at the door of Blackfield's Ale House. The outer wall was a charred ash black, and the door leaned crookedly against its hinges, a victim of the fire, but a survivor.

"I'll be right back. Stay here." He strode through the door into the ale house, and the men inside spoke to him with enthusiasm while he returned their greetings, calling them by name.

"They know him well. He must come here often," said Tansy, curling her lip into a sneer. "I don't mind if he has a mug of beer now and then. All men do. Alden and your father both would enjoy a mug, but for Gavin to be well known in this establishment means he drinks here frequently."

"Maybe he needs a drink after visiting The Burns," said Charles, leaning against a rare clean spot on the bricks with his legs crossed at the ankle and his arms across his chest. "How long do you think he'll keep us waiting out here?"

Before Tansy could answer, the door to the tavern swung open, and the largest man she had ever seen ducked under the door frame and out to the street. Charles bolted to his feet and put himself between the man and his aunt.

"Hello, I'm Brian," said the man, built like a draft horse with a powerful chest and strong muscular arms and legs. "Mr. Gavin sent me out to check on you. Are you all right?" His exceptionally low-pitched voice echoed against the wall.

"We're fine," said Charles, his eyes like saucers.

"Good. I'm Brian. I live here—well, I live upstairs. I take care of men who get too drunk and act up."

"Glad to meet you, Brian," said Tansy, leaning around her nephew. "My name is Tansy, and this is Charles. How long do you think Mr. Gavin will be in there?"

"Don't know. He never stays long, but he always talks to me. Most don't. They think I'm too stupid."

"Oh, I wouldn't think that was true," said Tansy.

Brian rubbed his beefy hand over his face, pushing his bulbous nose to one side, and blinked his round brown eyes. "I'm not smart like Mr. Gavin, but you don't have to be smart to be a bouncer, just big, and I'm big. That's why they keep me here."

He leaned closer to Charles and Tansy who both took a step back. "I been here since I was born, and I was born big. Too big for my ma. She died. Too big."

"I'm sorry for that," said Tansy. "But I'm sure she'd be proud of you now."

Brian stared at her for a moment. "You think so? You think she'd be proud? Mr. Gavin said you were a nice lady, but he said to be careful of the boy. Why don't you like Mr. Gavin?"

Before Charles could answer, Gavin reappeared on the street with a mug of beer in his hand. He staggered, and it sloshed out over his sleeve.

"Bye, Mr. Gavin," said Brian. "I'll see you next time."

"Of course you will, Brian," Gavin said in a slurred voice. "You better go back inside."

"Yes, sir!"

"You didn't get enough to drink in there?" asked Tansy as they walked away down the block. "You have to bring it home with you?"

Gavin's slurred speech and stumbling gait stopped. "This is for Jackson. He has no idea that I go to The Burns. He just thinks I'm a drunkard, so I bring him a mug, and he keeps his mouth shut. If anyone asks, I took you to the fabric shop and then made a stop here at the tavern. Now that's something you can tell." A sly smile crossed his lips. "On second thought, don't tell Nate. I'd hate to give him another reason to separate my head from my shoulders."

They walked the block to the alley, and as soon as they turned into it, Gavin started stumbling over his own feet again. He handed up the ale to Jackson, spilling even more of it on the seat.

"Thank you, sir," said Jackson, raising the mug high in a salute. "You always keep your side of the bargain."

Gavin's words came out like thick oatmeal. "You're my...I don't know what you are, but I'm glad you are. Drink hearty!" He staggered into the carriage.

Chapter Twelve

On the evening of the gathering for General Howe and his staff, Gavin Cullane approached the home of John and Matilda Duncan, dressed for the occasion in the outfit Duffy had sent over. It fit perfectly, but Gavin hated the insipid orange color of the vest and knee-length trousers with a color-coordinating jacket embroidered with flourishes, leaves, and, egad, even the occasional bird.

He waited to put on his wig and tricorne hat until he stood on the stoop of the stately three-story house with a brick façade painted a lush green with bright golden shutters gilding the four large windows on the first floor. The same bright gold highlighted the five smaller windows on the second floor and the three dormers across the roof line. The servants' door at the back of the house was the same lovely color. The only difference being that, upon entering there, one immediately left the charming décor to follow the stairs down to the basement into its dull shades of gray and brown where the servants worked and lived.

Standing at the massive front door of the Duncan house with his hand on the knocker, Gavin couldn't bring himself to lift it. This would be the first time he'd ever been admitted through the front door. For seventeen years of his life, he'd gone around on the side gravel walk and entered through the back, never through the forbidden front of the house. Even when he'd delivered Harriet's gown a few days ago, he went around to the back by force of habit.

He didn't belong here on the front stoop, and he fully expected to be ordered away at any moment. The atmosphere here seemed rarified, fresher, air that only the favored wealthy could breathe. He reminded himself over and over that his presence here tonight was acceptable as an invited guest. His position as colonial liaison gave him a step up in status, and the Duncans no longer treated him as their servant. He didn't have to carry food up from the basement kitchen or take the guests' coats to the guest closet on the first floor while trying to remember which coat belonged to whom, knowing that if he made a mistake, a tongue-lashing was on its way. Tonight, no one could require he clear away the leftovers tossed on the floor by privileged guests who never gave a thought to those who had to keep the house spotless.

His hand lay motionless on the knocker. He'd never walked through the front door, but tonight he resolved to do so in honor of his parents who never had that opportunity. Taking a deep breath, he raised the brass lion-shaped knocker bit by bit and let it fall. He raised it again and dropped it a second time. Just as the knocker sounded, the door swung open, and a man dressed in a black and white butler's uniform greeted him. "Welcome to the home of John and Matilda Duncan. Won't you come in?"

Gavin assumed a posture of superiority he didn't feel but held his head high. "Thank you," he said as he stepped onto the stone floored foyer. "My name is Gavin Cullane."

Susan Leigh Furlong

"Welcome, Mr. Cullane. Please sign in at the guest book. May I take your hat?"

"Of course," said Gavin as he handed his hat to the man. While most guests treated the butler as a piece of furniture, Gavin knew better. "What is your name?"

With a quizzical look on his face, the man said, "My name is Robert."

"Pleased to meet you, Robert."

"The same to you, sir. Your hosts, Mr. and Mrs. Duncan, will greet you in the front room. Right this way."

"Do you like working here?"

An even deeper look of puzzlement washed over Robert's face. He repeated, "Your hosts will greet you in the front room." The knocker sounded again, and Robert made a quick bow before taking a hasty retreat to the front door.

As Gavin stepped through the archway into the main living room, he paused before joining the dozens of other guests already there. Light from the forty-eight-candle chandelier hanging from the twelve-foot-high ceiling sparkled over the ladies bedecked in splendid gowns of gold, green, or blue and costly jewelry. The men wore equally fancy knee-length jackets over vests of contrasting colors, each adorned with gold or silver buttons. Their trousers fastened at the knees over white stockings, and their shoe buckles were as bejeweled as their ladies' necks.

Standing in small groups along the walls, they discussed politics or market prices. Gavin knew even more than some of these men about such topics from hours of standing waiting for requests for more food or drink. Tonight he would fit right in. No one could tell where he'd been born.

To keep the guests fed until serving the main meal close to midnight, assorted appetizers covered a dozen tables along the walls. Guests, not nibbling on the elegantly prepared tidbits, sat in the chairs scattered around the room for conversation or they moved into the ballroom to dance. The ten-piece orchestra played as the dance master instructed several couples on how to form their cotillion squares.

Gavin's eye caught Harriet Duncan standing in the center of the room wearing the beautiful gown Tansy had made for her. Surrounding her were a bevy of young men and several women, all bidding for her attention, so clearly, the gown did exactly the job it was intended to do.

Gavin leaned against the archway into the ballroom. As a child, he'd watched the dancing from the butler's pantry, which served as the staging place for the food before bringing it out for the guests. He had hummed along with the music and sometimes danced his way through the patterns as he waited for the food to be ready. He considered the steps for the minuet rigid and fancy, but he did love the country dances. Although he'd never actually danced with a partner, he felt sure he could do it properly if given the chance. Would tonight be his chance? His heart thumped in anticipation of fulfilling a wish he'd had since he was young.

Soon the dance master called out to Gavin. "Would you join us for this longways dance? We need one more man to balance out our numbers. Your partner is a lovely young lady. Join us?"

Gavin gave a generous bow and moved to the end

of one of the two long lines of men and women facing each other. The music began, and he was right, he could repeat the steps he had watched so often as a boy. But even more amusing was that not one of the other dancers recognized him as the one who had served their food ten years ago. He fooled them all!

That was until John Duncan came up behind him and tapped him on the shoulder.

"Mr. Travis is going to take your place, Mr. Cullane. Come with me." For a split second, Gavin considered refusing the order. He no longer had to obey this man, but rather than cause a scene, Gavin bowed to his partner and let Joshua Travis step into his place.

John Duncan led Gavin down a long hallway and opened the door to the billiards room. Gavin had never been in this room as an invited guest, but only to bring food to the men of Duncan's weekly evenings of billiards. After ushering Gavin inside, John Duncan closed the door and left.

To Gavin's surprise, standing on the other side of the green wool-covered billiard table with a cue stick in his hand was Simon Duffy, dressed in an impressive British uniform befitting his rank as a colonel. Gold buttons adorned his red jacket down the front with additional gold embellishments and braiding on the shoulders and cuffs. A white sash formed a cross over his chest that matched his bright white breeches tucked into tall black boots. On a chair, off to the side, rested a feathery pointed hat with Duffy's white wig beside it.

"Come in, Cullane," said Duffy. "It's only the two of us, so take off your wig if you wish. Mine is too hot."

"No, thank you," said Gavin. "Were we supposed

to meet here?"

"No, but we have something to discuss privately. Duncan was kind enough to let us use this room. Care for a game of billiards? Do you know how to play?"

"I've played in taverns, but I'm guessing the rules of this house don't involve whacking your opponent's head with your cue if he outscores you."

With a condescending sneer, Duffy sniffed, saying, "Correct." Lining up his cue stick, he sent the white ball into the red ball, which bounced off the rail, but missed the dotted white ball by an inch. "No point for me. Your turn."

Gavin walked deliberately around the table assessing his strategy, not just for his shot, but also for why he was here. This was the first time he and his handler had ever spoken outside of Duffy's official headquarters, and it made Gavin uneasy. He'd met with Colonel Duffy twice a week for months now, every Tuesday and Friday at two o'clock to report every detail of what he'd done and where he'd been. Duffy demanded precise details about the people he'd met, including particulars such as their eye and hair color, complexion, height, and weight, even what they were wearing. He wanted descriptions of the houses where these people lived and word-for-word retelling of all conversations Gavin had with them.

Duffy always sat in the same chair in his office with the half-opened curtains at the window behind his desk letting in an often-blinding stream of sunlight. The questions he asked always came in the same order. His patterns were the same, day in and day out, so why had he changed his routine tonight?

Gavin reviewed in his mind everything he'd told

Duffy and everything he'd left out. He'd reported his first visit to the Hemstead house with Charles because the soldiers were witnesses, but he left out seeing Daisy and Tansy scatter the envelopes on the street and about seeing the invitation on the Hemstead table during his second visit. He didn't report the loose stone in the wall or his encounter with Tansy in the park, and Duffy would never know that hidden in the bottom of his shoe under the inner sole was the coded message. He'd only bring it out if a patriot could safely decode it.

Leaning over the table, Gavin tried to ignore the cloud of doom hanging over his head. He took aim on the white ball and stroked his cue. The white ball hit the red ball, cushioned off the rail, struck the dotted white ball, and hit another side rail before driving both balls into the corner or the so-called crotch.

"You play well, Cullane," said Duffy.

"Knowing I won't get whacked on the head improves my game."

Instead of taking his next shot, Duffy tossed his cue on the billiard table and moved over to a small wooden table where the men sat to play chess or cribbage. "Enough billiards. Sit down. Have a whiskey?" He pointed to the decanter and the drink glasses. "I've already had a drink or two, but who's counting?"

"No, thank you," said Gavin.

Duffy downed the whiskey left in his glass in one gulp.

Gavin concentrated on relaxing his shoulders and his face as he took a seat across from Duffy, trying to appear unconcerned while facing the man who could send him back to the prison ship or hang him.

Crossing his arms over his chest, Duffy leaned back in his chair. "Duncan tells me you were a servant in this house."

Gavin nodded.

"You've moved up in the world from lowly servant to invited guest, but you still don't feel like you belong here, do you? Remember, it's all an act, a game. Did I tell you where I came from? A hovel next to the river, but I decided I wanted out and up, and here I am. It's all an act. Nobody can tell where you were born if you watch, learn, and play the game, and I've learned it well."

He flicked his hand as if to dismiss all the wealth and class of the Duncan house.

Pouring himself another drink, he said, "I do hate to miss a party, so I'll get right to the point. I have had several interesting conversations with your driver, Jackson."

"Really?" *What has that witless fool been up to?*

"Are you curious as to what he said?"

"I assume he told you about stopping at Blackfield's Ale House. Am I not allowed to have a drink in a place of my choosing?"

"Your drinking at such a vulgar place is of no concern of mine, but you're a terrible actor, making me wonder why you try to appear drunk in front of him. But it's not your drinking habits I want to talk about. It's what you're doing while you pretend to be drinking."

Gavin didn't move a muscle or change his expression. He waited for the ax to fall.

"I hear that you took a woman and a boy to The Burns recently. Distributing candy and medicine is not part of your job, and this isn't the first time you've been there, so I'm wondering why you went with two others. Care to elaborate?"

Gavin's mind raced. He always knew he'd be caught sooner or later. He was just hoping for later, much later.

"What makes you so certain that Jackson is telling the truth?" Gavin asked.

"Jackson's price is more than the mug of ale you bring him. He came to me a few weeks ago offering to sell what he knew, and being curious, I took him up on it."

Gavin cleared his throat. "So, what are you going to do about it?"

"I'm not going to do anything. It's what you're going to do."

****

Earlier that same afternoon, Tansy picked up Alden's canteen from the shelf and rubbed her thumb over it, pausing on the name scratched there. She shook it. The ring rattled inside, bringing tears to her eyes. Sniffing, she wiped her face with the edge of her apron.

Daisy, seeing her sister's tears, left the pudding she was stirring and came over to her side. "Tansy, that canteen will be something you can share with Young Alden, but if you're going to relive your grief every time you see it, it'd be better to put it in the trunk. I hate to see you like this."

"When Gavin gave it to me, it felt like Alden died all over again, like opening up the wound. I need more time to get used to having it here. I promise I'll try harder. It gets better every day, Daisy."

"I'm right here if you want to talk. A grief shared

is a grief cut in half."

"I know. I love you and everything you've done for me."

What Tansy couldn't share with her sister was that she thought about Gavin in a more positive light ever since she'd seen him at The Burns. His compassion for those people left in such dire straits moved her. He brought joy to the children who had little to look forward to, and he treated the men as equals. To her, he changed from a man she feared to a man she respected.

As daydreams filled her thoughts, she dropped a stitch on the dress she was hemming. In her mind, she could see her and Gavin sitting together on the park bench and talking about simple things like the weather. She even imagined him bouncing Young Alden on his knee as the boy laughed and giggled.

This won't do. I need to clear my head.

Setting aside the hemming, she asked, "Daisy, would you mind if I went to get the extra crocks we need to preserve the vegetables from the garden? I can pay for them out of the sale of Harriet's dress. The children are all busy with their schoolwork, and I just fed Young Alden, so he should sleep for a while."

"That's fine," said Daisy. "By the time you get back, our lessons should be over, and we can get started preparing the peas and the beans. It'll be good for you to get out of the house since this may be one of the last warm days before fall brings back the cool weather."

"Can I go, too?" asked Gideon.

"Young man, check your spelling and take your time with your handwriting. What you have to say is useless if no one can read it." Gideon grimaced, but did as his teacher told him.

Tansy, after picking up the crocks at McDean's general store, made a stop at one of her favorite places in the city, Mistress Abigail Mitchell's dress shop. Not only did Mistress Mitchell create beautiful dresses for women and girls, her shelves also offered spool after spool of colorful thread along with needles, buttons, and any other notions a seamstress might need. Tansy had spent hours here.

Today she decided to use some of the money from the sale of Harriet Duncan's dress to replace the sewing kit and the scissors she'd given to the woman at The Burns.

"Good morning, Abigail," she said to Mistress Mitchell as the bell on the door jingled to announce a new customer.

Abigail's shelves were bare! Only a single dress hung displayed in the window and maybe only a dozen spools of thread where there used to be over a hundred. "Your inventory is so low. Are you closing the shop?"

Abigail Mitchell, a woman in her eighties with a painful hunched-over back and bright white hair pulled back into a bun at her neck, showed her ever-delightful smile. "I may have to. The embargo makes it nearly impossible to get material and sewing notions. And the prices are so dear that few people are able to afford what I'm selling. Are you looking for anything in particular?"

Tansy's eyes scanned the shop's dwindling inventory. "I need to replace my entire sewing kit, so I'll take as much as you can sell me. I have money to pay."

"Bless you," said Abigail as she picked out a flowered sewing pouch and began filling it with thread, needles, pins, buttons, and a cloth measuring tape.

"I need scissors, too."

"You'll be taking my last pair. They're very fine, but also expensive. Imported from France before the British took over the city."

"I'll take them." The words "imported from France" made her think of the Second Church of England. Cyrus could help her replenish the cloth for Abigail's shop. She had money to pay for it, but she also had another idea. Not only would she give cloth to Abigail, but she'd see what she could donate to the people at The Burns. It would be simple enough to explain buying cloth for Abigail's shop and having Cyrus deliver it, but Nate and Daisy didn't know about her visit to The Burns with Gavin. She'd have to get the cloth there by herself.

Her lies were stacking up.

Chapter Thirteen

"What do you mean," Gavin asked Simon Duffy, "what I'll be doing?"

Simon Duffy steepled his fingers with a haughty look on his narrow face that Gavin had seen before. It meant he was about to say something Gavin wouldn't like, like the time he'd told the newly released prisoner he would have to be shaved from head to toe and drenched with kerosene and apple vinegar to get rid of bugs and lice. Duffy had given that order with the same thinly veiled smile he had here.

"I need something done, and since it involves some risk, I want you to do it."

"What makes you think I would?"

"Three things, a noose, a firing squad, and a prison ship."

Gavin felt bile rise up in his stomach.

"I have a question for you. What do you think Jackson does when he's not driving you around?"

"I haven't the slightest idea what that fart catcher does." The term for a footman or driver who walks behind his employer collecting his farts fit the sullen Jackson.

Duffy gave a gruff laugh. "He watches you, and he reports back to me, but we'll get to why that is important in a bit. First, do you know that George Washington's army is very short on gunpowder, in

114

particular the saltpeter to mix with the charcoal and sulfur? Washington is desperate to procure more before it costs him this war."

Gavin did not respond.

Duffy snickered. "Ha! An army without gunpowder! How many cartridges were you given as a soldier?"

Gavin kept a steady eye on Duffy, but again did not answer.

"I happen to know that you only got about twenty, which might last about ten minutes in a battle. Our troops crossing a battlefield found so many colonists dead with empty rifles across their bodies." He stuck out his lip in mock sorrow. "What a shame."

"I am well aware of the problem," said Gavin, keeping his expression as composed as possible. "Since King George refuses to share his saltpeter, Washington has to look elsewhere, either to get it from the French or go to the West Indies. So tell me how this concerns me?"

"There happens to be a large supply of saltpeter at a port in the West Indies, and that's where you come in."

Gavin asked, not even trying to keep the sarcasm out of his voice, "Do you want me to pick it up?"

"Don't be ridiculous."

"Well then, since I'm not permitted to carry a gun and therefore have no need of gunpowder, what could any of this possibly have to do with me?"

"I'm getting to that. Today is the fourth, and right now Washington is preparing to dispatch a ship on the fifteenth to pick up the supply in the West Indies on the eighteenth, but he needs to be told that it won't be ready until the thirtieth."

Gavin couldn't figure how this convoluted plan made any sense, so he returned a quizzical look with "And?"

Leaning forward in his chair, Duffy blew out his nose again with a whistle like a tea kettle. "Washington needs to be told that it won't be ready until the thirtieth so that Captain Reynolds of our own British Navy can pick it up on the eighteenth. Since we have it on good authority that Washington intends to dispatch a ship on the fifteenth, he must learn of the delay before that date. That is where you come in."

Gavin needed time to decide how to react. As the colonial liaison he should be happy to outwit Washington, but as a secret patriot he needed to thwart it, and as a man under the threat of noose or firing squad or prison ship, he needed to be cautious, very cautious.

"Nothing to say, Cullane?"

"Why can't you do this yourself?"

"I'm a well-known and high-ranking British officer, so a message from me or any other British operative would never be believed."

"But I'm an operative of the British army."

"That may be, but during your work, you have met people who are known to be loyal to General Washington. A message from them would be considered valid, especially if they received it from someone who, accidentally of course, had given away British intelligence secrets about saltpeter deliveries, someone who, for example, was the colonial liaison."

A thick, choking cloud of disaster fell over Gavin. If this plot were successful, it could mean George

Washington's defeat, the very thing he promised Alden he would avoid by doing whatever it took.

"I don't have the foggiest idea how you expect me to accomplish this. I'm already betraying the colonists by telling their secrets to you, and now you want it to appear that I'm also betraying the British by offering up information to the colonists. That makes me a traitor to both sides, and either way this doesn't turn out well for me."

Duffy walked around the billiard table while dragging his finger over the wool covering along the edge. "To be blunt, I am not interested in how this turns out for you, but I am getting to where Jackson comes in. He follows you every day and every night. Every place you've been, so has he. There is no place he hasn't told me about, and no person he hasn't seen you with. Right now, you may be thinking who could you persuade to send this phony message?"

"That crossed my mind."

"Are you familiar with a woman by the name of Carter who lives with the Nathaniel Hemstead family?" Without looking up, he continued, "Of course you are. You've kissed the lips of one and the arse of the other."

A dry, hacking cough came up in Gavin's throat. "I don't know who you're talking about," he said once he recovered his voice.

"I expected you to be more of a challenge, Cullane. After that guard on the prison ship, Peter Wright, chose to bring you to me, I really thought we would play this game of cat and mouse a little longer."

"Cat and mouse?"

"I told the captain that you would prove useful, but not with the ridiculous little bits of information you passed on, but in some larger, more important way, and now you will. You led us to a link in Washington's spy ring much sooner than anticipated. Good work, Cullane."

Gavin tried to maintain his expression of innocence by digging his nails into his palms.

"Are you telling me that you did not return a young thief, Mistress Carter's nephew, a Charles Hemstead, to the loving arms of his family even though he should rightfully be in a Sugar House prison? Or that you did not recover a coded message hidden in a stone wall by one Tansy Carter? And did you or did you not offer the name of this boy's aunt, the same Tansy Carter, as seamstress to sew a gown for Harriet Duncan of this house, and did you not take her to see Miss Duncan for a fitting for that gown in a carriage driven by one Richard Jackson? That seems like an awful lot of contact with a family you don't know."

Gavin wanted to melt into the carpet. He'd betrayed Alden and his promise by letting himself get caught in a trap of his own making, by leading Jackson right to the people he most wanted Duffy to stay away from.

"Jackson is very thorough. I'll see he regrets it," declared Gavin.

A vicious shout flew from Duffy's lips. "Jackson is the least of your worries! You will see that the printer, Hemstead, receives the message about the delay in the delivery of the saltpeter and that he believes it to be real. You will also see he sends it on through whatever spy network Washington is operating here in the city, and you will do it all without compromising your position as liaison. We may continue to have use for you."

Gavin stood up. "What if Hemstead refuses to cooperate?"

"As an incentive, we will allow him to continue his activities, under my direction and supervision, of course. I'm certain he could be very helpful in directing Washington in, shall we say, the wrong direction. Otherwise, we will hang him, his wife, that Tansy Carter, and the oldest boy for treason at a public execution."

"You don't mean it!"

"Oh, but I do, but just to show you that we British can be merciful, the other children, including the baby, will be dropped off at your beloved Burns. Hopefully, they will survive there."

Gavin's mind couldn't understand what his ears were hearing. *Please, God, this can't be happening.*

Struggling to keep his voice from cracking, he said, "What if I refuse to help you do this?"

"Then you will stand and watch the others hang right before meeting your own hangman."

Exuding a calmness he didn't feel, Gavin slid his chair back into place, picked up his billiard cue, and hung it on the rack. "I do need one thing in return. Do I have your word that if the message is delivered, the Hemstead family, including Tansy, won't be arrested?"

Tapping his finger on his chin, Duffy replied, "You're the one who makes promises, not me."

Gavin had to get out of this house! He bolted out of the billiard room and dashed down the hall to the front door. Leaving his hat behind, he swiped off his wig and tossed it into the bushes as soon as he stepped onto the street.

I thought I had been so clever. I deserve to be hanged for my arrogance in thinking I could hoodwink the entire British Army.

He would gladly give Duffy the pleasure of seeing him hang if it meant that Daisy, Nate, Charles, and Tansy would go free. But Duffy had made no such promises.

All it took to bring down his house of cards was Jackson, a man no smarter than a head of cabbage. He would see that lackey paid for his betrayal, but that would have to wait.

He had only nine days to save Tansy's life!

Chapter Fourteen

Day One of Nine—September 5

Gavin ran the five blocks to his room at the converted mansion, now a hotel for nonresident British subjects, and flopped on his bed. His thoughts ran wild.

Whatever he came up with next could not fail despite all his previous plans blowing up in his face. He'd left Tansy and the Hemsteads standing on the edge of a pit of fire. He had imagined himself to be so smart, so clever. When he wanted to trick and fool others, he'd massively underestimated the ability of others to trick and fool him.

How could I have been so stupid? He rolled onto his back and covered his eyes with his arm.

Among his many mistakes, he had believed the guard, Peter Wright, had been convinced of his change in loyalties. He had accepted the ship captain's offer of a way out of hell without understanding the price he would pay. But the worst of all was how he let Simon Duffy play him for the fool, and he'd led that vile man right to Hemstead and Tansy.

Twice a week, he'd sat facing the blinding sunlight of the window behind Duffy's desk to report little stories of "spying" activity, which he now knew Duffy hadn't the slightest interest in. Duffy's rasping laughter echoed in his head as he imagined Duffy telling the other officers how this man with the worthless title of colonial liaison strutted around the city thinking he could bring the British useful information. Duffy gave him enough rope to hang himself, and sure enough, he'd done just that. Hemstead was only a little fish in Washington's spy network, but this little fish could lead Duffy to hook all the others on the line.

Pacing, Gavin stopped to look out the window onto the street. Would his mistakes make all the people he saw walking past suffer? Duffy had to be so proud of himself. What a coup to mislead George Washington about the shipment of saltpeter for the gunpowder and to expose the general's spy ring at the same time. Having no gunpowder and no spy network would bring a quick end to the war in British favor. Any accolades and promotions Duffy earned while America lost its bid for freedom meant disaster for the country and all the people walking the streets now so unaware.

Think! Plan! This time be careful and thorough.

After spending a sleepless night formulating plans, rejecting them, and coming up with new ones, he settled on the only one he thought had even the slimmest chance for success. He risked everything, but so must Tansy and the others.

Seeing his plan written down on a scrap of paper helped him figure everything out.

By September 6, convince the Hemsteads and Tansy to trust him.

Create two messages about the saltpeter shipments. A fake one for Washington about the delay until the thirtieth to reach Washington any time in the next week.

A second true message about the British plan to steal the saltpeter on the eighteenth—to Washington to arrive no later than the thirteenth.

Get all the Hemsteads, including Tansy and Young Alden, out of the city as soon as possible and no later than the thirteenth.

But before any of this could happen, his enemies had to become his friends, despite knowing he had singlehandedly put them within sight of the hangman's scaffold.

As the sun came above the roofs and shone into his window, Gavin fell on the bed again and closed his eyes. Worn out and drained, his head ached and his empty stomach clenched.

I can't do this!

He opened his eyes and sat up, remembering Alden, lying in his arms, dying, pleading with him to do whatever it took. Knowing that Alden held out such desperate hope, Gavin had to play the game smarter, so much smarter, and he had to win quickly in as few moves as possible. *I won't give up, Alden, not ever!*

Then he remembered. Years ago, his father had taught him a chess strategy to ensure a win in only two moves. The problem was that the other side, Duffy's side, had to move first and had to make the move Gavin needed him to.

Duffy's first move was already done. He used his pawn, Jackson, to have Gavin followed. Gavin's countermove would be to catch Duffy off guard and use his own arrogance against him by making him believe Gavin was playing along. Duffy would then make another ineffectual move, thinking he'd caught Gavin in a trap impossible to escape. Gavin's final move had to be to put Duffy in checkmate, which was to get the correct message delivered and all the Hemsteads out of

Duffy's reach without compromising Washington's spy ring. Gavin had only two moves. He couldn't prolong the conflict any longer than that.

He'd make Duffy think he was following orders, so a complacent Duffy would wait until he thought Washington had missed the delivery of the saltpeter. By that time, Duffy's ineffectual move would be to tell the high command the delayed saltpeter had been his idea, and he'd try to collect his reward. The catch was that Washington would already have it, and Gavin's final move to checkmate would be that Tansy and the Hemsteads would already be safely out of the city.

One false step, one unexpected modification, if Gavin miscalculated even the smallest detail, all would be lost, so he spent the daylight hours of Day One planning for every possible scenario.

Day Two would come soon enough.

Chapter Fifteen

Day Two of Nine—September 6

Gavin devoted Day Two to convincing Tansy to support his plan. He had twenty-four hours to get her on his side, or eight days from now, they'd all hang.

He hadn't slept in two days.

Crouching out of sight across the street from the Hemstead house, he spent the morning watching the family's activity. He kept his eyes peeled for Gideon in the window, but the boy bolted out the side door and into his father's shop early in the morning and so far had not reappeared. A little later Charles and Lizzie left with cloth sacks in their hands, heading for the market, leaving Daisy, Tansy, Mercy, and the baby inside the house. He knew he could convince Mercy and the baby of his good intentions, but the women were another story. So, he waited a little longer.

Ten minutes after noon, Tansy came out the front door alone. Loose locks of her blonde hair blew back from her face as her steady strides took her down the block. He fell behind her, ever on the alert for a place where he could catch up and they could talk alone.

He scanned the street and every nook and corner of the buildings for anyone who didn't belong. He was certain Duffy had him followed, but so far no one looked out of place. Better not drop his guard. In this cat and mouse game, he was the mouse, and he never knew who his cat might be.

After about twenty minutes, he realized she was heading toward the Second Church of England.

What could she want there? It certainly wasn't more work for Harriet Duncan.

So he waited, nestled in an alley down the block from the misnamed fabric shop for over an hour until she came out with two bundles of cloth in her arms. Following right behind her came Cyrus and a young shop assistant carrying three larger bolts of cloth, which he placed in a small wagon out front.

"Mistress Mitchell used to be one of my best customers," said Cyrus to Tansy. "I'm glad to give her some of my high-quality cloth at a discount price, just for you. Lad, are you sure you know the way to Mistress Mitchell's shop?"

"I am, sir. I'll deliver these three bolts safe and sound, and I won't tell her who they're from. I'll just say it's from a friend."

Cyrus clapped him on the back, saying, "Be on your way."

The young man stepped to the front of the wagon between two long attached poles, lifted the poles to hoist the wagon into position, and pulled it around the corner in the direction of Mitchell's sewing shop. Tansy, on the other hand, walked in the opposite direction carrying two bolts.

"Are you sure you don't want me to go with you?" said Cyrus.

"I'm sure, but thank you for everything."

Gavin's heart raced. *Oh, no, she's heading toward The Burns!*

Just as Gavin stepped out to follow her, he spotted a man leaning against the wall in the alley directly across the street from him. Something didn't seem right about his presence. Although the man's eyes were closed and his body slumped as if he were sleeping off a drunken night, he was far too well dressed and too clean. All at once it came to him. He'd seen that man before. What a difference a bath and civilian clothes made for a fart catcher like Richard Jackson!

In long strides, Gavin crossed the cobblestones and stood in front of the seemingly sleeping Jackson. The man's eyes flew open, but he didn't have time to react before Gavin punched him twice squarely in the face. His legs buckled out from under him, and he landed in a heap on the ground, unconscious and bleeding from his nose.

Grabbing Jackson by the feet, Gavin dragged him farther into the alley and to the back of the building. Using the silk scarf and ascot around Jackson's neck, Gavin hog-tied his hands to his feet, and since no well-dressed man would ever be without a proper handkerchief in his vest pocket, Gavin wadded it up and shoved it into his betrayer's mouth.

After two more sharp kicks to Jackson's midsection, Gavin muttered, "There, that should hold you for a while," and he left to follow Tansy into The Burns.

She stood in the street across from the edge of the burned-out area. Several men living in The Burns straightened up to look at her, but none moved in her direction.

Gavin started running.

Tansy called out to the men. "I have something for

the woman I gave the sewing pouch to a few days ago. Is she here?"

No answer. She called out again. "I just want to give her this cloth. I thought she could use it."

"She's not here!" bellowed one man. "Go away!"

"It's nothing fancy, but very useable. It's strong and durable. The colors are pretty." She hesitated. "Can I speak to her? Or maybe to someone else?"

Three men in tattered coats and breeches stood, picked up broken pieces of the bricks scattered around them, and, raising their arms, stepped toward her with venomous looks in their eyes.

"Go away! We don't want it," said one.

"Don't come back," said another.

As the men got to the street, Tansy took a trembling step back and bumped right into Gavin. Wrapping his arm around her, he said, "She's with me."

The men stopped walking but stared at her like wolves stalking their prey.

"I told you not to come here," Gavin whispered in her ear.

"I just want to help," she whispered back.

"As you can see, this isn't helping."

To the men in The Burns, Gavin spoke louder. "We'll leave the cloth right here. Do whatever you want with it. She won't be back again."

"Now wait a minute," Tansy said. "This is a gift, and I expect nothing in return. I just thought it might make things easier."

"There's nothing easy about living here," growled the first man. "We don't want your pity."

Another man shook his fist, shouting, "What do you think we are, beggars?"

Tansy retorted back at him, "You didn't beg for it. I brought it. You need it."

In unison the three men started moving toward her again, each man raising his brick weapon above his head. In one quick shove, Gavin pushed the bolts of cloth out of Tansy's arms to the ground and pulled her back down the street.

She struggled against him. "Let go of me!"

Just before the men moved close enough to do some real damage, a woman's shout came from one of the tents. "Horace, stop! Stop! I want the cloth!"

Another female voice cried out right after her. "Percy, Edward, don't do it! I mean it! No, no, no!"

The three men stopped in their tracks. "Stay out of this," said one of them, turning back toward the women.

"I won't," said the first woman as she came up beside him. "This one gave me the sewing kit, and I stitched your jacket with it. I let out little Mabel's dress, so she could wear it a bit longer. Our clothes are in tatters, and the children keep growing. This cloth is a godsend."

To Tansy she said, "Miss, leave the cloth and if you see fit to bring anything else, please make it yarn for socks and mittens and caps for winter. And knitting needles, too."

Tansy nodded. "I will."

The woman said, "I'm grateful my husband is proud and brave, but he doesn't know everything. He's protecting his family as best he can." She bent down, gathered up the cloth from the ground, and walked back to her shack with it while several other women followed her inside the flimsy structure.

Gavin didn't wait to find out if the men had

anything else to say as he dragged Tansy down the street despite her continuing protests. Two blocks away, he stopped and pulled her into an alley. Pushing her back against the wall, he held her there with his hands on her shoulders and spit out the words, "Don't ever try anything so foolish again. Next time Agatha Marchand may not be there to rescue you."

"Marchand? The Marchands who owned so many of the Sugar Houses?"

"Yes, The Burns is filled with former rich loyalist families. You can see how far they have fallen despite expecting their loyalty to the crown to protect them. The longer they're forced to live in those horrible conditions, the angrier and more violent they become, especially the men who've had to swallow their pride and their bank accounts. They revert to the poor people they used to have so much disdain for. You were very lucky today."

Ducking her head, she spoke with regret and understanding. "I'm sorry for being so impulsive. Thank you for coming for me. How did you know where I was?"

The scent of whatever she used to wash her hair was perfect for her. Was it lavender? He leaned in slightly until his coat brushed against her breasts, and he felt her breathing on his neck. If Alden had survived the war, Gavin would have buried his desire for Tansy until he couldn't feel it anymore, but Alden was gone. He leaned his head until his lips were only a breath away from hers.

"What are you doing?" she said, putting her hands against his chest.

Stepping back with a jerk, he said, "I followed you

for a reason that had nothing to do with The Burns or the cloth."

She cocked her head, puzzled.

"Tansy, you and the whole family are in great danger."

Chapter Sixteen

Still September 6

"What are you talking about?"

"We need to find someplace to talk and not be seen. I was followed here. Believe me, Tansy, this danger is real."

"If there be snakes, it's because you put them there." Pulling out of his grasp, she walked away with long determined strides.

Following her, he said, "Tansy, you have to listen to me. You, Nate, Daisy, and even Charles will be hanged in eight days unless you listen to me."

She stopped and turned back to face him, giving him a withering stare. "If that's true, then it's your fault! What have you done?"

"Yes, it's my fault, my folly. I brought this down on your heads with my own arrogance, but I'm trying to make it right. You have to believe me."

"Why should I?"

"I've known you for a long time."

"What?"

He took a deep breath. "I'll start at the beginning. Alden told me all about you. We spent hours waiting for the next battle talking about you, and I felt like I knew you before I even met you. Once I did meet you, you were everything I hoped you'd be."

Her eyes blazed. "You hoped I'd be? You knew Alden, and now we're all going to be hanged! Tell me what you did."

"We have to find someplace else to talk, someplace out of sight."

She stomped her foot. "Tell me right now!"

"You can't be seen with me. My orders include providing the evidence that will lead to your arrest, and Nate's too. Please, let's get off the street."

All at once Tansy lifted her skirts and started running away from him. Taking chase, he caught up with her two blocks later. After shoving her, none too gently, into a recessed doorway, he held her against the wall.

"You have to believe me," he said. "I want to help you escape New York so Simon Duffy can't find you or any of the family. I'm telling you the truth."

"Who in the name of all the saints is Simon Duffy?" she asked with a sharp punch to his gut that made him double over, but he put his arm up against the wall and stopped her from running off again.

"He's the British officer I've been reporting to," he choked out, knowing what he would say next would damn him to Hell. "He's the one I've been giving information to about anyone not loyal to the crown." From the look on her face, he knew she'd sentenced him to Hell already.

"He knows about my visits to your house. He wants me to persuade Nate to send a coded message to George Washington that could be a turning point for the war in British favor."

She didn't respond.

"Then Duffy will arrest him and you, Daisy, and

Charles and hang all of you."

Her fist cocked. He prepared himself for her second punch to his gut by tightening his stomach muscles, but he flinched just the same, impressed by the strength in her arm.

"Traitor!" she shouted.

"Yes, it looks like I'm a traitor, but in truth I'm fighting for freedom."

She cocked her arm to hit him again, so he spoke quickly, "I made a promise to Alden. Let me explain. I can explain everything if we just get off the street."

She let her fist fly into his midsection. "Let me go!"

Coughing, he lowered his voice. "All right, I won't beg you. Either you'll listen to me or you won't, but I intend to do whatever I can to keep you and the family alive." Taking down the arm that blocked her from leaving the doorway, he stepped aside. "Go."

She hesitated. "You want me to trust a man who betrayed us and who has agreed to do it again?"

Rubbing his stomach, he said, "I know it's a lot to ask, but before Alden died, he made me promise to do whatever I had to in the fight for freedom. Made me promise to stay strong through everything to come. I've made mistakes, a lot of mistakes, but I swore to him that I'd do whatever it took or die trying. Alden believed in me. For Alden's sake, listen to me."

Her face fell, and her eyes misted over. "Alden believed in you?" she muttered. "Alden believed in you." Raising her voice, she said, "All right, I'll listen for Alden's sake, not for yours. Where can we go?"

"I know a place in a deserted part of The Burns. The building is burned out, but no one lives there. No one will see us. You won't run away again, will you?"

She shrunk from his touch, but her breathing steadied. "You want me to follow you to the place you just rescued me from? How loony do you think I am?"

"We can't stay here on the street. I can show you the way in, and you can leave anytime you want. I swear on Alden's soul that I'll escort you home whenever you say, even now if you want. If you won't listen to me, I'll find another way to stop Duffy, but please, just listen to me now."

She put her hand on his chest and took in two long, deep breaths while studying his face. "Take me home right now."

"All right." Taking her by the elbow, he started toward the Second Church of England. When they rounded the corner in the direction of the Hemstead house, she stopped walking and said, "I make no promises, but I'll listen. Lead the way."

He guided her back to a doorway directly across the street from The Burns, a block piled with jagged mounds of fallen beams, bricks, and collapsed buildings.

"Right after the fire," he said as he led her across the debris, "people made attempts to clear out the damage here, but after six months it became impossible. Too much had been destroyed to be saved, so this part of The Burns became a dumping ground for any rubble removed from the other sections. This three-block area has been abandoned to the rats and the ashes."

"We're so close to the Hudson River," said Tansy. "The Paulus Hook Ferry is just south of here. I took it once across to New Jersey to see my brother, Ash. He met me on the other side. The soldiers checked everyone out. They didn't want me to take the baby across for fear I wouldn't come back, but Daisy vouched for me. Had to give them her address, so they could check up on whether I came back to the city."

Gavin lifted her over a jagged wall of stone at the edge of the street. "They rarely patrol past the ferry station. We're safe here. Try to memorize the path, Tansy. It starts here and goes through these tall piles of debris that make a sort of tunnel. You can't see over the piles, so you have to go between them. You enter across from the store front with the red roof. See it?" He pointed back across the street.

She turned to look. "I see it."

"Can you see the green leaves from the top of that tree over there? That's where we're headed. Your first turn is left, followed by two right turns. See the Wall Street sign? Someone set it here as a joke, but use it as your marker to be sure you're headed in the right direction. Now do you see that big pile of brown bricks?" He pointed.

Tansy nodded as she lifted her skirt and stepped between the broken bricks, burned timbers, shingles, half-melted pots, pans, and legless chairs abandoned to the fire.

"Head straight for those bricks. It isn't a clear path now, so you'll have to make your way over the trash, but keep that brick pile as your header."

Tansy kept an eye on where her feet stepped, and twice Gavin had to tug on her arm to keep her going in the right direction. "You could get lost in here for weeks, so keep your head up and watch where you're going."

Dirt and ashes had left black streaks across their

clothes by the time they reached the massive brown brick pile, and Tansy breathed hard from anxiety and exertion. A large rat scurried in front of them, and try as she might, she couldn't suppress a scream while jumping aside and latching onto Gavin's arm.

Putting his arm around her to steady her, he said, "It's easy from here. You can see the house." The building he pointed to looked like a falling stack of a child's alphabet blocks, tall on one side with jagged edges down to the ground. The windows, charred and empty, added to the bleakness, but what surprised Tansy was a tall oak tree growing against the remains, untouched by the fire.

"How did that tree survive?" she asked as she struggled to keep up with Gavin's long strides over the uneven piles of trash.

"Trees can sometimes live through a fire because they're tall enough to reach above the flames. Also, their wood is wet with sap and water inside, compared to the dried-out timbers in a house. Plus they have that protection of bark around them."

Tansy gagged, covering her mouth with her hand. She leaned into Gavin's embrace, burying her face in his shirt, still gagging and trying not to throw up. "What is that?" she asked, pointing a trembling finger toward the ground.

He held her until her throat and stomach calmed down. "It's a human bone. Don't look at it. Just keep walking. A lot of people died in this fire, men, women, and children." He clasped his arm around her waist and guided her toward the remains of the house.

The formerly grand three-story house had collapsed into a partial wall on the first floor, a freestanding door frame, a scorched but intact floor, and a set of stairs leading to a basement level.

When they reached the archway of the door, Gavin said, "Go down the stairs to a room on the right. I've brought in a few supplies—lanterns, blankets, a bit of food and water, things like that—and I tried to sweep it out, but it's still pretty dirty. If we close the door to block the lamp light, no one will know we're there. Let me help you on the steps. These top few are almost burned through."

The room at the bottom of the stairs, or what remained of the stairs, must have been the pantry of the wealthy family who once lived here. Unrecognizable preserved food that had burst out of the jars and crocks from the heat of the blaze dripped over the shelves on the walls. Standing—in reality, more leaning—in the corner was a table with one burned-off leg, and on it were the supplies Gavin had brought in. He lit one of the kerosene lamps and closed the door. "I've walked around outside when the lamp was lit, and no light leaks out. We're safe in here. Do you think you can find this place again?"

"I think so, but I'm not sure I want to." Looking around, she said, "Gavin, I can't imagine how anyone or anything could survive this."

"Survival can mean different things to different people." He forced the images of the battlefield and the prison ship out of his mind, and whatever horror would come if he couldn't convince her to trust him.

She walked around the room, inspecting the damage. "I have followed you here to a place where no one can hear me scream. Was I foolish?"

"Please, Tansy, if you only knew how much I care

for…care about you and the family. It may have looked like I betrayed you, but I swear that was not my intention. Please trust me. Give me a chance to prove it to you."

"Don't make me regret this. Don't make Alden's soul regret that I followed you here."

"We don't have much time before it gets dark, and I have a lot to tell you." Taking a folded blanket from the table and spreading it on the floor, he motioned for her to sit. She did, and he sat beside her.

"Please listen, and don't judge until I tell it all."

"I'll try, but from what I know of you, it's hard not to judge."

"Do your best," he said, seeing her obvious scorn for him.

He kept his eyes on the wall while he recounted stories of the war and his friendship with Alden. "He told the silliest jokes at the worst times," he said. "Why did General Washington ride his horse into camp?"

She shrugged.

"Because the beast was too big to carry."

Her chuckle warmed him.

"That was Alden," she said. "If he wasn't the center of attention, he wasn't happy. I did love that about him, most of the time."

"Me, too. I think that's what made us such great friends. He brought out better things in me, and I did the same for him." Standing up, he paced back and forth across the small room. "I have something to tell you about how he died." He dragged his fingers through his hair. "It didn't happen the way I said it did."

Tansy stayed silent, but her eyes narrowed.

Turning his back on her, he said, "His hand was

blown off when he fell on me and saved my life. He died two weeks later in a prison ship in the harbor." When Tansy still didn't react, he kept talking. "The stump got infected. I did the best I could. He died a horrible death, but I held him the whole time. I never let him go." He choked on the words. "I'm so sorry." Swallowing a sob, he stepped farther away from her.

She stood. "I never blamed you. The truth is, it wasn't your fault that he died or even how he died. It was the war, and a war is made up of anonymous people. The problem is we just happen to be able to put a face on one of them."

With cautious steps, she moved closer to him. "I've had time to grieve for him, but obviously you have not."

Gavin led her back to the blanket. "Are you all right?" he asked. "Your hands are shaking."

"I'm suddenly cold, very cold."

Taking another blanket down from the table, he wrapped it around her shoulders. "Better?"

She nodded as he sat down beside her again.

"Before Alden died, I made a promise," he said, "a vow, to do whatever it took, so now I have to tell you the way I tried to keep that promise."

He told her about the guard, Peter Wright, the prison ship's captain, and about reporting to Simon Duffy. He told how he thought he was fooling them when in reality they were fooling him.

"I lied to everyone—you, Duffy, to everyone—and I take full responsibility for those lies, but I'd spent weeks on a prison ship in the harbor, and you'd be surprised how starvation and living in your own filth can make some decisions easier to accept. The captain said I could make the occupation easier for my friends and neighbors by being a liaison for the army, and I didn't care what I had to do to get off the ship, so I accepted."

He separated strands of hair exposing the scars on his scalp and pushed up his sleeves so she could see the ones on his arms. "Lice, rat bites, only bug-ridden gruel to eat, lack of water. It changes you inside and out. May you never know how many ways bugs and vermin can infest a man's body. May you never wake up in the morning to find more dead bodies lying around you than there were the night before. May you never know the smell of death. It can make you crumble into dust." He stared beyond her at something no one else could see.

When she touched his hand, he jerked it away. "I don't want your pity. I want you to understand why you have to listen to me. I've put your entire family in danger, and you have to help me do something about it."

Tansy whispered, "I'm sorry, Gavin."

His anger continued. "Don't be sorry! Listen to me and understand. Then we can do what we have to."

Without waiting for her to react, he went on. "Simon Duffy wants me to get a message to General Washington about a delay in a shipment of saltpeter for making gunpowder, but the delay is a ruse so the British can pick it up sooner. He knows that Nate has sent messages through Washington's secret spy network before."

Tansy's eyebrows shot up. "How does he know that?"

"He had me followed when I met you in the park.

The entire plan from the beginning was to set me up for something just like this. If I don't do what he wants, he'll have you, Nate, Daisy, and Charles arrested, and the little ones tossed in The Burns to fend for themselves." He swallowed the lump in his throat. "I was a fool, but I'm doing everything I can to right the wrong."

She stood up and bolted toward the door. "I have to warn them!"

Grabbing her before she could open the door, he twirled her around to face him. "No, Tansy. I have a plan. I know how we can get a true message to Washington and how the entire family can escape New York. Listen to me. I know it will work."

"Just like all your other plans have worked so far? Let me go!" She struggled in his arms, but he held her fast.

"Tansy, the family is being watched."

Her struggling increased. The pins flew out of her hair as she shook her head, and her fingers dug into his arms. "Let me go! You caught me at the message drop in the park so you could betray Nate to the British!" she cried. "You turned him in to save your own neck, and now you want us to help you? Are you out of your mind? Let me go! You're a beast!"

Gavin leaned toward her, pulling her into him. Speaking with calm determination, he said, "I am a beast. I'm every terrible thought you ever had of me, a liar and a traitor, but my heart is true. I will do whatever I must to save you from hanging. Even if it means being hanged myself."

Ignoring his words, she kept struggling, but he held her fast.

"Stop! Stop!" he shouted before he blurted out, "I love you!"

She stared at him as if a sea creature with six eyes and green skin had materialized before her eyes. "What?"

He wanted to stop talking, but he couldn't. "I'm in love with you, and I have been for a long time. Even before I met you, I was in love with you."

She locked her eyes on his and set her face with a deep scowl.

"I saw your portrait in Alden's watch, and I asked so many questions about you. He liked talking about you, and I liked hearing it. Then it happened. I fell in love with the woman in the portrait."

"Sounds like a fairy tale to me," she answered like a petulant child.

"It may have been a fairy tale in the beginning. Maybe my feelings were a way of coping with the horror of war, but then I met you. You were exactly as Alden said, and at that moment I was no longer in love with a painted image, but in love with a real woman."

He felt the tension leave her arms, but not the scowl on her face.

Neither of them spoke as a gust of wind made the unstable remains of the house quiver.

"Meeting Alden was the best, and the worst, thing that ever happened to me. The best because I felt the joy he had for life and learned to find some for myself. The worst because I knew you would never be mine, but I want you to know that if that kiss in the park is all I ever have of you, I will die a happy man."

****

The longer he talked, the more her heartbeat

143

slowed, the more her breathing calmed, and the safer she felt. Standing before her, she saw, instead of an American traitor, a man who defied his orders to bring Charles home after he stole the mail pouch. Gavin was the man who came with news of her deceased husband, not because he had to, but because he loved Alden. This man risked punishment to help the abandoned people of The Burns. His soul wasn't dedicated to the domination of the human spirit like the invading enemy from England, but instead dedicated to the deliverance of freedom and safety to anyone who needed it.

If she were to have a future, it stood right in front of her in the man Gavin Cullane. She would always love Alden, and she'd make sure that Young Alden grew up proud of his father. She realized, too, that Gavin, because of his deep friendship with Alden, would do the same. She had to listen to him and trust him. Alden had trusted him. She could almost hear Alden whispering in her ear, "Choose the man who knows you as I do. Choose my friend."

So she chose. "Tell me your plan, so I can see if I can improve on it."

He laid out his plans, and their escape began.

Chapter Seventeen

Day Three of Nine—September 7

"Nate," said Tansy as the family ate their early meal at the table by the fireplace, "I'd like you to take me to the Second Church of England this morning. I want to pick up some material for shirts for the boys while I still have money from Harriet's dress. Could you spare the time?"

Nate scooped a spoonful of cornmeal mush covered with maple syrup and milk out of his bowl and held it up in front of his mouth. "Why do you need me to go?"

"I don't like the neighborhood. I'd feel safer with you along. It won't take very long."

"I'll go with you," said Daisy while dropping another dab of butter into Gideon's bowl.

"Thank you, ma'am," said Gideon, stirring the mush.

"No," said Tansy. "Sorry, I want Nate's opinion on the material. After all, one of the shirts is for him, too."

"All right," said Nate. "It's not like I have any printing jobs. If we leave right now, we can be back before Daisy's done with the children's schooling, then Charles and Gideon can help me clean the press."

Both boys groaned.

As Nate and Tansy walked down to Princess Street

and the ridiculously named Second Church of England, pleasant conversation passed between them until Tansy said, "I want to say again how sorry I am that I couldn't get the message about the Duncans' party to the right people."

"It's probably a good thing," said Nate. "It would be a waste of time for anyone who went, nothing to be gained."

"Maybe we can find another way."

"Don't blame yourself. No harm done since Cullane hasn't done anything with it. I wonder why he hasn't."

"Maybe someday we'll find out." *Maybe sooner than you think.*

Three blocks away from the so-called church, Tansy put her hand on Nate's sleeve. "Let's go this way down the alley. It's quicker." Before he could answer, she turned into the alley and tugged Nate with her.

"Are you sure about this?" asked Nate, stepping over a small pile of rotting cabbage and moldy meat. "This alley is filthy."

"It leads to a back door."

That wasn't a lie. It did lead to a back door, the back door of Blackfield's Ale House. They crossed the threshold.

The only light in the narrow hallway came from sunlight streaming in through a small window in the door. The smell of ale and whisky was heavy as were the footsteps coming down the hall toward them.

"I don't like this," Nate said. "We're leaving." Grabbing Tansy's arm, he tried to pull her outside, but he felt a hand on his collar dragging him back in. He bumped into the chest of a man standing at least three inches taller and fifty pounds heavier, and the sheer bulk of the man stopped Nate in his tracks. The man put his hands on Nate's shoulders and pushed him farther inside down the hall, saying in an unusually low voice, "This way, if you please."

"It doesn't please me!" said Nate.

He turned back to punch at the man, but before his hand connected with the man's face, large puffy fingers engulfed his fist. Pushing Nate's hand down and around to his back, the man gave him another strong shove up the corridor. "This way, if you please."

"What's going on?" Nate called to Tansy over his shoulder.

"Please, Nate, don't struggle. We'll explain everything."

After five or six reluctant steps, the big man shoved Nate through a doorway on the right into a small room furnished with three round tables and six chairs at each table.

"This is our meeting room," said the man. "Take a seat."

Nate looked up into the eyes of a hulking man who could have been anywhere from thirty to fifty years old. Bushy salt-and-pepper-tinged hair grew to below his ears but still couldn't cover his protruding earlobes, and when he smiled, he was missing at least two of his front teeth.

The man pulled out a chair and forced Nate to sit. To Tansy he said, "Ma'am, he hasn't come yet, but he'll be here shortly. I'll be right outside the door. Just holler, ma'am, if this one gives you any trouble."

The door closed with a harsh click.

"Who was that?" snarled Nate with his hands

gripping the arms of the chair.

"Brian. He lives here at the alehouse. No family except the men here, and he's earned his keep as the bouncer ever since he was about thirteen and grew to his full height."

"Tansy, what is going on? Tell me, or so help me I'll...I'll..." he growled.

Tansy put her hands on her hips and stiffened her legs to face him. "Just what will you do, Nate? Brian will only put you back in that chair, and you will want to hear what we have to say." Her voice softened. "This is a matter of life and death."

The door swung open, and Brian entered again, pointing a finger at Nate. "Stay in the chair!"

Gavin Cullane followed the big man in.

Three hours later, Nate and Brian left the room in the alehouse, but Nate noticed Tansy's hesitation to leave with him right away, guessing it had to do with her changed relationship with Gavin Cullane. "I'll meet you at the end of the alley, Tansy," said Nate. "Don't be long. Then we can go home together."

After Nate was out of earshot, Gavin said, "I want to thank you. I want to thank you for believing in me...and trusting me."

"I do, Gavin. I do believe you...now, and I do trust you. If you can convince Nate to follow your plan, it has to be a good one. Nate's got a level head, and he thinks it will work."

"Thank you." Gavin never took his eyes off her. "There's something else. The last time I kissed you, I stole that kiss, and I hope you will forgive me."

"I do, and I have. I understand more about you now, more about why you've done the things you've done. And lest you think me too brazen." She reached up and caressed his cheek. "I see a different Gavin Cullane now, a man I appreciate and accept as true, and I can prove it." She stepped closer. "Kiss me again. This time I won't slap you."

He gazed at her face for a long time before tipping his mouth down to hers. When he was close enough to breathe in her breath, he said, "I've known you for a long time. I want you to know me."

Pressing his mouth against hers as a butterfly alights on a nectar-filled flower, he tested and enticed before she stretched up to take his lips in her own. She pulled him into her, and he went willingly.

Heat cascaded through her body, not the angry fury of the first time he kissed her at the park, but a slow, lingering heat that would last long after they parted. Rising up on her toes, she moved her hands across his cheeks and neck to wrap her arms around him. He responded by tugging her hips into his.

They shared soft, gentle kisses followed by strong, demanding ones. The world disappeared, leaving their jagged breath, their warm touch, and their soft moans to remain.

She lost all sense of how long they kissed until, in a gasp, she whispered, "Gavin." He lifted his head and tucked a strand of her sunlight hair behind her ear with a delicate sweep of his finger. His fingers grazed her cheek and slid around until they hid themselves in her hair at the nape of her neck.

"Things have changed so much from the minute you appeared at our door," she said, her lips still reaching toward his. "But I realize now that you haven't changed, only that I understand. Everything about you was wrong, but now I know why."

"I'm sorry for that." He kissed her again.

She murmured, "I want to start this moment like nothing came before, like everything is new."

"Our predicament doesn't hold much hope for ours to be a long courtship."

"Then a short one it will be." Putting her hands on either side of his face, she tugged him down to kiss her again and again and again. She wanted more from him, needed more of him, but they both knew that now was not the time. Too many threatened lives.

With reluctant sighs, they left each other at the door.

****

"They've taken Charles!" cried Daisy from the front step as soon as Nate and Tansy came within sight of the house. "They came while you were gone and took Charles!"

"Who took Charles?" said Nate, running toward his frantic wife.

"The soldiers! They took him to the Sugar House prison on Crown Street. They said he's held on charges of treason! Nate, treason! What are we going to do?"

Taking Daisy by the arm, Nate led her between the houses to the entrance of his print shop in the back, and she scurried to keep up with his long strides. He opened the door.

Gavin Cullane stood beside Nate's only remaining press.

"You!" she shouted. "You did this!"

Nate held her around the waist to keep her from charging at Gavin.

"What do you know about this, Cullane?"

demanded Nate. "Where is my son?"

Tansy said, "Daisy says they've arrested Charles and taken him to the Sugar House prison."

Gavin lowered his eyes to the floor and shook his head. "I was hoping it wouldn't come to this. I was hoping Duffy wouldn't do something like this to ensure I cooperated." Looking up, he said, "But it's something we considered."

"You knew he would be arrested?" said Nate, releasing Daisy, who ran at Gavin with her fingernails out ready to gouge. Gavin twisted her around and held her against him facing out, so all she could do was flail her arms and kick him in the shins. "Ouch!" he said.

Sobbing, she went limp against him.

"It doesn't change anything you need to do, Nate," said Gavin.

"It changes everything," answered Nate, seething. "My son is more important than sending a coded message."

"And that message is important to winning this war. I know how to get Charles back, but the coded messages must be ready first."

Daisy turned her rage on her sister. "You knew about this?"

"It's a contingency we took into consideration."

"Contingency? Consideration! My son's life is more than a consideration. How could you, Tansy? How could you?" She raced back to her husband and fell into his arms.

Long minutes passed before Daisy's sobbing eased and she swallowed her tears. She turned toward her sister, to see Tansy and Gavin standing with their arms locked around each other and Gavin kissing the top of her head.

Daisy spat on the floor, her anger raging again like a mad dog. "I warned you! He's a traitor, and he had our son arrested. It's a trap, Tansy. Don't be a traitor, too!"

Before either Gavin or Tansy could answer her, Nate said, "Daisy, I spent all morning with these two in a disgusting tavern that smelled like the sewer it was, but Gavin convinced me of his true motives. He was keeping a promise to Alden when he posed as the so-called colonial liaison, and now he's keeping a promise to Tansy and to me."

Daisy stared up at him unbelieving.

"I'll explain everything to you, but for now you have to trust me, maybe not Cullane, but me. I love you more."

She blinked away tears. "More than what?" she stammered.

"More than everything."

Falling into his arms again, she listened while Gavin and Tansy explained the plan to keep the family safe and how to return Charles home.

Chapter Eighteen

Day Four of Nine—September 8

Gavin's next move in the master plan was to make Duffy think he still had the upper hand, especially now that he'd had Charles arrested. Tansy prayed she had the courage to go through with it.

She smoothed down her skirt and took a deep cleansing breath before climbing the steps to the commandeered house Simon Duffy used as his headquarters. She wore her most flattering outfit, a blue-flowered cotton dress with dark blue accents at the sleeves, a split in the front showing her dark blue underskirt, and a revealing neckline designed to get Simon Duffy's attention. Her hair fell in a loose knot at her neck with no cap to cover it, so all could see its sunshine blonde.

A soldier at the top of the steps opened the mahogany door for her, and she stepped into a large foyer with a marble floor and a dazzling chandelier over her head. Just inside were two desks with a crisply dressed soldier seated at each one.

"May I help you?" asked one of them.

"My name is Tansy Carter. I am here to see Colonel Simon Duffy."

"He is not taking visitors today, ma'am."

"Please tell him that I have a message for him from

General Washington. Do you need me to repeat my name?"

"Uh…no, ma'am. Carter, General Washington," he mumbled before going through the doors to the right.

Tansy made her way to a chair against the wall, hoping the soldiers hadn't noticed her trembling legs or the quiver in her voice. Even though she and Gavin had rehearsed what she would say for as many scenarios as they could think of, she closed her eyes, she prayed for the family she'd come to rescue and for the man who had so unexpectedly entered her life.

The door to the inner office opened, and the soldier summoned Tansy to follow him inside. As soon as she stepped through the doorway, light streaming in from the south-facing window nearly blinded her. Putting her hand up to shield her eyes, she started across the room, but caught herself as she stumbled over a chair set right in the middle of the rug.

"Excuse me," she said, putting her hand on the back of the chair to steady herself. "The sun is very bright. Could you, please, draw the drapes?"

A thin, balding man in his middle forties with narrow gray eyes sat behind an ornate cherry wood desk. "No, I could not. Thank you, Corporal. I am not to be disturbed while Mistress Carter is here."

"Yes, sir," he said as he closed the door.

"What business do you have?" asked Duffy.

Tansy held her hand up to screen her eyes from the light, which she now realized was an intentional ploy on Simon Duffy's part to give him a distinct advantage, using the sunlight to make his visitors uncomfortable. Tansy sat up straight on the edge of the chair, refusing to let Duffy intimidate her.

Holding her head up, she said, "You know what business I have, so let's not waste time. My nephew, Charles Hemstead, has been incarcerated in the Sugar House on Crown Street. I would like to know when he will be released."

"He has been charged with treason, making release impossible."

"You know as well as I do that this charge is ridiculous. He is a sixteen-year-old boy."

"Boys much younger than that have been involved in treasonous activity against the British government...and hanged for it."

Tansy swallowed hard.

Duffy leaned back in his leather chair, steepling his fingers. "Will there be anything else, Mistress Carter?"

The haughty look in Duffy's eyes told Tansy that he had no respect for any woman. He wanted to master her, to dominate and force her to submit to his every whim, however vile, and all her tactics to make herself more attractive only increased his need. He was a man to be feared, and that was just the way he wanted it. Although she couldn't see the bulge growing in his trousers behind the desk, she knew it was there.

Be careful, she told herself. *Watch your every word.*

Tansy took a folded piece of paper out of her bodice, crossed the floor, and laid it on Duffy's desk.

He opened it and attempted to read it. "What is this gibberish?"

It was gibberish. Nate would never put even a false message of the Culper code into the enemy's hand, but Tansy said, "It, sir, is the coded message you wanted sent to General Washington."

Duffy's lips curled. "How do I know what this says?"

Sighing, she rolled her eyes as if anyone of adequate intelligence could read it. She tried to look self-assured as if she held the winning hand while on the inside she shivered, knowing she did not.

"It tells Washington to change the date of his pickup of the saltpeter."

"How can I be sure of that? I need to have it decoded."

"There's no time for that. Trust is a two-way street. I will trust you to release my nephew, and you will trust me that this says what you want it to and that I can get it to the appropriate people. My nephew is just as important to me as that message in the right hands is to you."

"It is risky to place my assurance in someone I have never met before," he said, continuing to stare at the message.

"I understand your concern, but think about it, which of us has the most to lose? I am risking my nephew's life while you risk only a missed opportunity to make a name for yourself."

Without warning, Duffy pushed back his chair, stood, and came around to the front of the desk. "I do not intend to risk anything."

Tansy willed herself not to move. If Duffy only knew how weak in the knees she felt.

He sat on the edge of the desk so close to her that his legs brushed against her skirt, but she locked her feet in place.

Holding up the coded message, he said, "May I keep this?"

"No."

He handed her the paper and let his fingers linger on hers a moment too long. "You have not mentioned Gavin Cullane."

"And why would I?" she asked, jerking her hand back and stuffing the message into her bodice, pushing it down farther than it needed to simply be out of sight.

Duffy's tongue peeked out of his mouth as he licked his lower lip. "Cullane has so little to offer a woman such as yourself. I could do so much more for you, give you a position in society and its accompanying wealth. Sadly, I find myself without a wife, and I do so enjoy having a woman at my side."

He didn't mention what Tansy already knew from the gossip that raged through a population with little else to take their minds off the war. Duffy's first wife had given him the prestige to secure a commission in the army and then disappeared without a trace while his second wife had left him with a fortune and then was found floating in the river. All investigations led to naught.

"I have no further need of Mr. Cullane's services nor yours after today," said Tansy. "Cullane wants to send this message on, and I want my nephew home. I am the one who knows how to get this to the proper people. Neither he nor you do. Release my nephew, and when he is home in the loving arms of his family, I will personally see that this message gets to General George Washington, and then the saltpeter will be all yours."

Duffy stood and looked down his nose at her. "If I send the boy home, how can I be certain that you will keep your word?"

Gathering all her courage, she pressed her hand to

his chest. "My word is as good as yours."

With a hearty laugh, he grasped her hand, squeezing it a little too tightly, and then put a wet kiss on the back of it. With a jerk, she pulled back her hand, and he laughed again.

"It will take three days to arrange for his release, and that is all the time you have to get this to Washington. The charge against your nephew is serious, and it will take a judge's order to vacate it."

"The three days to release Charles plus the two full days to reach General Washington is cutting the timeline very close. Are you sure you can afford to wait three days before I send the message?"

Duffy strode to the door and opened it. "Here's how it will work. I will start preparing the necessary paperwork today, and as soon as I hear that Washington has the correct message and is delaying his ships to pick up the saltpeter, I will have the boy released. You do your part, and I will do mine. Good day, Mistress."

"How can I be certain you will do as you say?"

"Our only choice is to hold each other accountable. You have my word as an officer in the British Army. I trust that I have yours as a citizen of New York. Good day, Mistress."

As Tansy swept passed him, he waved for the corporal to come inside and shut the door.

Tansy grasped the railing on the outside steps and took in several deep breaths before starting down the street.

She prayed she had convinced Duffy she believed he would uphold his part of the bargain and release Charles. At the same time, she also prayed he believed she would send a message to Washington to delay the saltpeter. If neither one was true, Charles would pay the price, and it would be her fault for not playing her role well enough. Her stomach clenched, and she wanted to vomit, but she put her hand on her mouth and held it in until she was out of sight of the house.

****

Duffy stood at the window and watched the young Tansy Carter walk away.

To the soldier, Duffy said, "Go to the Livingston Sugar House, and tell the captain to move Charles Hemstead into isolation in the tower and to keep a guard on him at all times. He is not to leave that cell for any reason whatsoever. Not for as long as he lives, which may not be long."

"Yes, sir!"

Chapter Nineteen

Day Five of Nine—September 9

Charles shivered.

Not from the cold—the fourth floor of the six floors of the Livingston Sugar House prison was stifling hot—but he trembled from his own nervous exhaustion. The sights and choking stench that greeted him when the soldiers brought him here two days ago overwhelmed him. Over a hundred prisoners covered the floor, starving skeletons, crawling with fleas and lice, and many too ill to even move, let alone make it to the overflowing slop bucket in the corner. The worst was that near the door lay the decaying bodies of eight men who had died the night before.

Two local women, paid a penny for each body, stitched blankets closed over the dead men and then dragged the bundles against the wall. Later in the day, two local men carried the corpses out to the yard to wait for the daily arrival of the death cart to take them to burial in a mass grave in the yard of the nearby destroyed Trinity Church. Like those on the prison ships on the river, their names would be known only to God.

Two Continental officers, Captain Lord and Lieutenant Drumgoole, had greeted Charles after the soldiers unshackled him and shoved him into the room.

"You're not a soldier, so what are you in for?" asked Drumgoole.

Charles rubbed his sore wrists. "I don't rightly know. I stole a mail pouch once, but they let me go for that. Today they said treason, but I didn't do anything. I swear!"

Captain Lord put his hand on Charles's shoulder. "None of us in here did anything, boy. At least not anything to deserve this."

"We'll show you the ropes, lad, although there's not much to it," said Drumgoole, a skinny, dark-haired man with haunting blue eyes. "The first floor of this building is for the British guards, and the other five floors are for the comfort and care of over five hundred colonial men. You can make yourself at home in any empty corner you can find."

Charles scanned the room. Men sprawled over every inch of space, looking like the piled-up foodstuffs his mother stored in the cold cellar.

"I don't see any place," said Charles. "I'll just stay here by the door."

"Not a good idea," said Captain Lord, whose ribs and collar bone poked through his threadbare shirt. "The soldiers can grab you too quickly. We'll find a spot for you. Move over, Dawson, give the boy some room."

An emaciated Dawson moaned but moved over, exposing a filthy bandage on a pus-filled wound on his leg.

Charles gagged.

"You'll get hardened to it, lad," said Drumgoole, "the longer you're here."

Lord and Drumgoole kept Charles close to them

for the rest of the day. They taught him how to stomach the scraps of pork and moldy sea biscuits brought up three times a day by washing them in water and scraping off the parasites. Baskets of baked rolls and other treats brought to the prison by two women in the neighborhood sometimes passed inside to the prisoners after a bribe for the guards. Men closest to death got the first servings, but Drumgoole managed to save Charles half of a houndstooth candy.

"Thank you, sir," said Charles after popping the candy into his mouth.

"Attention! Attention!" shouted Drumgoole. "The court is in session! Who will be convicted—I mean, who will stand accused today?"

To Charles's surprise, an uproar sounded among the men, all of them clamoring to be the accused.

"What is this?" asked Charles.

"You'll see," said one of the prisoners, clapping him on the back. "Come sit in the gallery with me. Name's Ned." He led Charles to the back wall and sat down, tugging on Charles's breeches to join him on the floor.

Captain Lord stepped forward, wearing a filthy towel with dried blood smeared over it on his head and holding a tin cup in his hand. Banging the cup on the wall three times, he said, "Hear ye! Hear ye! Court is in session! Mr. Prosecutor, who is on trial today?"

"Before we begin, your honor," said Drumgoole, his voice strong despite his famished appearance. "I must tell you that your judicial wig is crooked."

With a look of utter horror, Captain Lord straightened the towel until it covered his face. "Better?" he asked, peeking out from under the towel.

"Much, your honor. Who will bring the accused forward?"

A man grabbed another bony prisoner sitting next to him and dragged him to the front, forcing him to stand beside Captain Lord. To Charles's surprise, Ned burst out laughing along with everyone else. Nudging Charles with his elbow, Ned said, "Abel always puts on a good show."

Charles was more than a little confused, more so after he saw two English guards come inside the door and stand in the back.

"What is the charge?" said Lord in a nasal voice that brought more laughter.

"You may recognize the defendant from previous trials where he was convicted of becoming intoxicated on the fine wine we are served at every meal in this elegant establishment."

Judge Lord paced in front of the audience until the laughter died down. "I believe I sentenced him to serve three days in the luxurious king's quarters on the twelfth floor, did I not? As I recall, that sentence included sleeping on a down-filled mattress and drinking English whiskey from golden cups."

"Don't forget the doxy sent in for my pleasure," said Abel. He winked. "We done it five times." The other prisoners hooted, hollered, and made lewd gestures.

"Silence! Was that not enough to teach you a lesson?"

In all seriousness, Abel said, "It was hell, sir. I beg you not to punish me so harshly. Please, I could not stand to have a full belly." Just then he reached inside his mouth, jerked out a bloody black tooth, and held it up. "That makes three this week!" The crowd again burst into raucous laughter as Abel dropped the tooth into Judge Lord's tin cup.

"I'll save it for you," said Lord before tossing the tooth into a box on the floor. It clattered into the hundreds of rotted teeth already there.

"This time, your honor, the crime is much worse," said Drumgoole. "Abel Martin is charged with…" Drumgoole's voice choked with emotion. "The crime is so heinous I cannot bring myself to say the words." He buried his face in his hands.

"But you must," demanded Lord while dancing a little jig. "You must! It is your duty to do disgusting things."

Putting his hands to his heart, Drumgoole said, "I am distressed to say that he is charged with stealing the thick-cut beefsteak, dripping with gravy, right off the plate of inmate Peterson, who had only gotten one bite before Martin stuffed the entire thing into his mouth."

Peterson leapt up, holding his stomach and whimpering. "Thanks to him all I had left on my plate was a measly half a fried chicken, a bowl of savory beans, and a plate of cornbread. It was awful! Do you agree with me, boys?" The boisterous crowd agreed.

Charles leaned over to Ned. "When do these meals show up?"

"In your dreams, boy, in your dreams."

Four more men jumped up to testify in the most melodramatic style that Abel Martin had stolen over a dozen of their flapjacks, four cranberry tarts as big as your head, two loaves of bun bread with butter pudding, and thirty-five gingerbread cookies.

Charles's mouth salivated.

Prying open Abel Martin's mouth, Captain Lord said, "I am sorry, lads, but the food is gone. It can only be retrieved in an entirely different form later today in that bucket." He pointed to a stomach-turning slop bucket in the corner. The prisoners booed and gagged dramatically. "These are serious crimes. Do you have a defense?"

Sticking out his chin in defiance, Abel Martin said, "I'm not sorry. I'd do it again." Waving his finger across the audience, he said, "And if I get the chance, I'll steal your ration of salmon, clams, and catfish." He pointed at the English soldiers in the back. "That's the menu for tonight, ain't it?"

Both British soldiers laughed and nodded.

"So, guard your plates!" cried Abel. "Guard your plates!"

Drumgoole said, "As you can see, Magistrate, this man is unrepentant. His food thefts will continue unless his punishment is severe. Give him your worst."

The other prisoners cheered and chanted, "Your worst!"

Pacing again in front of the crowd, Captain Lord rubbed his chin as if in deep thought. After several minutes of grunts and groans to show he was taxing his brain beyond its capacity, he walked up to the defendant. "I have decided that you will be sentenced to..." Before he could finish the door slammed open, and two more soldiers marched in.

"Charles Hemstead, we want Charles Hemstead," one of them shouted. "We have release papers for Charles Hemstead."

Charles started to stand when Ned jerked him down and whispered, "It's a trick. There's no getting out of here alive. Keep your head down and be quiet." Charles obeyed.

Again, the guard shouted, "Charles Hemstead, where are you?"

To Charles's bewilderment a man with a scruffy beard, sunken eyes, and an ashen complexion forced himself to his feet, barely able to stand on emaciated legs. "I'm the one you want."

The guards grabbed him by his arms and dragged him out.

When the door shut behind them, Ned said, "That was John Barnes. He probably wouldn't have lasted the night anyway. Now you might think he did you a favor, but the truth is that in this place, you did him a favor by giving him your name. At least he'll have a few hours out of here, maybe even a bit of fresh air to breathe before he dies and gets out of here forever."

A low murmur floated through the men until one of them started clapping. Soon they all joined in. "They're hoping Johnny can hear them," said Ned. "That's their way of saying goodbye."

Trying hard not to be overwhelmed by the comradery in this terrible place, Charles clapped as loud as he could. The pain in his hands helped him hold back his tears.

"Gentlemen, I have reached my verdict," shouted Captain Lord. "I sentence this man to watch while the rest of us dine on large portions of plum pudding like Granny used to make. After our hearty meal of lamb, sausage, and braised carrots, we will watch while he licks all our plates clean."

"That's too good for him," shouted one man. "Make him eat the plum pudding, too."

"All right, Abel Martin, you will get the plum pudding followed by a hot bath scented with lemon verbena. Take him away!"

Martin sobbed loudly as two men dragged him back to his spot on the floor.

The laughter died out as the men wandered back to the spaces they claimed as their own, some against the wall, but most in tangled clusters across the entire room.

Charles shivered again.

Chapter Twenty

Day Six of Nine—September 10

Nate left the first coded message, the one Simon Duffy knew about, in a drop spot under a loose brick on Rutgers Street. It included the new false date of September 30 to pick up the saltpeter, along with instructions that Nate needed a reply at this same drop spot. The reply would be undecipherable twaddle because in asking for a reply, it became known that this drop could never be used again. It also alerted the colonial contacts to wait for a second message.

One of the soldiers who'd been watching the house followed Nate to the drop spot and stood nearby as Nate recovered the response. Duffy had made no attempt to hide any watchers, so Nate walked straight up to the soldier and handed him the message without ever opening it. *Let Duffy see what he can make of it!*

Nate then went home to prepare the second truthful message for General Washington that Nate would carry across the river to Continental-held territory in New Jersey.

****

Tansy tightened the ties on Lizzie's bonnet under her chin. "You look very nice, Lizzie. How do you feel?"

"I'm scared."

"Don't worry. Arrangements have been made for the whole family to take the ferry across the river to New Jersey, and you know what to do when we get there. Remember, you also know what to do if something doesn't go according to plan, so we're ready for anything. No reason to be scared, a little nervous maybe, but not scared."

"What if Mr. Gavin can't get Charles out of the prison? I don't want to go across the river without Charles."

"Mr. Gavin has given his word, and he'll bring Charles to safety."

Tansy said a silent prayer that Gavin could keep his promise and bring Charles to the rendezvous place on the other side of the river in time. He had told her he would not leave Charles in that prison under any circumstances, so they were not to wait for them, but to go on to safety on the Continental-held side of the river without them. If Charles was not there waiting in New Jersey, it meant they were both dead. Her stomach lurched at the thought. Mortal danger surrounded them on every side.

Their stolen kiss in the shadows of the print shop last night before he slipped away into the darkness had begun sweet and tender and then grew into an almost desperate passion.

"If tonight could last forever," he whispered in her ear, "I'd hold you and love you and never let you go."

"When this is over, we won't be separated again."

Softly rubbing his cheek against hers, he said, "This may be all we ever have. So many things could go wrong."

She leaned away. "No, I don't want to think about

what could go wrong. I have to keep my mind focused on when we will be out of New York and together. Otherwise, I can't breathe. We have each other now, and we will have each other again." Grabbing him by the ear, she said, "Do you hear me? We will have each other again!"

A sly smile worked across Gavin's face. "That's the spirited woman I've heard so much about." His lips fell on hers.

Late into the night, the family reviewed every detail of their escape and planned for every contingency until they left no room for error. Their journey would start as soon as the sun rose.

Nate printed four copies of the same message. The messages, written in Benjamin Tallmadge's code, had been signed with Nate's secret code name, Marshall Anderson. No one on General Washington's spy network knew his real name, but they would recognize his code name and accept the message as authentic.

yrjvgqus mjskksele 187 47 yickup 282 wjkt gndijk for 618 30 283 187 178 634 484 284 up 433 618 17 Mukt meeve 50 618 eo. Vqucgid fqr 50 m1rkh1mm 1pdjrkqp

Translation: Previous message false. Ammunition pickup in West Indies for September 30 is false. Enemy to purchase it on September 18. Must leave by September 12. Vouched for by Marshall Anderson.

Nate would carry one message, and Daisy cut the others into narrow strips and hid them in the children's clothing. They stiffened the brim of Lizzie's bonnet with thinly cut strips of one coded message laid across a thick paper and covered with clear glue made from fish scales. It took hours of soaking, boiling, and then cooling to get the scales ready to glue, making a stiff filling inside her cloth brim. Putting Lizzie's bonnet under her nose, Tansy sniffed. *Thank goodness. No fishy odor.*

Tansy arranged a second message, also cut into tiny strips, over the brass buttons on Gideon's jacket and then overlaid each button with a dark blue cloth, matching his jacket perfectly.

Mercy begged not to be left out of the message carrying, so Nate printed a third message in a special ink between the lines of a handwritten letter Daisy wrote. The letter was ostensibly from Mercy's grandmother, Daisy and Tansy's mother, and when held up to a heat source, such as a candle, the coded words became clear to anyone who could decipher the code. Mercy would carry this letter in her rucksack, after having rehearsed how it was the only letter she ever got and how she treasured it. Also inside the rucksack were some cookies, a slice of cornbread, and Mercy's doll, Gertrude.

"This puts the children at such risk," said Daisy.

Tansy said, "It's not likely the soldiers will search children, especially not in the places we're hiding the messages. However, it's a much greater risk that they will search or detain the adults, which would leave the children on their own."

"I don't know which I'm more afraid of."

"Your children are clever and resourceful, and we've trained them well. They know where the safe houses are. They know how to identify themselves so they can get help. We've rehearsed so many scenarios, even little Mercy could find a way, and with her brothers' and sister's help they'll be all right." Tansy touched Daisy's arm. "If I didn't believe that, I wouldn't trust them to take care of Young Alden."

With a sigh, Daisy said, "Your courage always astounds me."

She chuckled. "Courage or foolhardiness, who can tell which?"

Tansy and Daisy divided and then sewed what was left of the fifty pounds into the hems of their skirts and some of it into the hems of the children's clothing. Nate got a secret pocket stitched into the crotch of his breeches for coins. After wrapping each coin in cotton so it wouldn't clink, he slipped it into his hidden compartment. Each adult and child also carried two pounds in paper or coin in their pockets.

Since they would be traveling on their own in small groups to Tansy and Daisy's parents farm in western New Jersey, the adults and children alike studied and memorized the map Gavin drew showing landmarks, farms, and inns of known patriots. Every ten miles, he designated a meeting place where anyone who had gotten separated was to wait for two days for the others before moving on to the next landmark.

Gideon balked at having to learn so much in such a short time. He swore he could take care of himself until Nate spoke to him in a tone that commanded his attention. "First of all, Gideon, if you get lost, knowing this map is the only way you'll get back to the family. Second, you'll be responsible for showing Charles the way, and third, your life depends on knowing this." His finger hit the map repeatedly. "Are we straight, young man?"

"Yes, sir," said Gideon who immediately went back to studying the map.

****

A young girl of about ten years old stood outside the doorway of the fourth-floor room of the Livingston Sugar House Prison. "I have a basket for Lieutenant Drumgoole. May he have it?" she said in her quiet voice to the soldier stationed outside the door.

"I'll take it," said the soldier.

"Oh, no, sir. I beg you, it's for Lieutenant Drumgoole. He's my father, and it's his birthday. I beg you, please, let me give this to him." She bit her lip and looked up with soulful eyes.

"Let me see what's in it first." He lifted the cloth.

"One of the turnovers is for you."

After touching all the turnovers and taking out the biggest one, he said, "All right." Swinging the door open, the guard called out, "Drumgoole, I want Drumgoole here right now!"

"Is this your brat?" asked the guard after the lieutenant stepped over enough prisoners to make his way to the door.

"Hi, honey," said Drumgoole with a smile that, despite him being only in his thirties, revealed two missing teeth lost to starvation.

"This is for you, Papa. Happy birthday," said the girl.

"Why, thank you, sweet one." The child handed Drumgoole the basket and pulled on his tattered shirt to give him a kiss on his cheek. Whispering in his ear, she said, "When invited to supper, bring the boy Charles." In the loud voice she said, "I love you, Papa. When can you come home?"

"Off with you!" said the guard before Drumgoole could answer. The girl scampered down the stairs as

Drumgoole lifted the napkin covering the contents of the basket. Inside were three apples and three small turnovers.

Taking the basket back to Captain Lord, they used knives they had made from belt buckles to cut the apples and the turnovers into small pieces before passing them out to as many men as they could.

Chapter Twenty-One

Day Seven of Nine—September 11

With Young Alden safely wrapped in her gingham sling, Tansy took Mercy's hand. "Ready to go? I expect you will do just what we've practiced on this adventure."

Five-year-old Mercy nodded.

"We gave Young Alden a mixture of tart cherry and hops to make him sleep, but I expect you to be quiet all on your own. Do I have your word you will try your best?"

Again, Mercy nodded.

"Then we're off."

With Young Alden slung across her chest in his gingham sling, Tansy hoisted a smaller sling over her back filled with portions of food and Alden's canteen full of water, and taking Mercy's hand, the two of them stepped out on the front step. They waved to the two soldiers who had stood across the street all night.

For the soldiers' benefit, Tansy turned back toward the doorway and called out, "Nate, Gideon, we're leaving. We'll meet you at the park."

Neither of them answered from inside the house, but Tansy didn't expect them to. Nate and Gideon had left long before the sun was up to get to the Paulus Hook Ferry while it was still dark. They'd take a morning ferry across and camp on the other side until the rest of the family came across the next morning.

Tansy called into the house again. "Daisy and Lizzie, can you carry the other basket with the rest of our lunch?"

"We'll catch up," answered Daisy. "The picnic basket is almost packed."

A few minutes later, Lizzie and her mother were beside Tansy and Mercy. "I can smell the meat pies," said Lizzie in a loud voice for the soldier following them. "I hope they'll still be warm by the time we get to the park."

Their walk to the park in the less-stifling weather of September and the coming autumn was enjoyable, even if tension filled. Every once in a while, one of them looked back to see if the soldier named William lagged behind, and when Mercy waved, William cursorily waved back.

When they reached the corner by the tailor shop, Daisy said, "Lizzie and I want to go to Mistress Mitchell's shop to pick up some thread for her new dress. It's just up the way. How about we meet you at the park in a few minutes?"

"Fine. Gideon and Nate will have brought the rest of the food from the house by then," replied Tansy, "and we can all eat together. I'll set the blanket under the oak tree."

Tansy, Mercy, and the baby headed for the park while Daisy and Lizzie continued down the street.

"Is William following us?" asked Tansy.

Mercy looked back and waved again. "Yes, ma'am, just like we thought he would. Does he know about the loose stone in the wall?"

"Probably not, but Simon Duffy does, and he thinks I'm the one sending the message on. Now, quiet, no more talking about secret messages."

"Yes, Aunt Tansy."

****

Boarded-up windows to prevent escape on the fourth floor of the Sugar House Prison kept the air stale, thick, and hard to breathe while the 112 forsaken men on this floor slept or lay very still to conserve their dwindling strength in the heat. Over the last few days, desperation had consumed Charles, but he wouldn't complain in front of these men who'd suffered here much longer than he had. If they could bear up under these wretched circumstances, then so could he.

As noon approached, Charles closed his eyes and tried to sleep just to pass the time until he felt something hitting his shoes.

"Wake up, boy," said Captain Lord in a low, quiet voice. "Get up and come with us." Lieutenant Drumgoole crouched beside him.

Charles jumped to his feet, but Drumgoole put his hand on his shoulder. "Calm down. Don't wake the others. Follow me."

Stepping over other prisoners, Lord, Drumgoole, and Hemstead made their way across the room. Putting his mouth against the crack in the door, Lord said, "We're here," and the door opened just enough to let the three of them slip out.

In the hall, Charles took in a deep breath of the first fresh air he'd had in three days. "Ahh," he sighed.

"Shh," said Lord with a warning look.

Charles recognized the two soldiers as ones who had watched the mock trial two days before. The taller one beckoned them to follow him down the stairs, but as this was the first exercise these prisoners had had in a long time, they gripped the wall to keep their legs from buckling. Staggering down the steep steps, Charles lost his footing and fell forward, but unexpectedly, the British soldier behind him pulled him back by his shirt.

"Thank you," Charles said, looking back at the round-faced, dark-haired man.

The soldier smiled, a gesture Charles didn't expect from any of the English. That smile made him wonder if the executions of the three prisoners weren't far off.

Once on the first floor, the soldiers led the trio into a small room with a large table laden with yellow cornbread soaked with butter, soft baked apples covered in cinnamon, and mushy boiled potatoes dripping with gravy among the other food dishes. The delicious aroma filled Charles's nose, and his stomach rumbled.

"Sit," said the oldest of the two British soldiers. The three prisoners hesitated.

" 'Tis no worry," said the soldier in his Irish accent. "Sit, lads."

Charles followed Captain Lord and Lieutenant Drumgoole's lead and pulled out a chair. Trying not to grab the piece of cornbread set in front of him, Charles slipped his hands under his legs and sat on them while licking the drool off his lips.

"Go ahead, eat," said the Irishman, "but take it slow. You've no' eaten in a while, and it might take your stomach getting used to it. Start with the broth."

Between spoonfuls of beef broth, Captain Lord said, "Why are we here?"

"Watching you put on those plays to make yer men

laugh and maybe forget their troubles for a while, made us think about how we might be enemies, but we're still all men. We decided to give ye some of that food ye talked about so much."

" 'Tis what one decent man would do for another," said the oldest soldier. "What you don't eat, we'll put in this sack for you to take back to the others."

No one spoke another word until the three prisoners had eaten their fill. The food was soft, bland, and easy on their stomachs, but it gave them energy and satisfaction they hadn't experienced in a long time.

The soldiers began filling a cloth bag for each prisoner with the leftovers. When the bags stretched at the seams, the Irish soldier said, "I'm sorry, but ye have to go back. Follow me." He led them out into a small alcove before he heard the older soldier call from inside the dining room, "Furlong, come back here!"

"Wait here," said Furlong to the men as he hurried back to obey.

Lord, Drumgoole, and Charles eyed each other, wondering why they'd been left here alone, until they heard a loud whisper coming from the other direction, "This way! Hurry!"

Lord gave a quick nod of his head, and they all moved toward the voice. The side door stood open. Stepping out into the sunlight, they heard another whisper from a man hidden in the bushes at the back of the yard, "Follow me!" Again, without hesitation they headed in that direction. Once they were beyond the tall hedges, the man who had called to them stepped out into the light.

"Gavin Cullane," said Charles.

"Follow me," said Gavin. "Leave your sacks of

food here. Furlong and Smythe will make sure they get upstairs."

Charles hesitated. "I know him. This isn't good. He works for the British."

"I don't care who he works for," said Lord. "We're making a run for it."

Grabbing Charles by the arm, Lord and the others ran toward the freedom to be found inside the crowded city.

Chapter Twenty-Two

Day Seven of Nine—September 11

"This is a beautiful day for a picnic, right, Mercy?"
A delicate breeze swept over the park, and the lack of
rain for the last few days left the grass dry and soft.

"Yes, ma'am."

"I think we can put our blanket over there," Tansy
said, pointing to a spot just beyond the oak tree in the
center of the park.

Tansy unwrapped the carrying cloth around her
back to reveal three sweet cakes and some dried apples
rolled up inside a cotton rag. With the blanket spread
out, she unwrapped the sleeping Young Alden from his
sling and laid him in the corner, covering his face to
protect his eyes from the bright sun.

William took his post at the edge of the grass on
the walkway, never taking his eyes off them.

"Young man! Young man!" Tansy called to him.
"It seems we have foolishly let my sister leave with the
basket of food, but we have these cakes and apples, and
we would be more than glad to share with you."

William shook his head.

"Now," whispered Tansy to Mercy, and just as
they had rehearsed, Mercy picked up a dried apple
piece and ran over to William. "Please, eat with us. I
never ate with a soldier before. See my dolly, Gertrude,

over there? She wants to eat with a real soldier. Please!"

Taking his hand, she tugged him over to the blanket.

"I could get in trouble for this," William said.

"It's not shirking your duty," said Tansy. "We're right here beside you. You couldn't watch us any closer."

"I hope my commanding officer sees it that way."

The three of them enjoyed the cakes and the apples while Young Alden continued to sleep.

Mercy stood up to whisper in Tansy's ear. "Can't you wait?" asked Tansy.

"No, ma'am, I really have to go!"

"She has to relieve herself," said Tansy to William. "Will it be all right if we go to those bushes? If you could watch the baby, we'll be back as soon as we can. It won't take long."

"Well…" said William.

"We won't leave without the baby, and he won't be any trouble. He won't wake up until he's hungry again, and that shouldn't be for at least another hour. Do we have your permission?"

Jumping up and down and grabbing herself between her legs, Mercy said, "Please, Aunt Tansy!"

"All right," said William, "but be quick about it."

Tansy and Mercy, dragging her doll by the arm, made their way into the thicket on the opposite side of the park. After making certain the bushes had closed around them, Mercy said, "Now, Aunt Tansy?"

"Now."

Ten minutes passed before Corporal William Taggert looked in the direction of the thicket and wondered what was taking so long. He waited five more minutes before deciding to see what the trouble was. Checking on the baby first, he unfolded the gingham scarf to find a baby-sized cotton-stuffed doll with button eyes.

Chapter Twenty-Three

Brian wrapped his huge arms around Tansy after she and Mercy slipped in through the back door of the Blackfield Ale House. "We were getting worried you might not make it."

"We've been on the run ever since we left the park, darting in and around buildings in a haphazard pattern on the chance that William might have picked up our trail. We rested a couple of times behind garbage cans in alleys or in doorways to catch our breath."

"It's near three o'clock, and we were getting worried."

"Brian, this is Mercy," she said, hoping he'd release her from his bear hug. "Mercy, this is Brian. He's a good friend."

Mercy curtsied and said, "Glad to meet you, sir. Are my mother and sister here?"

"They are for sure," said Brian. "They got here a couple of hours ago. And the babe's been crying for his mother."

"I don't blame him," said Tansy, feeling the painful pressure in her breasts and the strong need to alleviate it by feeding her son. Young Alden giggled and wiggled as soon as she lifted him out of his cocoon of blankets in the picnic basket that Daisy and Lizzie had carried. Tansy kissed him on the cheek and, sitting in the chair Daisy slid under her, started to feed him.

"He was as quiet as could be until we got here," said Daisy.

"Did you have any trouble finding this place?"

"Not a bit. Your directions were perfect. Although," she whispered, "Brian was a little scary when we knocked on the back door, but now we know the kind of man he truly is."

"How long before Charles gets here?" asked Lizzie. "And Papa and Gideon?"

"We're meeting your father and Gideon on the other side of the river tomorrow, and hopefully Charles will be with them," said Tansy. "But tomorrow the rest of us leave for New Jersey. You've been very brave so far, and we can make it the rest of the way."

Brian carried in several warm biscuits covered with gravy and a pitcher of milk and set them on the table. Pulling spoons out of his vest pocket, he said, "Cook is packing you a couple of bags with food you can eat on the run. The girls can carry them while you and your sister take the baby in the basket."

"Thank you, Brian. Please thank everyone for sheltering us here. We're grateful."

"It's nothing, Miss Tansy. Mr. Gavin ain't cut from the same cloth as the lobsterbacks who come in here, drink our ale, and eat our food, and think that 'cause the king puts a tax on whiskey they don't have to pay."

At the mention of Gavin's name, the memory of the warmth of his chest against her surrounded Tansy, and she smiled. His arms had become a place of safety, confidence, and most recently love. The love she allowed to surface became a hunger that could only be satisfied by his presence. A simple glimpse of his face and all her fears disappeared, but without him she felt alone like she never had before.

Alden's love for her, although full and deep, had squirmed like an itch she needed to soothe, which she did with her quiet words and her lovemaking. Alden's restless soul needed her touch while Gavin was the salve that soothed her own uncertainties. A sense of calm flooded through her every time she looked into his eyes. Yes, they had a lot to learn about each other, but that learning would come. She did love Alden and always would, and she hadn't replaced his love with Gavin's. Instead, she allowed Gavin's love to flourish alongside it. Silently, she begged the Lord to bring Gavin back to her quickly.

"Are you all right, Aunt Tansy?" asked Lizzie.

"Yes," said Tansy, sitting up straight, "just remembering and hoping."

After eating and dosing Young Alden again with tart cherries and hops, everyone got ready for the next leg on their journey. Brian went ahead, making sure the streets leading to the entrance of the abandoned section of The Burns were clear of soldiers. When he was certain they were, he came back for the women and motioned for them to follow him. Racing across the street, they ducked between the mounds of debris and were soon out of sight.

They had made the first turn to the left and then two turns to the right when two women and three men stepped out from behind the rubble of brown bricks, blocking their way.

****

Nate and Gideon waited in the general store where passengers bought tickets for the Paulus Hook Ferry from Alice McGuire and her son, Amos.

A significant aspect of George Washington's spy network was that, while people might know the drop spots, they were unaware who picked up or delivered the coded messages. Today that secrecy might prove a problem for Nate.

It had been only by coincidence that Nate had been at the store several months ago when a young boy ran in with a book for the owner, Mistress Alice McGuire. The child was so excited that the book slipped out of his hand to the floor as did two bookmarks tucked inside the pages. Nate recognized that these bookmarks, decorated with tiny colorful patterns, held codes indicating pages and words in the book to reveal a message. The boy scooped up the book with profuse apologies and handed everything to Alice who accepted it as fast as she could. Nate continued to act as if he were engrossed in the packets of flower seeds on the counter and had not paid any attention to the boy or the book.

Today Nate had to hope he could convince Mistress McGuire and her son, Amos, that he, too, was part of the chain, so they might reveal who was next in line or at least the location of the next drop area. He had to deliver the truthful second encoded message to the right place so it could reach General Washington in time. He had two days before it would be too late.

"Can I have a licorice?" asked Gideon with his nose pressed against the jar on the shelf.

"We have to see how much it is first," said Nate.

Alice McGuire answered without looking up while she collected the fare for a box of farming tools headed across the river on the ferry. "A penny a whip."

"I can get it for you," said Amos, a man in his late

thirties with a leg missing at the knee. He'd lost it in the first battle for Bunker Hill and made no secret of the fact he had returned home a bitter, angry man eager to defeat the British. "See one piece in particular you want?"

"Any will be fine, sir," said Gideon as Amos reached into the jar and pulled out one of the black whips.

"My name is Marshall Anderson," said Nate, "and I have a fine supply of patent medicines that your customers will be clamoring for. Patent—that means each and every one of these elixirs has been authorized and approved. Care to take a look?"

He opened a wooden box filled with jars and vials of various shapes, sizes, and colors of liquids and several small boxes of powders. He'd printed the labels himself and tied them around the necks of the bottles, but what the jars contained was anybody's guess. Some had chicken broth mixed with horse manure. Others were filled with a combination of water and spit to give it texture, and others were nothing more than printer's grease and ink with a few drops of blood stirred in. The powders were mixtures of sand, baking soda, and ground up pencil shavings. What fun he and Gideon had creating them!

Amos shook his head.

Nate went on. "Like I said, my name is *Marshall Anderson*, and we carry a line of the finest quality medicines from abroad such as Daffy's Elixir Salutis, proven cure for colic and gripping, along with Dr. Bateman's Pectoral Drops and John Hooper's Female Pills, guaranteed to make any woman agreeable and happy."

"No," said Amos, looking at Nate underneath his eyebrows.

Getting deeper into his salesman spiel, Nate raised and lowered the timber of his voice and gestured with his arms. "Then how about Mr. Ben Franklin's own mother-in-law's salve for lice and itching? Widow Read's Ointment is the best bar none! See this advertisement? We couldn't print it if it weren't true. Swear to God!"

Nate handed Amos a flyer with a picture of the medicine bottle and a man smiling broadly, obviously free of lice and itching. "I call your attention to the ingredients printed at the bottom." Running his finger along the small print at the bottom of the flyer, he said, "Some of it is printed in the language of the ancient Mesopotamians who first discovered this wonderful elixir. Please."

At the bottom edge of the paper printed in the Culper code was *Nelubemm Ephiluqp jencms ~185 elliuv veocpa jills. Piih mqgevcqp 431 pizv uvqr cnrqlvepv niuueai 634 himcxil rmieui bimr*

Translation: *Marshall Anderson family facing arrest. Taking ferry. Need location of next stop. Important message to deliver. Please help.*

Amos nodded and showed the flyer to his mother before going into the back room. When he returned fifteen minutes later, he handed Nate back the flyer, saying, "I can't help you. We don't carry anything like this. Our customers don't like it."

Nate's face fell. "Are you sure?"

"Absolutely," replied Amos. "The licorice is on the house. Have a pleasant trip."

With a soft groan of defeat, Nate said, "Come on,

boy. We can have our lunch under the shade tree outside. When does the next ferry leave?"

"You got about an hour to wait. Two tickets will be four shillings British. We don't take money issued by the Continental Congress."

Nate handed over the money, took the tickets, and left the store with Gideon padding along behind him, chewing on his licorice.

Nate had failed. Without the next name on the spy chain, he had no way to get the true message to General Washington in time.

"We better destroy this flyer," said Nate. "We don't want it falling into the wrong hands." Pulling out the flint and steel from his bag, he started to spark it to light the flyer when Gideon called out, "Wait! There's writing on the back!"

Sure enough, in crooked handwriting was written *fwllqy'u cpp_g_ncmiu pqlvbyiuv euo jql 625 viegbil.*

With haste, Nate decoded it from his memory of the codes. "Burrow's Inn three miles northwest ask for the teacher."

Tousling Gideon's hair, he grinned. "We've got a place to leave your buttons. The plan says we're to wait for the others on the other side. We're not free yet, but we're on our way."

An hour later, two English soldiers on the dock asked Nate and Gideon to open their box of medicines for inspection. Gideon, imitating his father, convinced both men to tack a sprig of lavender on their hats to prevent headaches. The soldiers motioned for the male Hemsteads to take their seats on the ferry.

They both gave a sigh of relief once they reached the other side of the river, to the side not held by the

British, but Nate wouldn't relax until Daisy and his other children were with him and out of danger. The knots in his shoulders wouldn't ease until he saw them step foot on the shore on this side. He loved Daisy more than everything, and if he had to go back for her, even at the risk of being hanged, he would.

****

Also the seventh day, September 11

Gavin ran with Captain Lord, Lieutenant Drumgoole, and Charles away from the Livingston Sugar House Prison along a complicated, circuitous route, weaving in and out between houses and over fences and finally into a shed. Closing the door, Gavin whispered, "Quiet." After the several minutes it took them to recover their breath, Gavin cracked open the door. "I don't see anyone. Looks like we're all clear." He lit a small lantern.

Tools, shovels, hammers, several hatchets, and a variety of woodworking utensils lined the walls. Folded neatly on the workbench lay four sets of work clothes with a folded piece of paper on top of each.

"We don't have much time," said Gavin. "We have to get to the ferry and cross tonight. Find the pile of clothes with your name on the work pass on top. You've been cutting trees for the ship builders, and you're headed across to cut down more timber. All the details are on the passes. Hurry and change!"

"Where did all this come from?" asked Drumgoole as he stripped naked and pulled up the pants.

Gavin buttoned his new shirt. "I guess it would be your wife."

"My wife?"

"The mother of your darling daughter who

delivered the apples and the message. A lot of people don't like what they see going on at the prison, so they help whenever they can. Charles, roll up the sleeves on that shirt so it doesn't look so big."

"Tell her thank you from a grateful husband."

"I won't be seeing anyone in the city again. I'm on the run as much as you are."

"What about my family? Are they all right?" said Charles.

"Charles, I'm taking you to your father. Lord and Drumgoole, once we're across the river, you'll be on your own to rejoin your outfit or make your way home, whatever you want."

"What about my mother and my sisters?" pleaded Charles.

"You'll see them soon enough. Pull those caps down on your heads as far as you can to hide your faces. Grab an ax, and let's go."

Following another roundabout route, the four men made it to the McGuire store near the ferry. By now the day headed into dusk. Out of sight in a copse of trees, Gavin gave the men last-minute instructions. "When I went in to buy the ferry tickets, I told the woman you were all pissing in the woods. No sense letting any more people see you than we have to.

"Lord, you and Drumgoole go first. Tell anyone who asks that you were cutting down trees in the city just north of the Commons for new ships, and that you're headed north to work on fresh timber. Tell them a couple more of your crew are coming behind you. That should make it easier for Charles and me to get aboard."

Lord and Drumgoole nodded.

"They'll ask for your work passes. Memorize your new name, and don't make all my hard work in getting you out of the Sugar House wasted. Got it, Landow, Mullins, Rothchild?"

Each one in turn answered to their new name with "Got it!"

"This is a busy crossing point, but it's so near to the British-held fort of Paulus Hook on the other side in New Jersey, there will be redcoats crossing with us, so once you get on the ferry, sit separate and don't talk to anyone. Take a nap or twiddle your thumbs, I don't care, but as little conversation as possible. We don't want anybody to take notice of you."

"Yes, sir," the men said in unison.

"Charles, once we're aboard, you stay close to me. We'll go to the back of the boat and sit on the floor. Less conspicuous. Are we ready?"

Captain Lord reached out his hand to shake Gavin's. "We can't thank you enough for what you've done for us. For the rest of our lives, we'll be grateful for this second chance."

"I'm keeping a promise. Everything to come is up to you. Good luck."

Charles and Gavin watched the other two men board the ferry with only cursory questioning from the British guards. A few minutes later, Charles and Gavin walked toward the ferry boat with their tickets in hand.

"Good day," said Gavin to the two uniformed soldiers on the dock.

"Work papers," said the older of the two men. Gavin and Charles handed them over.

The guard asked, "Fletcher, where are you going?"

When Charles didn't answer, the soldier shook the

papers in his face. "Fletcher!"

"I ain't Fletcher," answered Charles. "I'm Thomas Mullins."

"All right, that's what it says here. Let me see your hands. Take off your gloves." After Charles tugged off his work gloves, the soldier inspected his hands. "These hands look pretty soft for cutting wood."

"I just started two days ago," said Charles, "and I've been driving the team and wagon. Not using the ax yet, but I expect I'll be doing a lot of that when we get north of here."

"He's apprenticed," said Gavin. "I paid his folks a pretty penny for him. Glad they were to get rid of him, lazy as hell, but I'll teach him the value of hard work, right, boy?" He cuffed Charles hard on the side of the head.

Charles nearly stumbled off the dock before saying, "Yes, sir."

Handing the papers back, the soldier said, "Give your tickets to that man and get aboard. You listen to your master, boy."

"Yes, sir."

They walked down the center of the boat, passing by Lord and Drumgoole who didn't acknowledge them, and then passing a dozen English soldiers who also didn't acknowledge their presence. Once seated on the floor at the back of the boat, Charles said, rubbing his ear, "You didn't have to hit me so hard."

"It got you aboard, didn't it? Now keep your mouth shut. That Brit is coming back here."

The soldier, after planting his feet in front of Charles to steady himself on the rocking boat, said to Gavin, "They need another oarsman. The lad will do.

All right with you?"

Again, cuffing Charles on the side of the head, Gavin said roughly, "Do as the man says, Mullins, if you want to eat tonight."

With a glare for Gavin that could set fire to kindling, Charles stood and followed the soldier who pointed for him to sit behind an empty oar with the three other oarsmen. At least the hard work distracted him from the danger they were still in.

Crossing the Hudson River was uneventful, and Gavin gave a quick nod to Captain Lord and Lieutenant Drumgoole as they walked off the ferry and into the town of several buildings, stores, and an inn. He continued to stand on the dock as new passengers boarded, but as the ferry prepared to return to New York City, Charles hadn't appeared.

Gavin began to pace. This was the last ferry back to New York City. He'd planned to hand Charles over to his father and then make the crossing back on this last ferry to get Tansy and the rest of the family.

"The boy who helped with the oars is mine," he said to the soldier in charge of the boarding. "I want him back."

"We'll be taking on another oarsman on the New York side, so he'll stay on."

"Isn't this the last boat of the day?"

"Aye, but he can ride back with the soldiers returning to the fort for the night on a smaller rowboat. You wait here for him."

But Gavin couldn't wait for Charles. He couldn't be trapped on this side overnight.

"I want that boy now!" he said.

After a hard shove sent Gavin sprawling, the

soldier said, "You'll wait for him here, and if you don't like it, I'll put you in chains. Now get out of the way!" He slid his musket off his shoulder and pointed it at Gavin. "On your feet! Get back on shore!"

Gavin had no choice but to obey.

Chapter Twenty-Four

Day Seven of Nine—Evening, September 11

"If Mr. Gavin says he'll be here, then he will," said Agatha Marchand, a sturdy, gray-haired woman who held her head high despite two years in The Burns. "I never met a man more steadfast to his word." She came to stand beside Daisy after handing the spoon to Lizzie to stir the stew on the small iron stove in the center of the room.

"Gavin sacrificed for us, and we will return the favor, regardless of the consequences. When he came to us two days ago with his plan to get you out of New York City, we told him not to worry, we'd take care of everything, and we have. Look what we've done.

"We met you at the bricks to make certain you didn't get lost. The floor is swept as best we could in this burned-out house, and we scrounged up as much fresh food as we could find, and the men carried in that small iron stove to cook on and keep us warm."

Brian's deep voice joined in. "I'll make sure Daisy, Lizzie, Mercy, and Young Alden get across the river on the ferry. I'll be proud to pretend to be your husband taking his family across, and if Mr. Gavin doesn't come, I'll take Tansy across, too."

Daisy stretched up her hand to put it on Brian's shoulder. "We will be forever grateful for your help."

"You'll need me on the other side. I'm never going back to the Ale House. I'm staying with Mr. Gavin, and I'll fight for freedom with him. I might not have the brains to put together an escape plan, but I have the brawn to make it work, and that's what I will do."

Daisy, peering out the door of the burned-out house, asked once again, "Where is Gavin with news that Charles is safe on the Jersey side?" Her anxiety reached a fevered pitch. "He said he would be here before sundown. Something's gone wrong."

Tansy, hearing the conversation, gave Young Alden to Mercy to rock and went to put her arm around her sister. "It's no more than a slight delay. He'll be here. Gavin will get Charles to safety in New Jersey with Nate and Gideon and be back here as soon as he can. I'm sure he will. We just have to be patient. Gavin's plan to get Charles out of the Sugar House depends a lot on what the nearby neighbors could do for him, but he promised he would get Charles to the ferry tonight, so we just have to wait."

Taking her sister's hand, Daisy said, "I know you're just as worried as I am, but thank you for trying to ease my mind." A cool breeze fluttered through their loose strands of hair as the night air signaled the end of summer and the first hints of the autumn to come.

Even as Tansy spoke the words, a deep dread settled over her that the worst had happened, that he and Charles had failed to escape. She and Gavin had just begun, and it couldn't end so soon. It couldn't! Where would their memories come from? They had so few. What would they have to remember each other by?

"Forgive me, Tansy," said Daisy, leaning her head against the door frame and putting her hand over her mouth to cover a sob. "I can't stay brave for very long. Gavin said if he doesn't come here to meet us, we should go on without him." She stumbled through her next words. "Because both he and Charles are dead." Her sobbing turned into wailing as Tansy pulled her sister into her arms. "And what about Nate and Gideon? How will we know if they're safe?"

Tansy held her until both their tears faded away.

After the sun set and the children were fed, covered with blankets, and put to sleep on pallets strewn across the floor, the adults soon followed suit, all except Daisy and Tansy who huddled against the wall and waited.

****

"Follow me," someone called out to a shuddering Charles standing alone in the dark on the shore on the New Jersey side just south of the British-held Paulus Hook Fort.

Charles spun around to see Gavin crouched in the bushes behind him. "How did you find me?"

"Pure luck and the grace of God. Follow me. Your father is waiting for you."

"I didn't know what I was going to do," said Charles as he trotted next to Gavin. "The soldiers just left me here after bringing me back to this side. How far is the ferry station from here?"

"About two miles. They wouldn't let me back on the ferry boat with you and said the soldiers would row you back to somewhere near the fort. I've been walking around in the dark for hours. Didn't you hear me whistling?"

"I heard whistling, but I thought it was just a bird."

"City boy...but no matter. We're together now. I'll leave you with your father and brother at a barn near the station, and then I'll go back to bring the rest of the family over."

"How will you get back across the river?"

"The only way I can."

****

Day Eight of Nine—After midnight on September 12

At almost three in the morning, the door leading to the basement blew open and a brisk wind swirled around the room. In walked a shivering and wet-to-the bone Gavin Cullane.

"Gavin!' cried Tansy as she rushed over to him. He held out his arms for her, but Agatha Marchand pushed her aside. "Get him out of these wet clothes," she said. "If he gets sick, all is lost."

Agatha and Brian quickly stripped a teeth-chattering Gavin naked, wrapped him in a blanket, and pushed him toward the stove. Brian stoked it with more wood until it blazed. "Over here, Mr. Gavin," he said.

"Drink this," said Agatha, handing him a ceramic cup. "The whiskey will warm you up, and put on these woolen trousers. They'll warm you, too."

"Where'd you get this?" Gavin asked between gulps of the amber liquor as he pulled the scratchy trousers up and tied them at the waist.

"A lady never tells. There, that's enough. Getting drunk won't help. Tansy's been worried to exhaustion about you. We all have. Sit over there." Pointing to the corner behind the stove, she gave him a little shove in that direction, but he barely made it to the corner before his legs collapsed out from under him, and he sat down with a thud.

"Where have you been?" asked Mercy as she crawled into Gavin's lap and rested her warm cheek against his chest.

"Charles was commandeered to help row the ferry from New York over to New Jersey, and then they kept him on to row back to the New York side without me."

Daisy was on her knees, her hands shaking. "So, my boy is back in New York? Where? We have to get to him!"

"No, Daisy, the British-held Paulus Hook fortress is spread across a couple of small islands in the river close to the Jersey side, so the soldiers returned to their posts at the fort in a rowboat and left Charles on the shore. Only by luck did I find him in the dark."

"So where's Charles?" pleaded Daisy. "Tell me where my son is!"

"He's safe with his father and brother on the New Jersey side of the river," said Gavin. "The three of them are in the barn of a farmer and his wife who take in passengers who can't afford the inn. He's tired but safe."

Daisy collapsed into Tansy's arms, and they both sat on the floor next to Gavin.

"Did they hurt him in prison?" asked Daisy, unable to control her tears of relief.

"He's a little worse for wear, has lost weight, needs a good washing up, and he's seen things no one should have to, but all in all he survived," said Gavin. "I told Nate to start walking to the next stop, but he won't leave until he sees all of you set foot on the other side. He, Gideon, and Charles won't head out until he sees your faces. He's so mulish."

"Papa is as stubborn as a mule," said Mercy. "Hee-haw!"

Gavin chuckled, despite his still-chattering teeth.

As Daisy's hand fluttered to her chest. "They're all safe on the Jersey side?"

Gavin nodded.

"Both of you were on the New Jersey side, so how did you get back here without the ferry?" asked Lizzie.

"I had to swim."

A gasp went up from all around him.

Wrapping her arms around Gavin, Tansy held tight. "How did you manage it?" she asked. "The current is strong there."

"I tied my shirt and jacket around my waist and walked into the cold water of the Hudson River. I made my way from island to island, resting when I could and avoiding patrols and places lit with torches. The swim was hard, the water cold, and that current tried to take me away more than once. The last leg to shore was the hardest and the longest, but every time I wanted to give up and let myself sink to the bottom, I remembered you were waiting for me."

He kissed Tansy on the forehead. "And here I am."

"We want to hear how you got Charles out of the prison, Mr. Gavin, sir," said Brian.

As his shivering slowed, and he could feel his fingers again, Gavin told of how he got to know some families living near the Sugar House Prison who helped him get information inside the walls.

"A brave little girl delivered the apples and a message," he said. "She was just as brave as you, Mercy."

"Good," said Mercy.

"It is known among the guards how two prisoners on the same floor as Charles, a Captain Lord and a Lieutenant Drumgoole, try to keep the prisoners' minds off their plight by putting on ridiculous little performances, so one of the neighbor men convinced a couple of the more sympathetic soldiers to feed Lord, Drumgoole, and Charles with food provided by the neighbors. That and ten pounds, generously offered by some patriots, was all it took. They ate, and we walked away."

"So you just slipped out the back door?" asked Agatha Marchand.

"Just about the size of it. Then, also with the help of some neighbors, the four of us disguised ourselves as work crews from the city who'd been cutting lumber for the shipbuilders. After we got to the ferry, Charles was right clever when the soldier at the dock asked why he didn't have proper calluses."

Again Agatha, a former society woman and used to being in charge, took over. "It's time to get back to sleep. It's going to be a big day for all of us, so back to your beds and close your eyes. You, too, Mr. Gavin."

"Yes, ma'am." Scooting deeper into the corner, he leaned his head back against the wall, grateful for Tansy's warmth when she snuggled up next to him.

"I've made a terrible mess of this," he said. "From the minute I got off that prison ship, I've brought nothing but trouble to you."

"Don't say that," said Tansy.

"I'm an arrogant fool. I almost drowned in that river because I hadn't anticipated the soldiers keeping Charles on the ferry. And, believe me, there'll be more things I won't have planned for, and everything could end up being for naught." He dropped his head to his knees. "I can't look at you. I brought you into this debacle."

"You listen to me, Gavin Cullane!" she said in a loud whisper. "You gave Alden a friendship like he'd never known. Everyone thought him a jokester and prankster, but you taught him how to be a friend. He trusted you with his family."

"And they might all hang because of me."

Tansy put her arm around his neck and ran her fingers through his still damp hair. "He told you all about me for a reason. So that if anything happened, you would take care of me. He trusted you. Alden was jealous of every other man, but not of you. He gave you his family, and he did it on purpose."

"But…"

"But nothing. Look at the Marchands and the rest of them from The Burns. You made a difference in their lives. You gave them hope. It might be a desperate hope, but it is hope just the same, something they didn't have any of."

"I did so little."

"They don't think of it as little. And Charles, a boy you didn't even know, you brought him home after he stole the mail pouch, and now he is safe with his father. You risked your own life to do that. No one else would, and what about Brian? Do you think he'd be here if he didn't think you made the sun rise in the morning? You're his hero. You treated him like a man instead of a dumb animal to be bossed around."

Gavin shook his head against his knees.

"And I love you."

Raising his head, his bronze-tinted eyes met hers. "How can you after all I've done?"

"How could I not?"

Brian's snoring burst into a sudden thunderous

snort before he settled back into his regular rough wheeze. At the same time, Mercy tossed and turned as if in the middle of a dream before she, too, drifted into her soft, steady breathing. Gavin and Tansy waited, her head resting on his shoulder and his arm around her.

Gavin's shivering stopped. "Even before I met you, I knew you were a remarkable woman, and I'll be forever grateful that you love me. When I can finally make love to you, it will be like this."

"Gavin," she whispered.

"When we're alone," Gavin began, "I'll put my hands on your cheeks this way." The movement of his thumbs matched his words. "I'll softly trace above your eyebrows with slow and steady strokes before moving along your cheekbones and down the line of your chin to your precious lips."

The tingling sensations on her face moved through her entire body.

Following the edges of her mouth, he glided the pads of his fingers over her soft lips. She opened her mouth just a bit and sighed before touching the tip of her tongue to his thumb.

"Then slowly I'll move down your neck to your collarbone." Sliding her blanket off her shoulders, he slipped his fingers under the bodice of her dress and over the tops of her breasts.

"Gavin," she whimpered as she draped her arms around him and nuzzled his neck.

"No, Tansy, this time is all about you." Pulling her close to reach behind her, he untied her dress in the back and pushed it down, exposing her taut nipples. With a light touch of his fingers, he massaged her breasts and then took each one in turn with his lips, leaving them wet and flushed.

She closed her eyes and inhaled the still damp masculine scent of him.

Kneeling in front of her, his legs on either side of hers, his hands skimmed down under the loose waistline of her dress to her stomach and hips where they explored every curve and indentation of her body, leisurely as if they had all the time in the world.

"Gavin," she moaned into his ear as she kissed him there. He drew his head away. "Only you."

His mouth found hers as he pressed her head back against the wall, and his right hand moved down her stomach, lower and lower. In one quick motion he pulled his hand out from her bodice and slid it up under her skirt and up her thigh. She arched trying to get his fingers closer to her core, but he held them away keeping his touch on the sensitive skin just below where she wanted him, where she needed him to be.

She reached between his legs, but he turned his hips away from her hand. "I am here for you tonight, only you." In one quick movement, he slid his finger inside her and at the same time circled his thumb over her womanly nub.

She gasped, and he smothered the sound with his lips. His tongue probed her mouth in the same rhythm as his fingers between her legs. His hand surrounded her core as his fingers moved faster and deeper within her, now with two fingers, and she grasped his arm, pushing his hand deeper.

She quivered with the powerful sensations building within her.

"Now, Tansy, now," he murmured. "Let it be now."

And it was. Her release enveloped her entire body, and she stifled her whimper of complete surrender.

Young Alden began to cry.

With both of them breathing hard, he pulled back and tugged up her dress and then the blanket over her shoulders.

"He needs you," Gavin said.

She slowly came to her feet to feed Young Alden some leftover mush, nurse him, and change his wet diaper before rocking him back to sleep. Laying him in the basket that served as his bed, she returned to Gavin to find him asleep as well.

Resting her head on his shoulder, she whispered, "Thank you, my love," closed her eyes, and was soon asleep herself.

Chapter Twenty-Five

Day Eight of Nine—Daylight hours of September 12

The sunrise came earlier than usual, or maybe it just seemed so with all the nervous energy bursting out of everyone, but Agatha Marchand soon harnessed that energy into action.

She began with Brian, Daisy, and the children. "We have created stories for each family group. Brian, you are a blacksmith. Do you know anything about smithing?"

He nodded. "A little. The horseshoes go on the bottom of the feet, right?" He grinned at his joke, but Agatha didn't.

"Jests like that could get you arrested, young man! Don't say anything. Daisy, you do the talking. Here are your clothes, and some for the rest of your family so you can pass for working class. And, Brian, go rub the soot from the stove around your fingernails. The rest of you need smudges on your clothes, but just enough to make someone think you don't care too much about washing, not enough that they think you've been through the coal bin."

She held up two outfits for Tansy and Gavin. "These are yours."

The man's consisted of worn overalls, a shirt with a torn left sleeve, and a straw hat that could have once

208

been a home for a family of mice. She also held up a leather cuff, closed at the end, to fit over his left hand and wrist.

"What in the world?" said Gavin, holding up the cuff.

"You are Hosea Bundle, a failed farmer who drinks away anything he gets," said Agatha Marchand. "You lost your farm and your hand in New Jersey and have been living with relatives in New York City who tossed you out. You're headed to other relatives who, fortunately for you, have no idea you are coming."

Gavin rubbed his hand across the leather sleeve until Tansy reached over and put her hand over his. "Memories?" she said.

He nodded with a wounded look in his eyes.

"My Alden, the baby's father, lost his hand at the Battle of Saratoga," said Tansy. "Gavin did his best to save his life, but he died on a prison ship with Gavin holding him."

"I'm so sorry," said Mistress Marchand. "I didn't know. You don't have to wear it. We can put your arm in a sling and have the same effect. I am so sorry."

"No," said Gavin. "I want to wear it as a tribute to Alden. I'm keeping my promise to him." Sliding the cuff over his left hand and wrist, he eased his fingers into it.

Agatha went on. "Now Tansy, you're his poor, overworked wife, Biddy Bundle. You've got a worn-out blouse and skirt and big hat to pull down over your hair and face. I've got dark hair dye to cover any loose strands of the lovely yellow hair and some gray dye for you, Gavin. Both of you will get some lines on your faces, too."

With an expert touch, she applied the hair dye and old-age makeup to both Tansy and Gavin. After stepping back to give them the once-over, she gave her approval. "Now for your missing hand, Gavin. Grab the bar inside this cuff and hold tight. Practice using your right hand to pick up things. And one more thing for each of you." In one hand she held the remains of a rotten cabbage. "Tansy, put this in your pocket."

"This stinks."

"Precisely. Now Gavin, you will be getting the very last of our whiskey. I hope you appreciate it." Pouring a bit of whiskey from a crystal decanter into her hand, she tossed it onto Gavin's shirt. When he flinched, she said, "Stand still. You not only have to look the part, but you also have to smell it."

Lastly, she held out two small pebbles. "Put these in your shoe, Gavin. They'll make you limp a little. Take a few laps around the room until you get the feel of it."

"I can feel it already," said Gavin as he paced across the floor, "and I don't like it."

"Would you like the hangman's noose better, young man?" she said with her hands on her hips.

He hung his head. "No, ma'am."

Agatha fed everyone thick slices of bread spread with jam before tying up small sacks of cloth napkins containing more bread along with slices of cold fried potatoes. "This will keep your bellies quiet for at least a day, maybe two. Daisy, your family has two canteens with water, which you'll have to drink sparingly. Tansy, I filled Alden's canteen and wrapped it with one of my handkerchiefs to cover his name. You and Gavin will have to share. Now let me look at you."

Daisy, Lizzie, and Mercy looked appropriately working class in their plain cotton dresses with aprons and bonnets that shielded their faces from the sun and from close scrutiny. Lizzie wore her dark blue bonnet with the coded message in the brim, and Mercy carried her doll and her letter.

Giving Brian some coins, Gavin said, "You can pay for the ferry at the dock instead of at the store."

"Now it's important to remember that you can use your first name, but not your last," Daisy said to the girls, "but our new last name is...Brian, what do you think our new last name should be?"

"I don't rightly know, ma'am."

Daisy folded her lips in, thinking. "How about Evergreen like that tree outside this burned house? Yes, I know it's an oak tree, but it is ever green." Everyone nodded. "So Evergreen it is. Now tell me your names."

"Brian Evergreen."

"Lizzie Evergreen."

"Mercy Evergreen." She patted both girls on the head while Brian beamed at his new adopted family.

"Mr. Gavin," said Brian, his broad shoulders nearly bursting out of his borrowed shirt and his pants with a wide swatch of a somewhat different color stitched at the bottom so they would reach his ankles. "I want to thank you for giving me this chance. I'll take good care of these girls and the baby, I promise."

"I know you will," said Gavin.

"Nobody ever gave me an important job like this before, Mr. Gavin. I won't let you down, no matter whatever comes."

"No matter whatever comes," said Gavin with a pat on the big man's arm. "I trust you, Brian."

Tansy nursed Young Alden one more time, fed him more soft mush, and gave him drops of the sleep mixture.

"Sorry about this," she said to him. "I promise once we get across, I won't ever dose you again. You can cry and carry on all you want." Kissing him, she tucked him in the basket and handed it to Brian. "You will take care of my baby, won't you?"

Brian smiled his toothless grin. "You bet, ma'am, like one of my own." And out the door he went with his new little family. "They are the first family I've ever had," he called over his shoulder. "You can be sure I'll protect them."

After making last-minute adjustments to Tansy and Gavin's outfits, Agatha smiled. "I wouldn't know you myself. Keep those hats pulled over your faces. Now let me see how you act. Gavin, stumble a bit and act stupid. Tansy, you have to act like you can't stand him."

"How do I do that?" asked Tansy, pulling a face.

"Just like this," said Agatha Marchand. "Watch me." She scrunched up her face, narrowing her eyebrows and sticking out her tongue to lick her lips every time she said his name. "The word 'Hosea' tastes like vinegar. He's lost you your happy home more than once, but you're stuck with him. A good punch in the arm wouldn't hurt either."

"Hey!" said Gavin, rubbing the spot where Agatha hit him.

When she was satisfied that Gavin and Tansy could do everything to be the Bundle family farmers, she kissed them both and sent them out the door.

"None of us will ever forget you, Mr. Gavin," she

said when he reached the top step. "My grandmother once said, 'You can always repay a gift of gold, but you will die forever in the debt of one who is kind.' We are forever in your debt."

"And I in yours."

Chapter Twenty-Six

Still Day Eight of Nine—September 12

This morning a crowd of about twenty people waited at the dock for the three armed British soldiers in full uniform to lift the gate so they could board the Paulus Hook Ferry. They were a cross-section of society from businessmen to chimney sweeps, from the idle rich to laborers, from the elderly to the very young, and the new Evergreen family fit right in.

Soldiers questioned each passenger about their destination, their reason for crossing the river, and demanding an assurance they would be coming back to New York. Then their persons and their satchels were searched. No one had been turned away until one of the guards dragged a teenage boy out of line despite the protests of his father.

Daisy clung to Brian's arm and struggled for a full breath. "They're looking for Charles," she whispered. He pulled her close with a reassuring hug, whispering back, "But Charles ain't on this side."

"Where are you headed and why?" demanded the soldier when it came the Evergreens' turn.

"We're going to my family farm in Monmouth County," said Daisy. "My mother is dying, and her last request is to see the grandbabies again. We'll be back as soon as she passes."

"Open your bag, girl," the soldier said to Mercy who untied her sack and opened it wide.

"Please, don't take my doll, sir. I love her."

"Everett," the man called to the other guard, "do we have use for a doll with no hair?"

Everett chuckled. "No, Sergeant Wright, we only take bald dolls every other Tuesday."

"What's in the basket?" Sergeant Wright asked Brian who had not let go of the basket carrying Young Alden since leaving the burned-out house.

Mercy piped up before he could answer. "That's my baby brother. He doesn't have any hair either. You're not going to take him, are you?" She stuck out her lip as a tear formed in her eye.

With a smile, Wright patted Mercy on the head. "You can keep your brother and your doll. On board all of you."

The five members of the Evergreen family stepped onto the ferry and hurried to find seats on the bench along the side.

Meanwhile, Gavin and Tansy left the cluster of trees about one half mile down the road. Gavin limped toward the dock while Tansy tugged on his arm.

When the pair got within clear sight of the dock, Tansy put her hand to her mouth. "There be snakes."

"What?" he said.

"There be snakes. Do you see him?"

Gavin squinted against the sun at the cluster of people ahead. "It can't be."

Colonel Simon Duffy dismounted his horse at the dock.

"We'll have to wait for the next ferry," said Gavin. "Quick, get out of sight over here."

While they scurried off the side of the road, they saw a soldier pointing down shore to where the young boy had been taken for questioning, and they watched as Duffy headed in that direction away from the ferry landing.

"Now's our chance. Step lively!" said Gavin.

"Where are you going and why?" asked the soldier at the end of the dock.

Sergeant Wright's eyes locked on Gavin's, and at the same time Gavin recognized his one-time captor from the prison ship.

There be more snakes!

"I said, 'Where are you going and why?' " repeated Sergeant Wright.

Now was no time to break character.

"What did you say?" said Hosea Bundle in a scratchy voice. "I can't hear you." Lifting his leather cuff, he scratched his neck.

At the same time, Tansy gave Gavin a sharp poke in the ribs. "Well, speak up, you old sot! You're the reason we're headed to New Jersey."

"It ain't my fault, old woman," said Gavin. "I have to drink to put up with you!"

"Don't you blame me for my sister kicking us out on the street!" She lunged at him with her filthy fingernails out ready to gouge. Gavin lifted his right arm in Tansy's direction as if to hit her, but Wright jerked it down and stepped between them.

"Tell me where you're headed," he said firmly.

"We're going to my uncle's farm and see if he'll take us in," said Tansy, brushing off her skirt and disturbing the rotten cabbage, releasing more of its smell. Glaring at Gavin, she added, "No thanks to you."

"I tell you what," said Wright. "I'll let you on board if you promise never to come back…And if you promise to stitch up his jacket."

Hesitating only a moment at the reference to his stay on the prison ship, Gavin said, "Done deal! Hurry up, old woman. Thank you, sir." He grabbed her arm and stumbled toward the ramp.

"Gladly!" she shouted, shaking him off. "Once we get across, I hope your other arm falls off!"

"Is there a problem here, Sergeant?" asked a voice from behind them. "Why are these two holding up the line?"

"No, sir, Colonel Duffy, no problem at all."

Gavin planted his feet, clenched his muscles, preparing to grab Duffy and throw him into the river to give Tansy time to escape in the chaos. Out of the corner of his eye, he saw Brian stand up from his seat in the boat.

"That boy is not the one I am looking for," said Duffy. "Are these two the last passengers for this trip? Get them aboard so we can leave."

In the split second before both Gavin and Brian moved, Wright said, "They were just about to take their seats, sir." Wright waved his hand toward the boat and ushered Tansy and his former prisoner onto the ferry. "Good luck," he said under his breath.

Brian sat back down.

Tansy and Gavin hurried to the back of the boat and found a bench along the rail. Pulling Tansy close, he felt her trembling. "We made it," he whispered in her ear.

Then he saw Duffy take a seat at the very front of the boat, facing away from them.

We're traveling with him, to the same place, at the same time. God, help us!

Chapter Twenty-Seven

Simon Duffy held his back stiff and resisted the urge to turn around and glare at the farmer and his wife seated in the back of the ferry. He recognized the pair as Gavin Cullane and Tansy Carter, despite their ridiculous disguises, which he had to admit might have fooled him, but he knew her from her voice. He would never forget that voice. Her almost musical lilt and pitch from the few minutes in his office haunted him, especially at night.

That day her tremulous fingers had given her away as terrified, despite the control she tried to present as she stood in front of him. Still, she held herself aloof, valiantly trying to appear confident, and her false attitude of arrogance aroused him. He loved a woman who challenged him, a woman he needed to conquer and force to submit to his will. Tansy Carter was such a woman, and he wanted to see her writhing beneath him, begging him to stop.

Gavin Cullane, on the other hand, had the cause of colonial freedom, and it made him weak. Duffy's ambition had nothing to do with any cause except to get himself on a pinnacle above everyone else. He curled his lip, thinking about how far he'd come from his wretched beginnings, but he had so much farther to go. If he could become king, he would, but since that wasn't possible, he'd settle for being a four-star general, the highest rank in the British army, and nothing less.

The two disguised bumpkins in the back of the ferry would make that happen for him. He licked his lips thinking about the glory he'd get from the capture of the two Continental spies who had made it possible for him to misguide Washington about the saltpeter supply. He was so close he could almost taste it!

Once he found the escaped prisoner, Charles Hemstead, he would delight in gathering a firing squad to shoot the boy while Cullane watched and waited for his own turn against the wall. He imagined Tansy begging for their release, and he would promise to free both of them in exchange for her favors. And the trusting soul she was, she, of course, would do it, maybe more than once.

These thoughts entertained him all the way across the river.

****

Nate Hemstead stood in the shadows behind a cluster of trees near the New Jersey-side ferry station on the Hudson River and watched the passengers disembark. An hour ago, he had sent his two sons down the road toward the house where he might deliver the true message intended for General Washington. He told Gideon and Charles to wait off the road near the house and not to go inside or approach anyone until Nate got there. Under no circumstances were they to turn over Gideon's buttons to anyone!

Nate peeked around the oak tree and surveyed the people coming toward him from the ferry. In the crowd he spotted a large man carrying a baby in his arms, followed by a woman with a basket and two girls. They were the right size for his girls, but their bonnets covered their faces. When the little one skipped ahead to take her mother's hand, she tugged on her bonnet, pulling it to the side, letting sunlight shower her face. Mercy! Nate's knees wobbled beneath him with relief.

He watched them until he was certain they were well away from the soldiers and heading toward the line of wagons for rent by passengers from the ferry. The big man Nate knew as Brian spoke to the driver of the third wagon in line as he lifted Daisy into the seat, handed her Young Alden, and lifted Lizzie and Mercy into the back. After a discussion about the fee with the driver, the big man paid him and took his place with the reins in his hands.

Breathing a sigh of relief, Nate darted farther into the tall brush on the side of the road and ran toward his sons.

****

Gavin and Tansy lingered at the rear of the ferry until they saw Simon Duffy walk off the boat and turn in the direction of the Paulus Hook Fort about two miles down the shore to the west.

"Come on!" ordered a soldier to the lingering couple. "These people want to get on!"

Gavin led Tansy off the ferry, moving as fast as he could with the painful pebbles in his shoe, all the while watching Duffy out of the corner of his eye. "I wanted to stop at the inn for a while to change our clothes, but I didn't count on Duffy being right behind us."

"Do you think he recognized us?" asked Tansy, stepping over and around the puddles toward the few houses and buildings on the shore.

"I don't think so, but with Duffy we can't be certain. Change of plans."

They walked toward a newly built structure. It

might soon be a thriving business, but for right now it advertised only two sleeping rooms and three tables for meals. Next door stood the shed of the wheelwright whose sign announced the rent and repair of available wagons and buggies.

"I'm renting the buggy right now, so we can put distance between us and Duffy. Stay close."

"I only have one buggy left," said the wheelwright. "I've been repairing it, but it'll do if you're not going too far. I can let you have it at a lower price, just make sure you bring it back here when you go back on the ferry."

"We'll take it," said Gavin, even though he intended to abandon the buggy when they were far enough away, hopefully where no one would find it.

Soon the farmer and his wife were on their way toward the first stop on the map everyone had memorized.

Simon Duffy rode on horseback at a safe distance behind them with four soldiers he requisitioned at the fort.

****

Charles and Gideon, much relieved when their father joined them at the Brownfield Inn, continued to crouch behind the house while Nate went inside.

Carrying Gideon's jacket with the coded buttons, Nate said to the man behind the desk, "My name is Marshall Anderson. I'm looking for the teacher."

"Really?" said the fair-haired man in his early twenties.

"Yes, is he available?"

"That depends. Are you willing to dig him up?"

Nate scrunched his face. "What?"

"My uncle died two days ago, and he's buried out back."

Nate's heart sank. He had no idea where the next stop on the spy chain might be, and it was too dangerous to ask. He had failed, and George Washington would not get the true message.

"I'm sorry. I didn't know," Nate said as he turned to leave.

"Wait," said the young man. "Do you have something for him? I can take it."

"There's nothing. I just wanted to talk to him. Again, I'm sorry about your loss."

Not looking up from his desk, the man stared at a piece of paper on top of his ledger. "My uncle was teaching me Phoenician. He was a teacher all his life, and he left this for someone to figure out, but it won't be me." He rotated the ledger in Nate's direction. "Can you tell me what this says?"

Nate stared at the pattern of letters and numbers, saying, "It looks like gobble-gook to me. What were you supposed to do if you found someone who could read it?"

"I have no idea. Maybe my grandmother does. Grammy, can you come out here, please?"

A woman with slate gray hair and a heavily wrinkled face came out of the back room. "Yes, Michael?"

"Uncle Caleb gave me this scribbled message just before he died and told me to look for someone who could read it."

The old woman glanced at the message before sticking out her hand and asking, "Do you have any spare buttons? I can always use some buttons."

"Ignore her," said the grandson. "She's getting feebleminded in her old age, always asking people for buttons or necklaces or hats with wide brims. What she does with them, we don't know. Pay her no mind."

Nate laid Gideon's jacket on the desk. "You're welcome to these."

Without saying a word, the woman took out scissors and sliced off the blue cloth-covered buttons, and then held out five other similar ones covered in green cloth from her apron pocket. "Here, take these extra ones I have. I can sew them on for you."

"I don't have time now."

"Still, take them with you, wherever you're headed."

Nate scooped up the jacket and the new buttons, saying, "Thank you very much, ma'am. Good day."

The coded message on the piece of paper had read, *"Grammy needs buttons for ship voyage."*

Chapter Twenty-Eight

The afternoon of September 12

As the buggy approached another turn in the road away from the ferry, Gavin said, "We have to get out of these clothes and me out of this leather cuff. We need to find somewhere to change into the other clothes Agatha gave us and get rid of these and the smell."

Gavin searched for a place far enough off the road to change without any passersby seeing them. "Look," he said, spying a small white-board church with a steeple atop a peaked roof with tall windows on either side of a black wooden door. Surrounding it were dozens of oak and maple trees laden with green leaves and a smattering of the rich colors of orange and red that signaled the coming change of seasons. The days stayed warm, but the nights told the true story of the end of summer.

"We can drive around back to hide the buggy while we go inside to change. It doesn't look like anyone's here, so we'll be fine. Afterward, we can find a place to get rid of these clothes."

Once the buggy was out of sight, they grabbed their small satchels and headed toward the back door of the church. Bit by bit, Gavin opened the door and peered inside. "All clear. No one's here."

Dropping their satchels on the pew, they helped

each other out of their pathetic outfits and slipped into the other clothes Agatha had packed for them.

"These feel much better," said Tansy as she wrapped and tied the sash around the waist of the simple brown dress with a matching jacket.

"What about me?" said Gavin, holding up plain blue trousers in one hand and a rope in the other. "These pants are too big for me. Help me keep these up so I can use this rope as a belt." They both started to giggle as Gavin wrapped the rope around his waist twice and folded the pants over to cover it.

A sound from the front of the church startled them.

A thin man with red hair and small gray eyes stood just inside the front door. He held a broom in one hand, but his knuckles were so swollen, he couldn't completely grasp it. It clattered to the floor.

"You surprised me," he said in a booming voice that seemed out of place in the slightly built man. "Hello, I'm Pastor Thomas Peterson. How may I help you?"

In a firm voice, Gavin said, "We want to be married."

Tansy's jaw dropped. "What?"

He turned his face away from the pastor to speak to her. "It's the only thing that explains why we're here."

But Pastor Peterson had not missed Tansy's startled look. "Do both of you want to be married?" asked the man, raising one eyebrow. "I won't marry anyone under duress."

"Of course we do!" answered Gavin.

"Do you, young lady?" asked Peterson. "Your face seems to say otherwise."

"Should we be married now?" Tansy whispered to

Gavin. "Is now the time?"

"If we wait, will that change anything between us? War makes everything move faster, but it won't make a difference for me. Is it too soon for you?"

She pursed her lips and studied Gavin's face before turning to Pastor Peterson. "Yes, I want to be married to this man. More than anything, yes, I do."

"Then come into my office so I can get some information and start posting the banns."

"We don't have time for posting banns," said Gavin. "We want to be married, today, right now. We don't have much time."

Pastor Peterson gave them a long questioning look before saying, "Is there a reason for the rush?"

"Yes," said Gavin, winking at Tansy. "I cannot wait another day to make her my wife, and our child is already eight months old."

"Nine months," corrected Tansy.

"Oh, yes, nine months." Then taking a bold chance that this pastor was not one of the remaining British sympathizers in New Jersey, he said, "Also the British army wants to hang us."

Tansy grasped his arm while Peterson gulped, his Adam's apple throbbing in his slender neck. "I do, of course, see the urgent need to marry if your child is nine months old, and even though this is Continental Army held territory, the king's men still attack and murder at will, so for the baby's sake, I'd better get you married as soon as possible. Step up to the altar." He waved his hand toward the carved wooden table at the front of the church. "Kneel down while I get my liturgy book."

When he returned, he carried two books. Placing

one on the altar he said, "I keep all my records in here. What names should I enter? You do understand that for the marriage to be legal I must have your true names. And you do understand that should the British invade this church, I will be obligated to turn over this book in its entirety."

"We understand," said Gavin. Taking a cleansing breath, he looked at Tansy. "I will have gained everything I ever wanted when you're my wife."

She laid her hand on his cheek, and he turned his head to kiss it. "My name is Tansy Johansen Carter," she said, never taking her eyes off her husband-to-be.

"I am Gavin Cullane. Please hurry."

Pastor Peterson wrote down both names and then asked them to sign next to it. "This will be the only record of your marriage. I will write out a certificate, but it is not considered legal proof in most courts of law with no banns and no witnesses except for myself."

Gavin's eyes stayed locked on Tansy's. "Our love is all the proof we need, sir."

Opening his second book, Pastor Peterson began reading, "Dearly beloved, we are gathered together here in the sight of God, and in the face of this congregation—well, in the sight of God and myself—to join together this man and this woman in holy matrimony, which is instituted for the procreation of children, as a remedy against sin, and in this case as a remedy against further sin, and for the mutual society, help, and comfort, that the one ought to have of the other, both in prosperity and adversity."

Tansy interrupted. "My son was not born from sin. I was married before, but my husband was killed in the war."

"And the child will be mine as truly and completely as he is hers once we are wed," added Gavin.

Reaching out, Gavin caressed her neck. She turned her head and kissed his fingers, remembering his touch during last night in the charred house in The Burns, anticipating his touch again, and more.

Peterson cleared his throat before going on. "Will you, Gavin Cullane, have this woman to be your wife, to love her, comfort her, honor and keep her, in sickness and in health? And forsaking all others, keep only to her as long as you both shall live?"

"I do, I will, I promise!" said Gavin.

Peterson chuckled. "It seems I can't get through this fast enough. To you, Tansy Johansen Carter, will you obey him and serve him, love, honor, and keep him, in sickness and in health? And forsaking all others, keep only to him as long as you both shall live?"

When Tansy hesitated before answering, Gavin cocked his head. "What?"

"I promise to love, honor, serve, and keep him through all that is to come, but to obey only if he is fair, just, and kind."

"Not the usual vows, but do you agree to that, Gavin?"

A sly smile crossed his lips for this strong-willed woman. "I do."

"Then repeat after me…"

In turn Gavin and Tansy repeated the vows Peterson spoke.

"Is there a ring?" asked the preacher.

"No," said Tansy. "Can we still be married?"

"I have something," said Gavin. Reaching deep

into the leather sleeve on the pew bench, he took out a gold band with a small single sapphire in the center. "Agatha Marchand gave this to me right before we left. It's her engagement ring to Mr. Marchand, and she made me promise to marry you with it as soon as possible. In fact, she was quite insistent that we get married. You know how she can be."

"The ring is beautiful," said Tansy.

"Slip it on her finger, Mr. Cullane," said Tom Peterson.

"May I say something?" asked Tansy as Gavin gently pushed the ring along her finger. It fit perfectly.

Pastor Peterson nodded.

"War is a terrible thing to witness. Both of us have known the horror and the loss it can create, but you, Gavin Cullane, bring me the most important thing of all, hope. When I thought I had lost everything, you came to me and whispered hope into my heart."

"I now pronounce you husband and wife."

"Wait," said Gavin. "I, too, have something to say." He lifted her hand to his lips and said over her fingers, "I am more when I am with you than I have ever been on my own. I used to dream of you every night, but you are more than my dreams. You are my living."

"Now I pronounce you husband and wife," said Peterson in a rush. "May no man put you asunder. Kiss the bride. Please, kiss her before I start to cry."

Gavin's palms caressed her cheeks as he leaned in and let his lips flutter over hers with soft, sweet kisses. He inhaled her breath, and she his, until neither could wait any longer to seal the vows they had spoken. Her arms wrapped around his neck as she melted her mouth into his. At the same time, his broad hands pulled her hips closer while his lips on hers spoke the wordless pleasure of knowing a deep, abiding love.

It took Peterson clearing his throat again for each to bring themselves back into the real world.

"We have to get rid of those other clothes," said Gavin, breathing heavily as they stepped apart. "Those over there."

"Yes," said Peterson. "We had a funeral this morning, but the grave is not covered over yet. Perhaps…follow me."

Mourners had lowered the casket of Mistress Jonathan Russell into the ground but had scattered very little dirt over it from the mound beside the grave.

"Stuff the garments around the casket as deep as you can. Then we can bury her completely," said the pastor.

Tansy handed Gavin the wretched garments and the leather sleeve as he lay on his stomach at the edge of the grave and pushed them down, trying his best to tuck them under the coffin. Lifting the two shovels sticking out of the mound of dirt, he and Peterson tossed the soil down until it covered the casket fully. They kept working until dirt mounded over the grave.

"That should do it," said Peterson. "Help me hide your buggy in the shed. I'll give you my horse, and each of you will have an animal to ride."

"We cannot thank you enough," said Tansy after saddling and mounting Peterson's horse.

Gavin would ride bareback on the horse from their buggy.

"I'll trust you to bring the animal and saddle back when this war is over. Now be off."

He watched them until they disappeared down the road.

They rode in silence for about two hours before Gavin's entire expression turned smoldering. His hazel eyes darkened and his lips parted as he took in an eager breath. "Would my wife like to rest for a time in that grove of trees up ahead?"

"Why, Mr. Cullane, I was thinking how I'd like to lie down and rest for a time, maybe not rest, but certainly lie down. Follow me."

He felt the heat in her own eyes nearly burn him.

He followed her deep into the grove, invisible to everything except the birds. He climbed down from his mount and dragged the blanket off the horse's back. Spreading it out on a small grassy area between two tall trees, he motioned to her. She knelt on the blanket and held out her arms, but he didn't come to her.

Still standing above her, he unhurriedly unbuttoned his shirt, saying in a smooth voice, "I hope I can live up to Alden's memory, to your memory of Alden and how he was...how he was...when he loved you."

"I don't want to talk of Alden." Tugging him down to his knees by the edge of his shirt, she slipped it off his shoulders and ran her palms over the dark hair on his chest. Her hands moved up to his cheeks. She moved to sit down on the blanket. "Undress me," she said in a voice thick with desire.

Gavin reached around her neck to untie the laces on her dress, and he pushed it off her.

Pulling his hands to the waist of her long slip, she whispered, "Your touch is warm." She encouraged him to slide the undergarment down and off as well. Her woolen stockings were next. His fingers delighted the skin along her inner thighs and calves as ever so slowly he pushed them down. Folding the stockings together and sliding them around her neck, he pulled her up to kiss her. She arched and lay back, now naked before him, her face flushed and her breathing jagged.

She murmured. "Let me see all of you."

Without a word, he stripped down and knelt before her, his desire for her obvious.

"This memory is for Gavin Cullane," she said. "Here in the woods, in this time and this place, and all the memories to come will be of Gavin Cullane. I want to see and feel the way he makes love, and I want him to see and feel how I make love to Gavin Cullane, my husband."

Cupping her head in his hands, he spoke her name, and then kissed her, delicately at first and then with desire that deepened each passing moment. She pushed him onto his back, never breaking their kiss, until she lay on top of him, covering him. Now his hands roamed up and down her back and bottom, caressing her until her entire body blushed with passionate sensations. She whimpered and pressed her hips into him. All the while their lips never parted.

A breeze wafted across her back, but it didn't shiver her. She was too heated by his body warmth and her own passion. One of his hands slipped under her to her belly and then moved farther down. Lifting up partially to her knees, she let him find her womanly nub and then he reached even farther to the ache between her legs, but still not leaving her lips.

When she did finally raise her head to look at his face, he lifted her off him and lay beside her, saying, "You deserve so much more than I can give you. If I could give you all the stars in the sky, I would, but all I can give you right now is myself. My whole being is yours, and it's been so since the first time I saw your face in the watch."

Her breath uneven, she lifted her hips to him, and he knelt between her legs and filled her up with himself. His strokes steady and smooth, deepened with each one. Her hands pulled him into her as she lifted her hips to join him. When both of them could hold back no more, he released, and she followed almost immediately.

"Don't leave me now," she whispered as he started to move away. "Don't leave me until...until..." Her voice choked with emotion. "My life is divided into two parts, and this one started today. I never want it to end...I never..."

He didn't let her finish her sentence. "For everything that is to come, for every desperate hope I have, I will be with you. Maybe not beside you, but with you. I'll never leave your heart, and you'll never leave mine."

As he let his hips move into her again, softly, his mouth locked onto hers. Making love this second time lasted until both were completely satisfied, completely.

"We'll be in a bed of our own soon, not this blanket," said Tansy as she dressed again after their lovemaking. Saying the word for "father" with the Swedish accent, she said, "Pappa will help you build a room onto the house that will be all our own. He can even help you build our very own bed."

"I'm no good with a hammer or a saw," said Gavin, tugging up the too-big trousers. "I did help build something once with the groundskeeper at the Duncan house. I liked deciding where the windows and doors should go, even the peak of the roof, but I bloodied all my fingers with the hammer. I'm more of a thinker and a planner."

"Pappa will tell you everything you have to do. And he can teach you all about the farming or you could work with Linden in the lumber business. There's an endless supply of trees between our land and the Delaware river."

Tossing the blanket over the back of his horse again, he said, "I can't see myself doing work like that. I nearly broke my back farming for my uncle, and I hated every minute of it. It's good work for some people, but not for me. I want to do something else."

"But farming and lumber are what we know. It's what we do. It makes perfect sense."

This time he turned to face her; his eyes narrowed. "Not for me."

"But Gavin, it's your only choice."

Picking up the reins of both horses, he handed hers to her and helped her into the saddle. "Tansy, I couldn't love you more, but all my life, I've had my choices made for me. As a servant in a rich house, as a soldier in the army, as a prisoner on that wretched ship, and now you want to make choices for me again."

"I didn't mean it like that."

"You want to go back to the life you had before, before the war, before Alden, before…me, but I can't do it. I can't, and I won't."

"What are you talking about?"

"You want me to be someone else, someone I'll never be, and I want you to stay the woman who lived in my dreams. I risked the lives of you and your family, all because of a portrait another man carried in his watch. Did I make a mistake?" He urged his horse ahead out of the grove toward the road.

"Mistake? How can you say that now? Not now. You said you knew me."

"I do know you. I know the real Tansy, not just the face in the portrait. I know the one who thinks for herself, the one who has wishes and dreams. But our future must be what is right for both of us, not just more of me being forced to accept what others choose instead of choosing for myself."

"You said you'd never leave me."

"And in my heart, I never will."

He turned south on the road, and for the rest of the day, they rode in silence while his mind churned.

Chapter Twenty-Nine

Days Nine and Ten—September 13-14

"May I help you?" Pastor Peterson asked the five men dressed in civilian clothing who came in through the front door of the church.

"I saw a buggy in your shed," said Simon Duffy. "Who does it belong to?"

"A buggy? I have no idea. Quite often people come to visit loved ones in the cemetery behind the church and put their buggy in the shed for privacy. I never see them. Perhaps it is someone like that." He picked up the broom he left leaning against the pew and began sweeping again.

"I followed that buggy here, and now you have a buggy but no horse."

"I'd rather walk," said Peterson. "I can tell by your accent that you're British soldiers out of uniform. Doesn't that make you spies when you're on this side of the fighting lines? I can shoot you on sight."

"But you won't," answered Duffy. "A man of God is a pacifist. Search the place," he ordered the other men.

"What are you looking for?" asked Peterson as the four men roamed between the pews and onto the upper platform.

"Not what, who. A man and a woman. Are you

going to tell us which way they went?"

"I don't know who you're talking about."

An hour later, Pastor Thomas Peterson lay unconscious on the floor with his bloody broom stick beside him.

****

Brian slowed the wagon as they approached a line of several other wagons loaded with farm goods waiting along the side of the road for a company of Continental soldiers to pass.

"Where are they going?" asked Mercy.

"They're on their way to more battles," said Daisy. "New Jersey still has places where the soldiers have to fight."

"Are we going near a battle?" asked Lizzie, her eyes opening wide.

"New Jersey can still be a dangerous war zone, but we're not going anywhere near the fighting. The farmer we passed a while back said the war had moved to the west, and that George Washington had won the battles of Princeton and Trenton, so he's proved to the world he can turn farmers and shopkeepers into a unified army. We don't have to be afraid."

"I'll keep you safe," said Brian. But Daisy, despite what she told Lizzie, still had doubts. They couldn't expect help from either side if they were captured, not without exposing the elaborate spy system.

"We don't have to be afraid," she repeated to the girls.

"I see Mr. Nate in the back of that wagon over there," Brian said. He started to point, but Daisy held down his hand. Her husband and sons stretched out across the back of a wagon loaded with bushel baskets of vegetables. "Should I stop?"

"No," said Daisy. "We don't want anyone to think we know each other. We've got a ways to go before we get to the safe house near Woodland."

"But wouldn't the girls like to see their father and their brothers?"

Daisy smiled at Brian's concern for his new "family." She would not make the same mistake people had for all of his life by overlooking his gentle spirit and loving heart.

"All right. Lizzie, Mercy, look ahead, but be quiet about it. It's your father and your brothers on that wagon up ahead." When Mercy jumped to the side of their wagon, her mother stopped her. "No one can see that we know them. Just smile and wave politely so they know we're all right. I'm not quite sure how far it is to the next safe house, but when we get there, we can hug and kiss them all we want."

Gideon first noticed his sisters' discreet waves. "Look!" he said, tugging on his father's sleeve. "It's—"

"Quiet," said Nate. "Give them a smile so they know we saw them, but nothing else. Remember, we don't know them until we get to the safe house, and at the soonest, we won't get there until late tomorrow."

Both Hemstead boys grinned as big as they could as the girls waved, keeping their hands close to their bodies.

Nate gave a slow-moving salute as Daisy passed by, and she put her hand on her heart before turning away so no one would see the tears spilling out of her eyes. "They see us," she said in a low voice to Brian who kept his eyes straight ahead.

"They surely do," he said.

From the back of the wagon, Lizzie said, "Mama, Young Alden's been sucking on my finger something fierce. He's starting to whimper. I think he needs to eat again."

"Oh, dear," said Daisy. "Brian, look for some cows with full udders. It's getting close to the time the farmer will be taking them in to milk, so we better hurry. It seems we can't steal enough milk to keep that boy fed."

****

Several miles ahead, Tansy hid in some bushes, milking her breasts, which were so painful and swollen the milk leaked out several times a day, ruining the front of her dress. She used their only blanket to cover herself, hoping no one would notice.

"We should be to the safe house in Woodland in Burlington County late tonight or early tomorrow. Can you make it until then to feed the baby?"

"I'll have to." A squirt of baby's milk landed in the puddle underneath a red oak sapling.

Gavin and Tansy arrived at the small burg of Woodland first. The safe house belonging to Malcom and Martha Whitfield sat to the east of town on thirty acres of farmland—thirty burned-out acres.

The travelers waited hidden by a small grove of trees, staring at the extent of the devastated land in front of them. Vines, once covered with blueberries and raspberries, were nothing more than stubs. The chicken coop was empty and silent as were the barn and horse paddock, and just two trees stood tall in the apple orchard, both barren of fruit. The rest were stumps.

"Did the British do this?" asked Tansy.

"It could have been either army," said Gavin. "Soldiers have to eat, and they take whatever they can get. Let's hope the Whitfields are still here and surviving. I'll ride up first to look around and signal for you."

"I'll go with you."

"No, you won't. If, as you say, there be snakes, you need to go back and warn Daisy and Nate and the others not to come here. Just tell them to keep going to Swedesboro."

Tugging his hand to her lips, she kissed it. "I love you, Gavin Cullane. Take care of yourself."

"I do love you, Tansy Cullane. I do love you." Smiling, he urged his horse on with his heels. Ten minutes later, he waved to Tansy, and she rode up to the house to be greeted by Malcom and Martha Whitfield standing on the porch.

"The word came that you and several others would be arriving," said Malcom, a man in his fifties with salt and pepper hair and a long black beard. "Someone leaves messages in an abandoned well about a mile from here. The coded message was signed 'Grammy.' It didn't say how many were coming, only that some were on their way. Don't tell us where you're headed. What we don't know, we can't betray. Have you news of General Washington's progress against the redcoats?"

While Gavin and Malcom talked in the front room, Martha and Tansy went into the kitchen to cobble together a meal from what the soldiers hadn't stolen. "Thank goodness they didn't find the trap door to the cellar," said Martha. "I've got about two years of preserves and canned goods down there, even some dried meat and bacon. Ever since the war started, I've been hoarding whatever I could. I'm about out of flour, but everyone around here is more than willing to share.

Yesterday I traded four jars of blueberry jam for a pound of flour. Here, stir this for biscuits. No eggs, the soldiers took all the chickens, but we'll make do."

Two hours later Brian, with his "new family" of Daisy, Lizzie, Mercy, and Young Alden, walked into the house to find an abundant meal on the table, just waiting for them.

Gavin helped Brian guide their wagon into the barn. After he unhitched the horses and got them settled in their stalls, he said, "These spokes on this back wheel look near split through."

"Yeah," said Brian. "I'm sorry, but I don't know about repairing wagons. Daisy said we should tie up the spokes and the rim as best we could, and by the grace of God we got here. The spokes'll have to be replaced before we leave again."

Gavin smiled at the big man's modesty. "You did a fine job of getting the family here safe and sound. I'm proud of all you've done for us."

Brian beamed as he dragged the wagon by the hitch into place in the barn.

The moon was up by the time Nate, Charles, and Gideon walked up to the house and knocked on the door. Daisy, bumping over her chair in her rush to get to her men, sobbed with relief, hugging each one of them and saving the longest and strongest hug for Nate.

"Come in! Come in!" said Malcom. "Got any buttons? Take a seat. Eat your fill."

"I've got these." Gideon held out the buttons Nate had gotten from Grammy at the inn.

Malcom tore the pieces of cloth off each button to reveal slivers of paper with coded writing on them. He slid the papers into a small jar, tightened the lid, and left the house.

"How did he know there'd be messages in the buttons?" asked Gideon.

"Any time anyone comes he asks if they have buttons," said Martha. "If they do, he knows there'll be messages in them. Nobody carries around extra buttons unless they picked them up from someone on the spy chain."

"Where's he going?"

"To deliver the message," said Martha. "It's too dangerous to keep it in the house. Eat up. He'll be back soon."

Everyone ate their fill of the first good meal they'd had in days. After the table had been cleared and the dishes washed, Martha announced to the guests in the front room, "Let's get a surprise ready for Malcom when he comes home. How about a sing-along? Got a favorite?"

"Yankee Doodle Dandy," called out Gideon.

"All right. I'll get us started. Here's the pitch." She hummed a note, and everyone started singing. Brian's booming, off-key voice overpowered the lighter and higher timbre of the children, who also had trouble finding the exact notes. Only Tansy and Daisy could match Martha's pitch, but everyone's enthusiasm was impressive.

"Well," said Martha at the end of the song. "That was brilliant in its…uh…cacophony."

"What's cacophony?" Mercy whispered in her mother's ear.

With a wink at Martha and a smile for her youngest daughter, Daisy said, "Beauty."

"Another one!" called out Gideon.

"Let's try the hymn 'Be Thou my Vision,' " said Martha. "You should all know that one." This time Daisy's and Tansy's lyric voices led the singing of the familiar hymn.

Be thou my vision, O Lord of my heart,
Naught be all else to me, save that Thou art
Thou my best Thought, by day or by night
Waking or sleeping, Thy presence my light.

In the middle of the third verse, the door blew open and Malcom burst in. "I heard the music. How about we try 'Chester'? It's brand new, and getting real popular around here. It sets the redcoats' ears on fire whenever they hear it. I'll teach it to you."

He belted out the words and the others followed as best they could. After the third time through, "Chester" became everyone's all-time favorite.

Let tyrants shake their iron rod
And slav'ry Clank her galling Chains;
We fear them not; we trust in God—
New England's God forever reigns.
When God inspir'd us for the fight,
Their ranks were broke, their lines were forc'd;
Their Ships were Shatter'd in our sight,
Or swiftly driven from our coast.
The Foe comes on with haughty Stride,
Our troops advance with martial noise;
Their Vet'rans flee before our Youth,
And Gen'rals yield to beardless Boys.

Gavin's stomach tightened at the words "beardless boys." Memories overflowed of him and Alden marching into battle, and then sitting together on the prison ship. They were "beardless boys" no more.

****

It would be dawn in a few hours when Simon Duffy and four other men bedded down just beyond the burned-out apple grove, wondering what all the racket was coming from the house.

Chapter Thirty

On September 15, General Washington dispatched a ship to the islands to pick up a shipment of saltpeter. When the British discovered their plan to steal the saltpeter had been foiled, they searched for someone to blame, and their search eventually led them to one Simon Duffy who was last seen on the Paulus Hook Ferry.

****

Martha and Malcom spread out pallets and bundles of blankets in every nook and corner of the farmhouse for their ten visitors. Malcom then laid a loaded musket or pistol next to both Nate and Brian.

"I never used one," said Brian. "Don't know how."

"Keep it just in case. I keep mine beside my bed," Malcom said. "This war has taught me to always be ready. Gavin, take one with you to the barn."

Tansy and Gavin had eagerly accepted the privacy of the loft in the barn for the night. Spreading out on top of the soft worn quilts Martha had lovingly made over the years, the newlywed couple snuggled into each other to stay warm. Young Alden slept contentedly in his basket tucked against the loft wall with his full belly and the soothing tones of his mother's voice close by.

"We haven't talked much since the last time we were alone like this," she said without looking at Gavin. "Do you still intend to leave after we reach

Swedesboro?"

He cleared his throat. "I don't know what will happen after we get there. I'm the kind of man who thinks about things. I churn ideas around in my mind, and while I may think it's one way in my mind, it often turns out to be another way in real life."

"But have you decided to leave?"

He didn't speak for a few long minutes as he stared at the roof. "The truth is I would die inside if I left you. I love you, Tansy, the real you. If I leave, I'm a broken man."

Tansy brushed her hand through the hay, saying, "I will go with you wherever you go, whatever you decide to do." Gavin rolled over to face her as she went on. "When you are beside me, my love is stronger than anything that may come between us. I won't be separated from you. I can't. So whatever you decide, I'll be with you."

"Please, understand. I know what family means to you, and I want you to be where you can be happiest, but I can't, I just can't, be a farmer. It's not who I am or who I want to be. I wouldn't let the prison ship break me, and I'm trying not to let anything else do it now. I know who I am. I just don't know what I want…besides you and the baby."

A rat scurried through the hay and burrowed itself into a loose pile for the night. Tansy shivered at the sound, and Gavin pulled her into his arms, kissing her on the forehead. "If it could always be only you and me together, I'd be content for as long as we lived, wherever we lived, but I cannot face a life that's not of my choosing."

She interrupted. "The world is a troubled place

because of this war, but let's not talk about it tonight. Let it just be the two of us. We won't even think about Young Alden." She added with a wink, "Unless he cries again. Tonight it's just the two of us. Let's talk about anything and everything as if there will never be anyplace but this loft. No decisions to make, no place to be but right here. The world is complete in this loft, complete with just Tansy and Gavin. All right?"

His face softened. "We should seal our treaty with a kiss. Maybe seal it with many kisses."

And they did. They talked. They kissed. His hands stroked her body from her neck to her toes, and she did the same for him. After their hands, came their lips, and when both of them could barely stand their separation, they made love, passionate, abiding love, the fire within them burning deep and lasting.

The next day, the sun had peeked above the horizon and made its way upward by the time Tansy and Gavin, carrying Young Alden, wandered into the house. They had been fully sated with each other, and now they craved food.

****

The shadowy haze right before sunrise found Martha, Daisy, and Lizzie scurrying to put a morning meal on the table. Preparing enough for twelve people, including several hearty men and growing boys, took a huge chunk out of Martha's hidden larder.

Daisy protested, "It's important to leave you and Malcom enough food to feed you through the winter. We'll soon be in a safe place where there would be plenty to eat."

"I won't hear any more about scrimping on the food in my larder," said Martha. "It may be a few days before you get a square meal again, so you'll fill up this morning and be on your way with my blessing."

When the platters had been cleaned of the butter biscuits, the blueberry and strawberry preserves, the fried sausages, canned peaches, and applesauce, a loud wailing sounded from outside the house.

Nate, Gavin, and Malcom grabbed their weapons and ran to the windows while Brian shepherded the women and children into a back corner. Brian who had never handled a gun in his life, no need to with his size, shielded his new family with his body.

"Where is Mercy?" cried Daisy. "Mercy! Where are you?" She started out of the corner before Brian put his hand on her shoulder and gently pushed her back. "I have to find Mercy!"

"She went to the outhouse," said Lizzie, her voice cracking. "I thought she could go by herself."

The wailing got louder until three men stepped through the door, one of them carrying a screaming Mercy over his shoulder.

"Put me down!" cried Mercy, kicking her legs as hard as she could and pounding the man on the back with her fists.

"Gladly," said the man as he dropped her in a heap on the floor. When she tried to run, he grabbed her up by the hair. "You're going nowhere, you little brat!"

"I peed on him," Mercy announced as she kicked him in the shin.

"Served him right," answered Daisy, still pressing against Brian's firm grip. "Now stay still. Stay still, I tell you."

Mercy quit wiggling, and the man loosened his hold on her hair but didn't let her go.

"What do you want?" asked Nate while keeping his musket pointed at the three men who also held their weapons high, ready to fire. Gavin and Malcom stood poised with their own guns.

A sinister, yet familiar voice came from the porch. "I can tell you what I want."

Simon Duffy stepped between the strangers into the room. "I'm here to arrest the traitorous turncoat and the mistress who helped him deceive the British army."

"You're in General Washington's territory now," said Malcom, waving his musket in Duffy's direction. "You have no authority here."

Duffy lifted his chin and nose into the air. "I have all the authority I need. Now!"

The man holding Mercy by the hair lowered his pistol, aiming it directly at Mercy's head.

"Mercy, don't move!" called out Daisy.

"I could take you out right now," said Nate, aiming his musket at the man.

Duffy sniffed. "Before or after he pulls his trigger?"

With a heavy sigh, Gavin lowered his musket and put his hand on the barrel of Nate's, pushing it down. "It's me he wants, and it's me he'll get. Let the girl go, and I'll come without a fight."

Malcom interrupted, "You'll not go without a fight from me."

"Or me!" said Brian.

"There'll be no fight," said Gavin, laying his gun on the floor and raising his hands in surrender. "It's me he wants. Let the girl go."

Simon Duffy tapped his foot against the wooden floor while everyone waited without moving.

To Malcom and Nate, Gavin said, "He wants you to put your weapons down, too."

"You are a very bright man, Cullane," said Duffy. "How smart are your friends?"

"Put your weapons down," said Gavin. "Then he'll let Mercy go. He'll take me, and it'll be over."

After a long hesitation, Nate laid his musket on the floor with Malcom reluctantly following suit.

"Now the woman," said Duffy with a twisted sneer.

Gavin said, "No."

"Your choice."

The British soldier jerked Mercy closer.

Immediately, Tansy pushed her way out of the group of women and children. "No! I'm here." Moving quickly she stood next to Mercy, giving the man's gun a firm shove away, and tugging the girl out of his hand. "Go to your mama."

Mercy ran to Daisy.

"Well, well," said Duffy. "I've thought about you often, Mistress Carter, thought about how it would be when we met again." He looked at her from under hooded eyes, and Tansy shuddered.

Gavin lunged forward, but before he could reach Tansy or Duffy, two of Duffy's men moved their weapons, both of them pointed at Tansy, one pressed against her chest. Gavin stopped in his tracks.

"There's nothing to be gained by capturing us," said Gavin. "We're in Continental Army territory, so we're not guilty of anything here. You'll have to take us all the way back to New York, and for what? I doubt anyone in the British army cares about us."

"But I care," said Simon Duffy. "No one bests me,

especially not an inept spy and a woman who will soon regret her lies to me, and, look, I see an escaped prisoner standing in the back. Come here, boy." Duffy pointed to a spot on the floor in front of him.

"Leave him be," said Nate and Gavin in unison.

Duffy sniffed loudly again. "Come here, boy!"

Charles sucked in a heavy breath and started forward, but before he took two steps, Brian reached out and pushed him back toward his sisters and brother. "No," said Brian. "Mr. Gavin said 'Leave him be.' "

"I could have you shot, big man," snarled Duffy.

"Would be no matter," said Brian. "Mr. Gavin said 'Leave him be.' "

A stiff breeze swirled through the house from the porch before Duffy said, "I think I'll do just that. To return with an escaped prisoner, especially this brat, is of little consequence, but I can make the capture of a couple of spies into quite a coup for me. They sent messages to Washington so he could pick up the saltpeter before the British, and they will expose Washington's entire spy network after I turn them in. It will be a feather in my cap, followed by accolades and a promotion."

He moved toward Tansy and stroked his hand across her cheek. She shuddered.

Duffy said, "Tie them up." Two soldiers grabbed Tansy and Gavin by the arms and tied their hands behind their backs while the others watched helplessly. The soldiers dragged their prisoners out of the house and lifted them into the wagon from the barn. The fourth soldier already sat in the seat waiting, reins in his hands.

"Now get rid of the rest of them," muttered Duffy

as he walked out of the house to his horse and mounted up. "Let it be a lesson to anyone still supporting General Washington. Burn them out." To the soldier driving the wagon, and the one riding beside him, he ordered, "Move out!"

Back inside the house, Duffy's two remaining soldiers aimed their weapons at the men, women, and children crowded into the corner. Young Alden cried and wailed while one of the pair edged his way to the fireplace, picked up a burning stick, and held it to the curtains at the window, setting them on fire. He tossed the stick onto the woven carpet and watched the flames grab the linen tablecloth.

Flinging the burning tablecloth into the corner, Brian laid the table on its side. Platters clattered to the floor as Brian pushed anyone near him behind the cover of the table.

Lizzie screamed and hid her eyes.

In the confusion, Nate picked up his musket, sweeping it across the wood floor into the legs of the soldier nearest him and brushing him onto his back. The man's musket fired, sending the shot into the ceiling. Fumes joined the thickening smoke from the burning curtains and rug as the room became engulfed by the deadly blaze.

The remaining soldier took a step backward as Brian leapt over the table and ran straight at him. Brian grabbed the muzzle of his gun and smacked the stock of it into the man's head while at the same time the man's finger jerked off the trigger. The weapon fired, but the shot buried itself in the floorboards.

Malcom cocked and aimed his pistol, wounding one of the soldiers in the shoulder, and Nate did the same with his musket to the other one. Both soldiers lay face down on the floor.

****

At the sound of the shots and the rising plume of acidic black smoke from the house, Tansy buried her face in Gavin's chest and cried. He gritted his teeth and nuzzled against her to comfort her as best he could with his hands tied behind his back.

Simon Duffy leaned over the side of the wagon from his horse and yanked Tansy up by the hair. "Dry those tears," he said, smiling a wicked smile. "You and I will have a fine time when we get someplace, shall I say, more comfortable."

Gavin lurched up on his knees and leaned over the side of the wagon toward Duffy, giving the man a withering stare. His eyes filled with contempt as his mouth ground out the words. "Let…her…go."

With another sniff, Duffy released Tansy, sat up, and shifted uncomfortably in his saddle. He shouted to the driver of the wagon, "Get those horses moving!" before taking his place in front of the team.

Gavin slumped back in the wagon. "I'll never give up," he muttered under his breath. "I'll do whatever it takes."

Chapter Thirty-One

Choking smoke filled the front room of the Whitfield house as the flames crisscrossed the floor, slithering like hundreds of snakes, toward the kitchen at the back. Martha, barely audible over the roaring fire and the shouts of the others, bellowed, "Follow me! This way!"

When Daisy realized Martha wanted them in the kitchen, she lifted her skirt, tied Young Alden into its folds while urging the children toward the back of the house. "This way!"

Martha flung open the larder door in the floor and herded the children down the steps, and then giving a hand to Daisy with Young Alden, followed them into the underground larder.

Malcom, overcome by the smoke, collapsed on the floor in the front room. Brian, gripping the older man by the shirt, dragged him into the now also smoke-filled kitchen, handed him down to Nate on the ladder, stepped into the dark hole, and with a mighty heave pulled the door closed behind him. Just as the larder door closed, a tremendous sucking wind sounded as the fire consumed the rest of the house in one blast. A deafening noise shook the ground below, and Brian felt the heat on his back against the larder door.

The two British soldiers made a dash out the front door.

The families, forced to press themselves into the dirt walls of the small larder, surrounded the children in the center while Brian wedged himself on the ladder.

"Follow me," shouted Martha. "We haven't much time." Grabbing onto one of the wooden shelves built into the wall holding foodstuffs, she pushed it to one side. When she had it open a bit, she pushed Gideon and Lizzie into the exposed tunnel. "This way!"

One by one the children, and then the adults with Nate and Charles carrying Malcom, crawled into a dark, dugout tunnel. Brian came at the last, his shoulders and back scraping the walls, disturbing the already unstable passageway and shaking dirt loose in thick clumps down on top of them.

In the complete darkness, Mercy started to cry. "I can't see!"

Charles, reaching out blindly until he found her, wrapped his arm around her waist. "Stay with me," he said. "I'll get you there."

The group crawled forward until they started bumping into the ones stopped at the end of the tunnel.

"Help me," called Martha at the front of the line. "It's right here." The children crowded around her on their knees and tried to help her push up on a metal covering. The cover creaked but didn't budge. "Harder! Stronger!"

Nate, still dragging Malcom, said, "I can't get up there to help. Charles, Lizzie, Gideon, give it all you've got. You can do it!"

With their next push, the cover shifted and more dirt fell in.

"Again," he said. "All at once." Four pairs of hands of different sizes squeezed close together and, on the count of three, pushed upward.

The cover gave way, letting a stream of fresh air, light, and clumps of hay fall into the tunnel. Now able to stand up in the opening, Martha said, "We're here. Everybody out."

"Where are we?"

"It's the barn," called Lizzie as Charles lifted her out.

"It's our escape route," said Martha, tugging Mercy up by the arms. "We haven't used it since General Washington pushed back the redcoats around here. Nate, climb out and help the rest of us."

Brian came last, lifting his arms out one at a time and then his shoulders until Nate and Charles could pull him up. By this time Malcom began to rouse, coughing and wheezing. "The smoke…might be worse…than the fire," he sputtered.

"The house is gone," said Nate, looking out the barn door. "A pile of coals and ashes."

"No worries," said Martha. "We can all stay here. Look." Squeezing behind a line of wooden barrels stacked against a wall covered with numerous farming tools hanging from nails, she slid open a hidden door. "The soldiers couldn't be bothered moving the barrels or taking so many tools down, so they ignored this wall."

One by one the children peeked in.

"Hey, it's filled with stuff," said Gideon. "Even a bed."

"Blankets, water barrels, and all kinds of jars," said Lizzie. "Just like the larder."

"This land has been a battle ground for a couple of years now, and we expect it will be for a few more before General Washington sends those redcoats home, so we needed to be prepared. We used the tunnel twice before and hid here once for a week until the soldiers left. I restock it as best I can every time."

"I married a wise woman," coughed out Malcom.

"And we thank you more than you know," said Daisy. "I wish you had a cow to get some milk. Young Alden is hungry again."

"One of the first things the soldiers took was the cow, but that boy needs to start on soft foods to keep him filled up. Let me see what I can put together," said Martha as she slipped into the hidden larder.

Brian, covered in dirt from head to toe, wiped it off his eyes, saying, "We have to get Mr. Gavin."

"You're right," said Nate. "You and I will go after him and Tansy."

Charles stepped toward his father. "I'm going with you," he said.

"I need you to stay here."

Charles's mouth tightened into a stubborn line. "He came for me at the prison, and now I'll come for him."

Laying his hand on his son's shoulder, Nate said, "Gavin would want you where you are most needed. Malcom is still weak and coughing from the smoke, and you are the only one who can protect the others." He added in an even voice, "And they'll need someone to take them to Swedesboro if Brian and I don't make it back."

Charles's shoulders slumped, but he straightened them up again. "I will take care of them until you get back."

Nate drew his oldest son into a tight hug. "I'm trusting you with a man's job, and I know you can do it."

Charles chewed on his lip and, looking into his father's face, said, "Please come back."

Nate nodded. "Brian and I are going for Gavin and Tansy. Do you have any weapons in that hidey-hole, Malcom?"

"Sure do."

An hour later, Nate and Brian, armed with a musket, two pistols, and a knife for each, left on foot to follow Simon Duffy and his prisoners.

****

Five hours and twenty miles after leaving the Whitfield house, the broken spokes on the back wheel of the wagon had had enough and split apart, tossing Gavin and Tansy to the ground as they slid off the collapsed back end. The British driver barely held on to the reins as he toppled off the seat while the second soldier reached over and struggled to help keep the horses under control.

Almost foaming at the mouth with spittle, Simon Duffy shouted, "Fools! Get that wagon fixed! We'll camp here for the night. Tie them to the wagon wheels. Not together. I don't want any more of his stink on her before I'm ready for her."

Chapter Thirty-Two

Nate and Brian chewed on hardtack and gulped back swallows of water as they traveled. The wagon tracks weren't hard to follow, but the closer to sunset, and the darker it got, the more difficult it became to see the trail and the slower they went. In order to keep up their endurance, they set a pace of running for three minutes, then walking for three minutes to catch their breath. They covered a lot of ground, but their sense of urgency increased with each mile. If Duffy got too far ahead, they'd never find their friends.

Along the way the two men formulated several plans to overpower Duffy and rescue Gavin and Tansy. Nate began to realize Brian understood a lot more than people gave him credit for. He wasn't dim-witted, only uneducated. He easily memorized each scenario and often offered suggestions for each possible circumstance, and even though they were both worn out, the thoughts of eventually finding Gavin and Tansy gave them hope and strength to keep moving. They knew what they had to do.

All at once Nate put his arms out in front of Brian, stopping him. "Hear that?" he whispered.

The sound of a nickering horse came across the wind again, followed by three more horses doing the same.

Brian nodded in acknowledgement.

The night left a lone sliver of moonlight across the campsite along with the fading embers of a cooking fire. The pair crouched behind two large oaks as Nate pointed to a small pup tent and mouthed the words "Simon Duffy." Brian gave a curt nod. Then Nate pointed to one British soldier in plain clothes patrolling in front of the broken wagon where Tansy and Gavin slept, their heads bobbing against their chests. Their hands had been stretched out and tied to the wheels, Gavin to a front wheel and Tansy lashed to the back one. Nate jerked his head toward the four horses on a picket line behind the wagon. A second soldier lay snoring loudly in his bedroll close to the fading fire in the center of the camp. Again Brian nodded.

"When I am in position near Gavin, I'll shoot the patrolling soldier, and that will be your signal. Gavin will have to cut himself free while I reload and wait for Duffy."

After shaking hands with Brian for encouragement, Nate edged around the campsite toward Gavin while Brian moved silently, despite his size, to the tree closest to the sleeping soldier.

****

Tansy awoke from a restless sleep. Shadowy movement flickered among the trees. Just the wind, she thought, but a shape stopped at the front of the wagon while another moved behind a tree opposite her. The larger figure at the tree seemed familiar.

Brian!

A musket shot echoed in her ears, and the patrolling soldier fell to the ground. He lay motionless as a pool of blood formed under his chest.

Nate!

They had come to rescue her and Gavin. Galvanizing fear surged from her gut to her throat.

She furiously rubbed the ropes around her wrists against the rough edges of the wheel. Out of the corner of her eye, she saw Gavin struggling with his own bonds. A knife glinted in the moonlight. Her right wrist bled while the rope on the left twisted and tightened. Her hand went numb.

The soldier by the fire pitched off his blankets just as Brian lifted him off the ground, blankets and all, and whipped the rope he carried over his shoulder around the soldier's chest and yanked. The man thrashed, but Brian clipped his jaw, and he collapsed unconscious.

Simon Duffy scrambled out of the pup tent and aimed his pistol at Gavin. "Stop or I'll kill him!"

Brian charged toward Duffy, shouting, "No!"

A dull click sounded. "Misfire!" cried Nate as he hurled his now-worthless weapon at Duffy.

Duffy fired.

Gavin flung the knife.

Tansy screamed.

Brian fell.

Gavin scrambled to kneel at Brian's side just as Tansy tore her bindings loose and raced toward them. Gavin pressed his hand against the blood gushing from the bullet hole in Brian's neck. "Brian! Brian!"

In a gurgling voice, Brian said, "Mr....Gavin," before closing his eyes forever.

In a daze, Tansy scanned the clearing. Simon Duffy was nowhere in sight, the only trace a trail of blood from the knife wound in his stomach.

****

A fitting place to bury Brian seemed best near the

abandoned well on the Whitfield farm where messages were hidden and then sent on. He had surrendered his life in the name of serving his country and his friends, so here was where he should be remembered.

Malcom and Nate built a huge wooden coffin to accommodate Brian while Daisy and Tansy laid him out on a makeshift table of a board slid between the slats of a stall in the barn to wash his body. Gently Lizzie brushed his hair until it lay neat and shiny on his head. Tansy and Martha had spent the night sewing a blue linen shirt and dark brown woolen trousers for Brian, but the best they could do for his feet was to stretch two pairs of Malcom's socks over each foot, one over the toes and the other at the heel. The women decided his shoes were in such bad shape, he would prefer to walk the clouds of Heaven in his stocking feet.

"He held my hand once," said Mercy. "His hand was so big, but he made me feel safe."

Lizzie wiped her tears as she kissed him on the cheek. "I always wanted to do that. He was so sweet."

The next day at the gravesite, everyone gathered around the coffin beside the open grave the men had dug that morning.

Gavin cleared his throat and moved closer to the coffin to speak when Mercy stepped up and took his hand. "Can I say some words?" she asked.

"Of course you can."

"He always lifted me out of the wagon with only one hand."

"He was a big strong man."

"He told me he had a cat named Perkins, and he kept him in his room. Nobody knew but him."

Gavin lifted her into his arms. "I didn't know he

had a cat."

"He was afraid they'd make him get rid of it. He didn't want to lose his only friend…until he met you."

"He said I was his friend?"

Mercy nodded. "He talked about you a lot. He was so proud that you chose him as a friend. It made him feel special."

"Perkins is an unusual name for a cat," said Gavin.

"Not to Brian. Perkins was his last name. Brian Perkins."

Gavin's features fell. "I didn't know his last name. This man protected and saved the lives of my family. He called me his friend, and I didn't even know his last name." As he lowered Mercy to the ground, the wounded look on his face pained everyone who saw it.

Turning to speak to the people around the grave, his eyes filled with tears he hadn't cried since Alden died. "I knew him best, but I hardly knew him at all. In the tavern, all anybody noticed about him was his brute strength. He never talked much because no one ever talked to him. The first time I asked him how he was, he shook my hand nearly off my arm, telling me he was fine, there hadn't been many drunks that day, that he was getting fried chicken for dinner, and how was I? He said it all in one breath."

Gavin put his hands on the edge of the coffin and leaned over, tears dropping from his cheeks onto Brian's new shirt. "Brian, my big man, you say I treated you better than most, but the truth is that I didn't treat you well enough, not like you deserved. You gave your life for mine, and you deserved so much more." A choking sob left his throat.

Tansy wrapped her arms around Gavin's waist and

leaned her head against his back. "You trusted him with the important job of bringing Daisy and the girls to safety. That made him so proud. The first part of his life may have been hard, but these last few weeks he knew family and people who loved him. You gave him that."

Daisy said, "Every day he'd say, 'One day closer to seeing Mr. Gavin.' He could hardly wait to see his best friend."

Gavin's shoulders shook. Nate and Charles eased him away from the coffin as Malcom laid the lid on the box and nailed it shut. All the men, including Charles and Gideon, lowered the big man into the opening. Each shovelful of dirt splattered on the lid until soil filled the grave and mounded over the top.

"I'll carve a stone," said Malcom, "and I'll make sure to put his whole name on it, so everyone will know. Brian Perkins. Mr. Brian Perkins.

Chapter Thirty-Three

October 11-20

The trip to Swedesboro was delayed by three weeks to help rebuild the Whitfield house with the help of the nearby neighbors. Martha declared the new place even better than before, and she thanked everyone the best way she knew how with good food and plenty of it.

The rest of the trip to southwestern New Jersey and Swedesboro by the Hemsteads and the Cullanes was uneventful, although as they neared their destination, Nate asked Tansy why Gavin was so sullen. "Shouldn't he be excited to be somewhere safe at last? A place where he can start again with a new wife, a new son, and a new life?"

Tansy pulled Nate aside to talk to him away from the others. "Gavin has choices to make about this new life, and he wants to make the right ones. Working at farming or lumber is not for him. Gavin's not like Alden who made decisions in a split second. Gavin needs time, and I've been trying to give it to him."

"Is everything all right between you two?"

"I've made up my mind that whatever he chooses, wherever he goes, I will be with him. I don't know what will happen in Swedesboro, but I've tried not to pressure him. I've been just as unsettled as he has, but one thing is certain. My heart is his, and, no matter what, his heart is mine."

Autumn had settled in to stay by the time the families reached the Johansen farmhouse. They stayed warm wearing an odd collection of handmade sweaters and cloaks Martha Whitfield had insisted they take with them, and huddling in the Johansen yard, they let Mercy walk up to the front door by herself and knock. When her grandfather opened it, she said in her small but determined voice, "Do you know who I am?"

Lars Johansen answered curiously, "No, young lady. Who are you?"

"Your granddaughter!"

At that moment, the entire Hemstead and Cullane families, except Gavin who held back, jumped up on the porch, laughing and shouting their greetings.

Elsie Johansen hugged, kissed, and cried over everyone, smothering the grandchildren with her love before she asked, "Who is that handsome young man over there?"

Taking her mother's hand, Tansy said, "That's my husband, Gavin Cullane."

As Gavin stepped forward to shake his new father-in-law's hand, Lars shifted his feet back. "New husband? Who is left to grieve for Alden?"

Handing Young Alden to her mother, Tansy enfolded an arm around her father's waist and looked up into his deep blue eyes. "We have a long story to tell you, but Gavin knew Alden in the war, and he rescued us from being hanged by the British as spies. I love him and I married him, and I am certain he loves me and my son. More than once he offered to give up his life for mine. I want you to get to know him, but if he is not welcome here, neither am I."

Lars's eyes flickered back and forth between his daughter and his new son-in-law.

"We like him," said Mercy, tugging on her grandfather's pant leg.

Lars, reaching down to pat Mercy on the head, said, "Then so do I."

He hesitated only a moment before kissing Tansy on her forehead and stepping off the porch to grab Gavin's free hand for a vigorous shake. "Forgive me, young man. I spoke too soon. If Tansy chose you to be her husband and to care for our grandson, then I know it was a good choice. Welcome. Come in and sit down while Elsie gets you something to eat."

****

Meanwhile

Simon Duffy, his gut torn by the knife, moved from one British encampment to another over the next six months. Along the way, a sympathetic country doctor treated his wound, but could do no better than to leave him with a jagged stitched-together stomach, unable to eat a proper meal, and in constant pain.

Duffy eventually found British troops east of Philadelphia near Monmouth County, New Jersey, as the soldiers marched in retreat after their defeat by Continental troops at the Monmouth Creek battle.

Demanding to be taken to British General Clinton, Duffy prepared himself to receive accolades for escaping from dangerous patriot spies, only to find chains being locked around his wrists and himself under arrest for his role in the saltpeter fiasco. He marched the rest of the way toward the coast where he was imprisoned until the end of the war when any record of him disappeared.

Chapter Thirty-Four

Five years later—November 25, 1783

The door to the house on Franklin Street in New York City creaked open as Gavin peeked into the front room. Everything stood just where they had left it, except now covered with dust and cobwebs and with an empty bird's nest in the rafters. He opened the door wide enough to let Tansy, and his sons, Alden, age six, and Brian, age four, inside. Tansy, heavy with child, grabbed Gavin's hand for his help to pull herself up the step into the house.

"It needs a good cleaning," she said. "Cobwebs and dust everywhere. We'll see if anything else decided to use it as their home since we left."

"Is this where I was born, Mama?" asked Alden.

"Yes, it was. I used to rock you right over there in that corner in that chair."

Alden, a fair-haired version of his birth father, ran over and pushed the chair to start it rocking. A cloud of dust and dirt billowed up, setting off a coughing spell in the boy.

"Leave it be," said Gavin. "We have time to get at least this room cleaned up before the Evacuation Ceremony at Fort George. Cousins Charles and Linnea went on ahead to the fort. Charles especially wants to be there for the raising of the Stars and Stripes as the last of the British occupation force sails out of sight."

"He's going to show Linnea the prison, isn't he?" said Alden. "Can we go see it? I want to see where Charles was a prisoner."

"I don't think so," said Tansy. "I'm not even sure Linnea should go. They say ghosts of the prisoners haunt the building, and people are afraid to go past it at night."

"She'll be fine," said Gavin. "She's a farm girl. She's seen a lot. Besides, Charles will be right there beside her. It might be more upsetting for him to see the prison than for her. He was actually in there."

"I want to go and see the ghosts," said Brian.

"No, Brian. They're just stories, no ghosts," said Gavin, carrying in the buckets, brooms, and mops from the front step. "Help me with these, boy."

"Charles and Linnea have only been married a few months," added Tansy, "and this is the first time she's even been to a big city. Being born and raised in Swedesboro doesn't give a girl much experience with life here, so I'm glad they'll be living with us until they can get a place of their own."

Handing Alden a broom and Brian a dust rag, she said, "Let's get this front room cleaned up. The wagon with some of our furniture from Swedesboro is due to arrive tomorrow morning, so we have to sleep on the floor tonight. Alden, help your father bring in the blankets and supplies, and Gavin, please, open the windows. I think we'll need all the fresh air we can get in this dusty place."

Two hours later the front room was presentable, at least for today.

"When are Aunt Daisy and Uncle Nate coming?"

asked Brian.

"Remember what we talked about," said Gavin. "Onkel Nate and Tant Daisy with Lizzie and Mercy are staying in Swedesboro so he can run the lumber mill, and Gideon is studying to go to the University of New Jersey. Charles, Linnea, and the four of us came to New York to help rebuild the city now that the war is over. Remember the trips I made here to get things organized, so I could design buildings and set up neighborhoods just like I did in Swedesboro?

"Remember how I designed the houses and shops after your grandfather introduced me to people who wanted them? I designed them, and Charles learned how to do the actual building. We're going to do that here."

"Your father never wanted to be a farmer," said Tansy, "so he leaves that work to my brothers, Ash and Linden, and to your Onkel Nate, but now he's going to use his abilities here in the city."

"And don't forget, your mama is going to turn the print shop into a place where she can design and sew her own clothes. Do you remember now?"

"What about Grandpa Cullane?" asked Alden. "Where will you build his house?"

Gavin lifted a letter from his vest pocket. "His house will be the first we build. The house across the street burned down, so we'll put a new one for your grandfather on the lot." He pointed to words on the letter. "See it says, 'I can hardly wait to play with Alden and Brian, my very own grandboys, and be back in New York City.' Remember?"

Brian's auburn hair fell across his face. "I remember, and I want Grandpa to come, but I don't like

271

the city. It's noisy and too big. There's no woods to play in."

Tansy pulled her youngest son into her arms and rocked him in the chair in the corner. "I remember when I first came to the city, I felt the same way you did, but I learned to like it. The best part is that here is where I met your father."

Brian lifted his head to look at his mother's face.

"And this is also the place where the Brian you are named after lived. You will make new friends. I promise."

Gavin, leaning against the front door, said, "We'd better get moving if we want to be at the fort for the flag raising by noon. It'll be exciting, Brian."

Brian jumped up and dashed into his father's arms.

"This is the most important day of the war. The British are gone from New York City for good. There's bound to be a big crowd for the raising of the Stars and Stripes flag and watching George Washington come into the city. So, boys, I'm tying one end of this rope to your wrist, Brian, and the end of another rope to yours, Alden, not too tight, and the ends of both ropes to mine, one on each hand. That way you won't get lost. When we get down to the fort, you can take turns sitting on my shoulders so you can see better. All right?"

****

A constant undertone of excitement filled the crowd in the yard of Fort George at the oceanside tip of Manhattan Island. Here on Evacuation Day, the last of the British occupation force would leave the island, and George Washington's triumphant return would signal the finest victory of all. The peace treaty had already been signed in Paris, even though the Constitution for the new country was still being debated, but that didn't matter to anyone in the crowd today. This was a new country, free and independent.

Charles Hemstead gripped his wife, Linnea's, elbow as he pushed his way through the crowd. More than anything he wanted to see the last symbol of occupation, the hated British Union Jack flag, replaced with the Stars and Stripes. Memories of his time in the prison still haunted him, but seeing the new flag would be the end to all that.

"Look!" he shouted when at last he and Linnea made their way forward. The British flag still flew!

Someone standing on the wall of the fort shouted, "I can still see the British ships! Hurry! The redcoats are thumbing their noses at us from the stern. Hurry, while they can still see our flag fly!"

The men surrounding the flag pole hurried, but to no avail. The Brits' last nasty trick had been to nail their flag around the pole and then grease the pole, making it impossible to shinny up and take the flag down. Four men gave it their best effort but now lay on the ground with various injuries from their fall, one broken leg, one broken arm, and two with severely bruised backsides.

"We have to get up there!" shouted one man. "The ladder's not tall enough. Climb on my shoulders. Maybe we can make a human ladder."

After the second human ladder toppled to the ground, Linnea shouted in Charles's ear, "What can we do?"

"I have an idea." Charles patted the string of wooden cleats he carried around his neck. "Good thing I brought these to throw in the ocean as a good riddance gesture." He shoved his way through the masses to the pole. Holding the cleats high, he shouted, "I can do it with these!"

An older man flung two men out of his way. "What have you got there?"

"Wooden cleats!" shouted Charles. "I work cutting lumber with my father and uncle in New Jersey. I can climb any tree with them." Sitting on the ground, he tied the cleats onto his boots with the straps buckled around his shins. Standing he said, "Give me a hand to get me started."

Two men hoisted him up until he could dig his cleats into the wooden pole. One foot at a time he jammed the cleats into the pole while the crowd cheered. His hands slipped on the thick layer of axle grease with each step, but he eventually made it to the top. Digging his fingers under the cloth of the Union Jack, he tore at it, sending it down in pieces until all that remained were a few scraps and the nails. Charles saved one large piece of the hated English flag to wipe off as much grease as he could from the top half of the pole. "I can still see the last of the British ships. Hurry!"

"The honor of hanging our flag should go to John Van Arsdale, a veteran from our fair city," shouted someone from below.

"Send him up!" called Charles.

Van Arsdale tied one end of a rope to the corner of the flag of this new country and looped the other end around his arm. He went up the ladder now leaning against the pole until he stood on the top rung with Charles gripping his jacket to keep him steady against the wind.

"Here, lad, tie the flag up there," said Van Arsdale.

"No, sir," said Charles. "This honor is all yours."

Together the two of them stretched up until Van Arsdale looped the rope around two of the nails jutting out from the pole. With a strong tug on the rope by both of them, the Stars and Stripes billowed in the wind.

Cheers of the liberated United States citizens floated on the air for the next hour even after the last of the British ships sailed out of sight.

HISTORICAL INFORMATION

The inspiration for *Desperate Hope* came from the fascinating book *George Washington's Secret Six: The Spy Ring That Saved the American Revolution* by Brian Kilmeade and Don Yaeger. Major George Beckwith, a British Intelligence officer from 1782-1783, said, "Washington did not really outfight the British, he simply outspied us!"

The British invaded and captured New York City in 1776, and George Washington knew that to win this war for freedom, he had to regain control of the island. He first sent Nathan Hale, an inexperienced young man with no training in the business of spying. Within a matter of days Hale had been captured and hanged, thus sending the message, "You spy, you die."

Washington had to find another way, and he did so with the help of the Culper Six, five men and one woman who designed a convoluted system of coded messages, secret operatives, and hidden delivery places that led to, among other things, uncovering a British counterfeiting scheme, preventing an ambush of French troops, and even the smuggling of a British Naval code book. These patriots never told their stories, but a persistent historian uncovered them over 150 years later. Please, read this spellbinding book to learn more.

The main characters in *Desperate Hope* are entirely fictional, but there exists a kernel of truth in all the events. The horror of the prison ships on the river was real, as were the bodies washing up on shore and creating a serious health hazard. The fire that burned over one-third of New York City is also true, although naming the burned-out area "The Burns" was wholly my idea. I also adapted the true story of how Washington got the saltpeter ahead of the British.

Smuggling coded messages in the buttons of a boy visiting his grandmother is also true. He crossed the river on the ferry, visited her where she removed the buttons and sewed on identical ones, then sent him back to the city until the next trip. Captain Lord and Lieutenant Drumgoole were actual prisoners in the Sugar House Prison and put on mock trials to entertain the other prisoners. It is also true that sympathetic British guards invited them to dine, but in reality, the prisoners escaped with the help of a slave, not our clever hero, Gavin Cullane.

A plaque now hangs at Police Headquarters that marks a window from the Sugar House Prison. It says: "This window was originally part of the five-story Sugar House built in 1763 at the corner of Duane and Rose Streets and used by the British during the Revolutionary War as a prison for American patriots. The Sugar House was demolished in 1892 and replaced by the Rhinelander Building, incorporating this window in the façade as an historical artifact. The Rhinelander Building was demolished in 1968, and the site is now occupied by Police Headquarters."

Three months after the British surrender, the last of the occupation force left New York City. Evacuation Day had been set for November 25, 1783, at noon, and a crowd of patriots gathered at Fort George on the tip of Manhattan to tear down the last British flag and fly the new Stars and Stripes. However, as a dirty trick, the British soldiers nailed their flag to the top of the pole and then greased the pole. The British fleet sailed away as the Americans struggled to get the enemy flag down.

Eventually, someone made wooden cleats, climbed the greased pole, and John Van Arsdale, a war veteran, hung the flag of the new country just as the last of the British ships sailed out of sight.

A word about the author...

Susan Furlong always wanted to be a writer, writing and directing her first play when she was nine years old. With research and imagination, her favorite thing is to drop her hero and heroine into the middle of a true historical event to see how they survive. She has written two non-fiction books about her hometown and co-authored a full-length play—*The Twelve Seats at the Table*. *Desperate Hope* is her fourth book published by The Wild Rose Press, and it takes the Cullane family "across the pond." Raised a big city girl, she now lives in small town Ohio with her husband and her two cats, Calvin and Hobbes.

Visit Susan at
www.SusanLFurlong.com
Facebook.com/SusanLeighFurlong
Twitter@FurlongLeigh